P9-CFL-523

"Bite me," he said grimly.

"Same to you," she muttered irritably.

Paul blinked, and then a surprised laugh slipped from his lips. "No. I wasn't— I mean, really go ahead and bite me, Jeanie. You need to feed. Feed on me."

"Oh," Jeanne Louise said on a sigh, and then frowned at him. "Not ten minutes ago you were upset with me because I was going to bite someone. Now you want me to bite you?"

He grimaced and glanced away. "Yes, well . . . I shouldn't have reacted as I did. I guess I was a little jealous when I saw you cuddled up to that hunk in the parking lot. I suppose after that kiss earlier today I feel a little possessive." Paul shrugged uncomfortably, and then rushed on, "Besides, you shouldn't have to feed on others. You're only without blood because I kidnapped you. If you have to bite anyone it should be me. No one else should have to pay."

Paul shifted a little closer, and turned his head to offer her his neck.

By Lynsay Sands

LYNSAY SANDS

THE LADY IS A VAMP

AN ARGENEAU NOVEL

AVON

An Imprint of HarperCollinsPublishers

This is a work of fiction. Names, characters, places, and incidents are products of the author's imagination or are used fictitiously and are not to be construed as real. Any resemblance to actual events, locales, organizations, or persons, living or dead, is entirely coincidental.

AVON BOOKS
An Imprint of HarperCollins*Publishers*
10 East 53rd Street
New York, New York 10022-5299

First Avon Books mass market printing: August 2012

Avon Trademark Reg. U.S. Pat. Off. and in Other Countries, Marca Registrada, Hecho en U.S.A.
HarperCollins® is a registered trademark of HarperCollins Publishers.

Printed in the U.S.A.

10 9 8 7 6 5 4 3 2 1

THE LADY IS A VAMP

One

'Last day, Fred,' Jeanne Louise commented, offering a smile to the guard as she approached the security station. The mortal man had worked the exit of the science division of Argeneau Enterprises for nearly five years now and was being rotated out to another area to prevent him from noticing that many members of the staff didn't age. She would miss Fred. He'd been a smiling face wishing her a good night and asking about her family for a long time.

"Yes, Miss Jeanie. Last day here. Off to one of the blood banks next week."

Jeanne Louise nodded, her smile fading slightly and expression sincere as she said, "They'll be lucky to have you there. You'll be missed."

"I'll miss all of you too," he assured her solemnly, walking around the counter to the door to unlock it for her. He pushed it open then and held it, turning sideways to let her slip past as he said, "Night, Miss Jeanie. You enjoy the long weekend now."

"I will. You too," she said, smiling faintly at his calling her Miss Jeanie. He always made her feel like a child . . . which was impressive since he was only in his late fifties and she was more than forty years older than he was. Not that he would believe that. She didn't look over twenty-five. It was one of the benefits to being a vampire, or immortal, as the old timers preferred to be called. There were many such benefits and she was grateful for every one. But it didn't stop her from feeling bad for mortals, who didn't enjoy those benefits.

Great, a guilt-ridden vampire, she thought wryly and gave a chuckle at the cliché. Next she'd be angst ridden, mopey and whining about her long life.

"Yeah, not gonna happen," Jeanne Louise muttered with amusement and then glanced around at the sound of a stone skittering on pavement. Spotting one of the guys from the blood division entering the parking garage behind her, she offered a nod and then turned forward again to make her way to her car. Slipping into her convertible, she started the engine and quickly backed out to head out of the garage, her mind distracted with considering whether she should stay up and take care of some chores today, or just go home to bed.

That was one problem with being a vampire, Jeanne Louise acknowledged as she turned out of the garage and started up the street. The hours were off-kilter with the rest of the world. Her shift generally ended at 7 A.M., but she'd stayed behind to finish up when the others had left. It was now 7:30, which meant that to perform some of those chores she was thinking of, she'd have to stay awake for another two hours and then head out to those places that weren't yet open. Under a hot, beating sun.

Frankly, at that moment, staying up another two hours was an exhausting thought.

Home to bed, Jeanne Louise decided, taking one hand off the steering wheel to stifle a yawn as she slowed to a stop at a red light.

She'd just come to a halt when movement in her rearview mirror caught her attention. Glancing toward it sharply, Jeanne Louise caught a glimpse of a dark shape popping up in the backseat and then a hissing sound was accompanied by a sudden sharp pain in her neck.

"What the—?" She grabbed her neck and started to turn at the sound of the back door opening and closing. But then her *own* door was opening and the dark figure was reaching past her to shift the car into park.

"What?" Jeanne Louise muttered, frowning at the garbled word and how slow her thought processes suddenly seemed. And then the man was scooping her up to shift her into the passenger seat and sliding into the driver's seat himself. Vision beginning to blur, Jeanne Louise watched him shift the car back into drive, and then she lost consciousness.

Jeanne Louise stirred sleepily and tried to turn onto her side, but frowned as she found she couldn't. Opening her eyes, she stared at the ceiling overhead, noting that it was a plain white, not the pale rose of her bedroom at home and then she tried to sit up and recalled what had woken her. She couldn't move. Because she was restrained, Jeanne Louise saw, gaping down at the chains crisscrossing her body from her shoulders to her feet. Good Lord.

"It's steel. You won't be able to break it."

Jeanne Louise glanced sharply in the direction the voice had come from, her gaze sliding over what was a very small room, all white with nothing but the bed she lay on. The only interesting thing in there with her was the man addressing her from the doorway. He wasn't overly tall, perhaps four or five inches taller than her own five feet six, but the man was built with wide shoulders and a narrow waist. He was also rather attractive in a boy-next-door sort of way, with brown hair, a square jaw, and eyes a brighter green than she'd ever seen . . . and she'd seen a lot of mortal eyes in her one hundred and two, almost one hundred and three, years of life. These easily beat out every other set she'd ever seen.

"How do you feel?" he asked with what appeared to be real concern.

"I've been better," Jeanne Louise said dryly, glancing down to the chains again. Steel, he'd said. Cripes, he had her bound up like a crazed elephant or something.

"The tranquilizer I used on you can cause headaches and a fuzzy feeling as it wears off," he announced apologetically. "Are you experiencing anything of that nature? Do you need an ibuprofren or something?"

"No," Jeanne Louise said grimly, knowing it would go away quickly on its own thanks to the nanos. She then narrowed her eyes on the man's face as she instinctively tried to penetrate his thoughts and take control of him. She intended to make him get her out of these ridiculous chains, explain himself, and then she would call her Uncle Lucian and have him send someone to deal with the man. That was the plan anyway. It didn't go that way, however—because she couldn't penetrate his thoughts, or take control of the man.

Must be the drug he gave me, Jeanne Louise thought with a frown and gave her head a shake to try to clear it a little more before trying again.

"Nothing," she muttered with bewilderment. The drug definitely had to still be affecting her, she thought, and then scowled at him. "What did you give me?"

"The latest tranquilizer we've been working on in R and D," he said mildly, and then disappeared out the door and briefly out of sight.

Jeanne Louise frowned at the empty space, his

words running through her head. "R and D" was research and development. But R and D for where? It couldn't be a normal tranquilizer for mortals; that would have hardly slowed her down let alone knocked her out. But—

Her thoughts scattered as he returned and approached the bed.

"Do you work for Argeneau Enterprises?" Jeanne Louise asked, eyeing what he held in one hand with interest. He was holding a tall glass of what appeared to be ice water and she was suddenly terribly aware that her mouth and throat were parched.

"I do. I'm in R and D like you, only I help develop new drugs while you have been working on genetic anomalies, I believe," he said easily as he paused beside the bed.

Jeanne Louise frowned. Bastien Argeneau, her cousin and the head of Argeneau Enterprises, had hired her directly after she'd graduated from university seventy-five years ago. She'd worked for Argeneau Enterprises ever since. At first she'd actually been in the department this man claimed to be in, but twenty-five years ago, Bastien had asked Jeanne Louise to choose who she wanted from R and D and form a team. She would be heading up a new branch of the department, one dedicated solely to the task of finding a way to allow her cousin Vincent and her uncle Victor to feed without the need to bite mortals. They desperately wanted to be able to feed off bagged blood like everyone else did. It made life much simpler. However, both men suffered from a genetic anomaly that made bagged blood as useful to them as water. They would starve on a diet of bagged blood. She was supposed to figure out why and if they could be given some sort of supplement to prevent that. She'd been heading up the team working on the problem ever since and they still hadn't figured out what the exact anomaly was that caused it, let alone how to fix it.

Sighing at what she considered her failure, Jeanne Louise glanced to her captor again, noting that he was standing beside the bed glancing from her to the water and back, his expression troubled. Catching her questioning glanced, he asked, "Can you drink water? I mean, I know you people can eat and drink, but will it help or do you need blood only? I have some laid in for you."

Jeanne Louise stared at him silently. I know you people can eat and drink? You people? Like she was another species altogether. An alien or something. The man knew she wasn't mortal. But what exactly did he know? She eyed him solemnly, once again trying to penetrate his thoughts, and once again failing. Then her gaze slid back to the water. It looked so damned good. The glass was sweating, rivulets of water running down the outside and Jeanne Louise would have paid a lot just to lick up those drops. But she had no idea what was in the glass besides ice and water. He could have drugged it. She couldn't take the chance. If he worked in

R and D at Argeneau Enterprises, he had access to drugs that could affect her.

"It's not drugged," the man said as if reading her thoughts, which she thought was rather ironic. He was mortal, one glance at his eyes proved that, and mortals couldn't read minds. Immortals could, yet she couldn't read his while he seemed to be able to read hers. Or her expression, she supposed.

"There's no need to keep you drugged," he added as if to convince her. "You'll never escape those chains. Besides I need you clearheaded to consider the proposition I'm going to put to you."

"The proposition," Jeanne Louise muttered with irritation, giving a tentative tug on her chains. With a little time and effort she might have broken the chain . . . if he hadn't gone crazy with it, wrapping it around her and the bed like it was linen around a mummy.

"Water or blood?"

The question drew her gaze to the glass again. There was no guarantee the blood wouldn't be drugged too. She debated the issue briefly and then gave in with a grim nod.

He immediately bent, sliding one hand beneath her head and lifting it, then placed the glass to her lips and tipped it. Jeanne Louise tried to just sip at the water, but the moment the liquid touched her tongue, so cold and soothing, she found herself gulping at the icy drink. Half of it was gone before she stopped and closed her lips. He immediately eased the glass away, laid her head gently back on the bed and straightened.

"Are you hungry?" he asked then.

Jeanne Louise considered the question. Her last meal of food for the day was usually breakfast in the Argeneau cafeteria about an hour and a half before heading home. She wasn't hungry . . . but he'd have to unchain her to feed her and that thought was appealing enough to bring a smile to her lips.

"Yes," Jeanne Louise said, quickly hiding her smile when she noted the way his eyes narrowed.

He hesitated, and then nodded and turned away to leave the room once more, presumably in search of food for her.

Jeanne Louise watched him go, but the moment the door closed behind him, she turned her attention to the chains, trying to sort out if they were one long chain wrapped around her and the bed over and over again, or several of them. She supposed it wouldn't make much difference. Bound up as she was, she couldn't move enough to get the leverage to try breaking one let alone several lengths of chain.

Her best bet was for him to unchain her so that she could sit up and eat. She could overpower him easily then. Of course, it would be easier all the way around if her mind wasn't still affected by the drug he'd given her and she could just take control of him. She'd just make him unchain her then and save herself a lot of bother. Jeanne Louise had no idea what this proposition of his was, but mortals who knew about them were few and far between. They were either trusted retainers, higher-ups in Argeneau Enterprises, or exceptionally brilliant scientists who had to know what they were dealing with to do their jobs. He was obviously one of the latter—a brilliant scientist working on drugs in R and D. But no matter what group they belonged to, mortals in the know had tabs kept on them. They were given sporadic mind checks to see that they were okay mentally and not planning anything stupid like going to the press about them. Or kidnapping an immortal, chaining them to a bed and propositioning them.

Somebody had obviously fallen down on the job here, Jeanne Louise thought grimly. The knowledge didn't worry her much. She wasn't scared, she was just annoyed that her routine was being disrupted this way and that she'd probably be up most of the day as this mess was cleaned up. They'd have to find out what the man's plans had been, who else, if anyone, he'd told about them, then the man's mind and memories would have to be wiped, and the situation set to rights. Jeanne Louise wouldn't have to take care of all that. The Enforcers were in charge of things like that, but she'd probably be kept up for hours answering questions and explaining things. It was a huge inconvenience. Jeanne Louise disliked having her routine disrupted.

Her thoughts scattered and she glanced expectantly toward the door as it opened, satisfaction curving her lips when she saw the plate of food her captor held. He would definitely have to unchain her to eat. However, she soon figured out that the guy wasn't just smart at his job, when he shifted the plate to one hand and bent to do something beside the bed that made the top end rise with a quiet hum.

"Hospital bed," he said straightening, a grin claiming his lips at her vexed expression. "They're handy."

"Yes," she said dryly, as he paused and glanced around with a frown.

"Be right back," he announced and set the plate on the floor beside the bed before heading out of the room again. He wasn't gone long. Not even a minute passed before he reappeared with a wooden chair in hand. He set it down beside the bed, then scooped up the plate again and settled into it. The fellow then immediately scooped up some food on a fork, but when he held it toward her, she turned her head away with irritation.

"I'm not hungry."

"You said you were," he pointed out with surprise.

"I lied," she said succinctly.

"Come now, I warmed it up and everything. At least try it," he coaxed as if speaking to a difficult child. When she merely cast a scowl his way, he smiled charmingly and held the fork of food up. "It's your favorite."

That drew her attention to the plate and her eyebrows rose slightly when she saw that it was indeed her favorite, a cheese omelet and sausages. It was what she had for breakfast in the cafeteria at work each morning. When her gaze shifted to his face in question, he shrugged.

"I thought you should be comfortable while you're here. I have no desire to make you uncomfortable or unhappy."

Jeanne Louise's eyes widened incredulously and then dropped meaningfully to the chains. All she said, however, was a sarcastic, "Helloooo?"

"I'll remove those after you've heard my proposition," he assured her solemnly. "I just needed them to keep you in place until I do."

"You can stick your proposition," she growled and then narrowed her eyes on his face again and tried to slip into his thoughts, but again came up against a blank wall. The drugs were still affecting her. She fell back on the bed with annoyance, and then scowled at him.

"Fine. Tell me about this proposition of yours," she said finally. Anything to get out of there.

He hesitated, but then shook his head. "I don't think you're in a state of mind to listen. You seem rather annoyed."

"I wonder why," she said dryly.

"Probably because you're hungry," he said mildly and held out the forkful of food again.

"I told you I'm not hun—" Jeanne Louise paused, scowling as her stomach gave a loud rumble. Apparently she was hungry after all. It was probably the smell of food causing it, and the fact that she'd been so wrapped up in work she'd only eaten half her breakfast that morning. At least that's what she'd told herself when she'd pushed away her half-eaten meal. Forget the fact that she'd been skipping meals a lot, and only eating half meals when she did bother with food recently. It just didn't seem to be quite as flavorful or tempting as it used to be. Even chocolate didn't seem as yummy as it had once seemed.

In truth, Jeanne Louise suspected she was reaching that stage where food lost its appeal and became more a bother than anything else. Mind you, while her breakfast had seemed bland and boring that morning, the same thing smelled damned good now and she actually was feeling a bit hungry, she acknowledged, eyeing the forkful of food. When he began to move the fork from side to side as if trying to tempt or amuse a child, she turned narrowed eyes his way. "If you start making airplane sounds I'm not eating for sure."

A startled chuckle slipped from his lips and he grinned. But the fork steadied. "Sorry."

"Hmm," she muttered and accepted the food. It was as good as it smelled, and after chewing and swallowing she asked reluctantly, "How did you know it was my favorite?"

"I've had breakfast the same time as you in the mornings for years. Well, I did until a month ago," he added and then shrugged. "It's what you always get."

Jeanne Louise peered more closely at him now, noting the buzz cut hair, dark brown eyebrows, green eyes and pleasant smile. He was a good-looking man. It was hard to imagine she hadn't noticed him in the cafeteria at some point over these supposed years they'd had breaks together. But then she did tend to get into her work and walk around a little oblivious a lot of the time, she supposed. Jeanne Louise wanted desperately to find the cure for her uncle and cousin and even took her notes with her when she went for her breaks so that she could glance over them while she ate. As focused as she was on her obsession, Jeanne Louise supposed Uncle Lucian himself could have been in the seat next to her and unless he said or did something to catch her attention, she probably wouldn't notice.

Her eyes shot back to his as something he'd said caught her attention. Eyes narrowing, she asked, "Until a month ago? Don't you work for Argeneau Enterprises anymore?"

"Yes, I do," he said quietly. "I took a couple months off."

Jeanne Louise stared at him silently, processing this information. If this plan, whatever it was, hadn't been in his mind before he'd taken the break . . . well, it may be that no one had messed up after all. There wouldn't have been anything for one of the team who kept tabs on mortals to find.

"Eat?" he asked quietly, urging the forkful of food closer to her lips.

Jeanne Louise's eyes dropped to the fork and she almost shook her head in refusal on principle alone, but it seemed like cutting off her nose to spite her face when her stomach was rumbling eagerly and her mouth filling with saliva at just the prospect of the food he offered. Sighing, she opened her mouth somewhat resentfully, closed it around the fork when he slid it carefully inside, and then drew the food off with compressed lips as he removed it. They were silent, eyeing each other as she chewed and swallowed and then he scooped up another forkful for her.

"It would be easier if I could just feed myself," she pointed out dryly when he raised the next forkful.

"Yes, it would," he agreed mildly and when she opened her mouth to snap a bit impatiently that she'd prefer that, he slid the fork in, silencing her before the first word could leave her lips. As she chewed, he added, "But I know your kind are very strong and I don't want to risk you trying to escape. I'm sure once you understand the situation, there won't need to be such caution. But until then . . . this is just the better way to handle things."

"My kind," Jeanne Louise muttered the moment she'd swallowed. "We *are* human, you know."

"But not mortal," he said quietly.

"The heck we aren't. We can die just like you can. We're just harder to kill. And live longer," she added reluctantly.

"And stay young, and resist disease, and can self-heal," he said quietly, slipping another forkful of food into her mouth.

Jeanne Louise eyed him as she chewed and swallowed and then said, "So let me guess, you want that. To be young, to live longer, be stronger, be—"

He shook his head and silenced her by slipping another forkful of food past her lips even as he assured her, "I don't."

"Then what do you want?" Jeanne Louise asked with frustration when she could speak again. "What is this proposition?"

He hesitated and she could see the debate going on behind his eyes, but in the end he shook his head again. "Not yet."

This time when he raised the fork to her lips, she turned her head away and muttered, "I'm not hungry," and meant it. She was too frustrated and angry to care about food anymore. Besides what she'd eaten had taken the edge off her hunger.

He was silent for a minute, but then sighed, set the fork on the still half-full plate and stood. "I'll let you rest for a bit. The drug should be out of your system by the time you wake up again. We can talk then."

Jeanne Louise didn't even acknowledge his words with a glance, but stared grimly at the wall as he bent and did something to make the bed slide back into a flat position. She didn't move until she heard his footsteps cross the floor and the door open and close. Then Jeanne Louise slowly allowed herself to relax and let her eyes slip shut.

She wanted out of there and back to her own life. But she was also tired, and there was little she could do until the last of the drug wore off. The moment that happened though, she would take control of the situation and make the man release her, Jeanne Louise promised herself. He wouldn't be expecting that. While there were mortals who knew about them and knew some of their skills and strengths, the immortals' ability to read and control minds was not usually one of the skills revealed. Mortals didn't take the knowledge of those attributes well. It tended to freak them out to know their thoughts could be heard, and "her kind" had learned over the years to just keep that bit of knowledge to themselves. Of course if his job had depended on that knowledge, he might have been given it. But Jeanne Louise doubted that was the case or he would keep her drugged rather than wait for her head to completely clear to make this proposition he had.

Whoever *he* was, she thought with a frown as it occurred to her that she had no idea what his name was or much of anything else really. All she knew was that he worked in R and D at Argeneau Enterprises and took the same breakfast break as she did.

Which meant he probably worked the night shift too. That was interesting. Mortals usually didn't like the night shift. It was usually full of immortals, while the mortals stuck to the day shifts. She wondered briefly why he would work the night shift, and then let the matter go. She needed to rest. Jeanne Louise wanted to be awake and alert when he returned.

Paul pulled the door closed behind him with a little sigh and moved up the hall to the stairs, his mind running over everything he'd done so far, looking for any problems that might arise, but he didn't see any. He'd waited until she was off Argeneau property and away from the cameras on the grounds before making his move and it had all gone as smoothly as he'd hoped.

Hers had been the only car at the traffic light when Paul had hit her with the tranquilizer. That, of course, had been pure luck. God or the Fates had been smiling down on him this morning.

The tranq had worked as quickly as it did in testing and it had only taken seconds for him to get out of the backseat, shift her to the passenger seat and slide behind the wheel himself. The whole thing had been over within a moment.

The only place where he could see a problem was when he'd crawled out of Lester's trunk and got into the backseat of her car at Argeneau Enterprises in full view of at least three security cameras. But he'd worn dark clothes, and a balaclava to cover his face. There wouldn't have been much for the cameras to catch. Paul had snuck onto the property in the trunk of Lester's car, but there wasn't anything the other man could tell them. Paul had broken into Lester's garage, jimmied his trunk open, got in, and hitched a ride into Argeneau Enterprises. It meant he'd had to hold it not quite closed until the end of the long night shift.

Moments before Lester had returned to the car, Paul had slid out of the trunk and made his way to Jeanne Louise Argeneau's car. His main concern had been that it might be locked, but few bothered in the parking garage. It was so well patrolled and had so many damned cameras, no one would try anything there as a rule. Much to his relief, Jeanne Louise hadn't had her car locked, and she hadn't worked past her usual half hour after end of shift but had arrived just moments after he'd gotten in. If Paul was spotted moving from one car to the other on the cameras and security had been on their way, they'd been too late. His only worry now was that Lester might be thought of as a co-conspirator in the whole business and get in trouble. That would make him feel bad. Lester was a good guy.

Aware that he couldn't do a damned thing for the man right now, Paul pushed that worry away as he mounted the steps out of the basement. They came out in the kitchen, and he headed for the sink, intending to dump the food Jeanne Louise had left unfinished and rinse the plate. But halfway there he changed direction and instead walked out of the room and up the hall to the stairs to the second floor. Paul mounted those quickly, slipping one hand under the plate as he went to check that the food was still warm. It was and still looked fresh and tasty enough that it made him hungry.

He only hoped Livy would think so too, but feared she wouldn't. Nothing seemed to tempt her appetite anymore.

"Daddy?"

Paul forced a smile at that soft query as he crossed the pretty pink bedroom to the canopied bed to peer down at the little blond slip of a girl who almost disappeared in all the soft fluffy pillows and comforter. "Yes, baby. I'm here."

"Mrs. Stuart said you went to work last night," she said with a hurt expression.

"Yes, baby. Just for a bit. I'm back though," he said quietly, not surprised that she knew. Paul had driven Jeanne Louise's car to the parking lot where his own car had waited, relieved to find it empty. He'd quickly switched her to his car, then had driven straight home and into his garage. He'd carried her down into the basement through the garage door to chain her up before heading into the house proper and finding the babysitter.

Mrs. Stuart had reported that Livy had suffered a rough night then. He'd been disappointed but not surprised by the news. They all seemed to be bad lately. But not for long, Paul reassured himself and then tipped the plate of food slightly for her to see. "Are you hungry?"

"No," she said dully, turning her head away from the food he presented.

Paul hesitated, but then said gently, "Sweetie, you have to eat to keep your strength up so you can get healthy again."

"Mrs. Stuart said I wasn't going to get healthy again. That God was . . ." Livy frowned as if trying to recall the exact wording and then said, "calling me home to be with Him. She said if I was very good and He liked me, maybe I'd get to see Mommy. But she doubted He would 'cause I was naughty and crying. Do you think God will like me even though I was crying?"

Paul simply stood frozen. All the blood seemed to have slid from his head and down his body to pool in his feet, leaving him empty and weak. His brain was having trouble processing what she had said. And then the blood came pounding back, rushing up through his body and slamming into his brain, bringing a burning rage with it.

He didn't say a word; he didn't dare. The expletives roaring through his head were not for a child's ears. After a moment of struggle, Paul managed to bark one word, "Yes." Then he turned stiffly and simply walked out of the room, straight downstairs and back into the kitchen. His movements were jerky and automatic as he scraped the food off the plate into the garbage pail. He then walked to the sink, but rather than rinse it under the tap as intended, Paul suddenly found himself smashing the empty plate across the top of it. He didn't even realize he was going to do it, and hardly noticed let alone cared that bits of shattered glass flew up to spike his face and neck.

The stupid vicious, nasty old cow. He never should have had Mrs. Stuart watch Livy. He'd known she wouldn't be able to keep her Bible-thumping to herself, but he'd had no choice. Mrs. Stuart used to be a nurse before retiring, and there was no one else he'd trusted to know what to do if there had been a problem. But he'd never let the old bitch near her again. If she was good, God might like her? But he probably wouldn't because she'd cried? The child was dying of cancer, being eaten alive, wasting away and suffering a pain that he couldn't even comprehend, and couldn't prevent. They had given him a prescription for pain meds for Livy, and the strongest dosage they could, but they did little for the girl. The only other option was to keep her sedated in hospital until she died and he refused to do that. He wouldn't simply watch her die. He wanted her cured, but until then, nothing seemed to ease the pain she was suffering and for Mrs. Stuart to suggest that her crying because of that excruciating pain might make God not like her so she wouldn't see her mother—

"Daddy?"

Stiffening, Paul sucked in a breath to calm himself and then turned to peer blankly at the five-year-old girl standing in the kitchen doorway. In the next moment, he was rushing forward to scoop her up. "What are you doing out of bed, baby? You shouldn't be up."

"I'm tired of staying in bed," Livy said unhappily and then reached up to touch his chin. "You're bleeding. Did you cut yourself?"

"No. Yes. Daddy's fine," Paul assured her grimly,

carrying her back to the stairs and up. She was all bones and pale skin and his heart ached as he held her. The child was precious, the most precious thing in his life. Paul lived for her, and he'd die for her too if he had to. But for now, he'd put her back to bed and then catch a couple hours of sleep himself. He'd stayed awake all night and needed to be alert and on the ball when he talked to Jeanne Louise Argeneau. He needed to be clear and persuasive. He needed to convince her to make his child one of her kind. He'd give her anything she wanted to get her to do that, including his own life, just so long as she turned her and taught her to survive as a vampire. He'd give anything and everything to know she lived on. He'd failed her mother, his wife, Jerri. But he wouldn't fail Livy. He had to convince Jeanne Louise to save her life. She was his only hope.

Two

Jeanne Louise woke to the awareness that she wasn't alone. It wasn't instinct. It was the hum of a mortal's thoughts playing on the periphery of her mind. They buzzed there like a bee by her ear, soft and, at first, not entirely intelligible as she slid back to consciousness, and then she opened her eyes and turned her head.

She wasn't surprised to find a child standing at her bedside rather than the man who had left her there. It was something about the thoughts, their tempo and lightness, she supposed. The thoughts she'd awakened to had been soft, questing, curious like a child's rather than heavy and defensive and even fearful like an adult mortal's usually were.

Jeanne Louise stared at the girl for a moment, taking in the pallor to her skin and thinness of her body. The child looked like a stiff wind would take her away, and one inhalation told her the child wasn't well. She caught a strong whiff of the sickly sweet stench of illness coming from her. The child was dying, Jeanne Louise realized, and found the thought troubling. Mortals died much younger than immortals, but rarely this young. This was a tragedy. All that hope and promise snuffed out before it had been allowed to bear fruit. It was an abomination.

"Hi," Jeanne Louise whispered, the word coming out almost a croak. She should have drunk more of the water her captor had offered earlier, she supposed. As he'd promised, it apparently hadn't been drugged, and it might have eased her condition. Without it, she was now parched either from the tranquilizer dart he'd shot her with or from the nanos' efforts to remove it from her body as quickly as possible.

Jeanne Louise took a moment to work her tongue in her mouth, building up saliva and swallowing to try to ease the dryness, and then tried again, "Hello. Who are you?"

"I'm Olivia Jean Jones," the little girl said solemnly, one hand rising to fuss nervously with a strand of her long, lank blond hair. "But everyone calls me Livy."

Jeanne Louise nodded solemnly. She hadn't really needed the child to tell her her name. She had already plucked it from her mind along with the name of her father, who was also the man who had kidnapped and chained up Jeanne Louise. Paul Jones.

Leaving that bit of information for now, she quickly rifled through the girl's mind to see if she would be of any use in getting her free. But the child didn't seem to even know there was a key to the chains, let alone where it might be. Disappointed but not terribly surprised by the knowledge, she said, "Hello Livy. My name is Jeanne Louise Argeneau."

Olivia's eyes widened. "You're Jean like me."

"Close," Jeanne Louise said with a smile.

Livy didn't question that, but announced, "I'm five."

When Jeanne Louise merely nodded, she added earnestly, "And I am always polite to my elders, and I'm nice to everyone, and—" She paused and frowned. "Well, except Jimmy down the road, but he's always mean to me first," she added defensively before rushing on. "And I don't cry much, except sometimes my head hurts real bad and I can't help it. But I try not to, and I try not to lie either because that's a sin, and I like flowers and puppies and . . ." Livy paused and bit her lip and then asked, "Do you think God will like me?"

Jeanne Louise stilled in the bed at the question and the worry behind it, and then slipped into the girl's thoughts, sifting for the source of it. Her mouth tightened as she touched on the memory of a tired and cranky older woman warning this small waiflike child that she wouldn't get to see her mom in heaven if God didn't like her and He didn't abide crybabies. Jeanne Louise didn't even hesitate, but quickly eased the child's fears, fading them in her mind even as she said, "I think He will love you, Livy."

"Oh." The girl smiled widely, the worry dropping away under her influence. "I hope so. Then I can see Mommy."

Jeanne Louise hesitated, unsure how to respond to that, but finally said, "I'm sure your mommy would like that." She then asked, "So your mother is in heaven?"

Livy nodded and moved closer to the bed. "I don't remember her much. I was little when she went to the angels. But we have pictures. She was beautiful and she used to sing to me to make me sleep. I don't remember that but Daddy said she did."

Jeanne Louise nodded. "Did she have blond hair like you?"

"Yes." The girl beamed happily. "And she had pretty blue eyes, and Daddy said I got her smile and it's the prettiest smile in the world."

"No doubt," Jeanne Louise said solemnly. "You're very pretty."

"You're pretty too," Livy said kindly, and then suddenly seemed to become aware of Jeanne Louise's state. "Why do you have all that chain on you?"

"We're playing a game."

Jeanne Louise glanced sharply to the man who had spoken: her captor, Paul Jones. Better known as Daddy in Livy's mind, she read even as the girl smiled at the man.

"You're awake," Livy said simply.

"Yes. But you shouldn't be out of bed," the man said solemnly, moving to scoop up the child.

"I went to see you when I woke up, but you were snoring, so I came down to find the picture books," Livy explained.

"I moved my office upstairs," the father said quietly. "And you don't need the photo albums."

"Yes, I do, Daddy. I forget what Mommy looks like and I need to remember so I can recognize her when I get to heaven," Livy said worriedly.

Paul flinched at the words, terror and pain stark on his face for one moment, and then determination replaced those emotions and he turned abruptly away to carry his daughter out of the room. "I will bring the albums to you after I put you back in bed."

Jeanne Louise watched them go, her concentration on the back of Paul's head as she tried to ignore the envy slipping through her. The bond between her kidnapper and his daughter was one she'd never gotten to enjoy with her own father. Her mother had died when she was just a baby, and circumstances had forced Armand Argeneau to place Jeanne Louise with her aunt Marguerite. It had been an effort to keep her safe, which she now understood and appreciated. But she hadn't known to appreciate it as a child. All she'd known was that while her aunt had showered her with love and attention, and her brothers—both much older than her—had visited and treated her with caring and affection, she hadn't had parents of her own to love her. That being the case it had been the one thing she'd most yearned for.

Pushing those thoughts away, Jeanne Louise closed her eyes and turned over what she'd learned. Livy was dying of cancer. The word had been in the child's mind, a word she didn't understand except that it meant sick and her head hurt. Jeanne Louise could only speculate that the child had some kind of brain cancer, a tumor or something, though whether that was the primary problem or the cancer had started elsewhere and metastasized to the brain she didn't know. All she knew was that the girl was resigned to "going to heaven" and the father was not. From that she suspected Livy was the reason she was here. Paul Jones didn't want her to turn him, he wanted her to turn and save his daughter.

That was just a guess. Jeanne Louise hadn't read the thought from the father's mind as he'd left. She hadn't read anything. She'd tried though. She'd tried to slip into his thoughts not just to read him, but also to take control as she'd planned . . . and she hadn't been able to. His mind was a blank wall to her.

Jeanne Louise wanted to think that it was the tranquilizer still affecting her, but she'd been able to read Livy's mind easily enough even with possible brain cancer, which could often make doing so difficult. That being the case, she was pretty sure the drug she'd been given was no longer in her system. Which meant she simply couldn't read Paul Jones. Which left her in one hell of a spot. And not just because she now couldn't simply take control and make him release her. That was no longer even a concern in her mind. Not being able to read Paul meant that for her he was a possible life mate.

"Dear God," she whispered, opening her eyes and staring at the ceiling as the term reverberated through her head. A life mate. Someone she couldn't read or control and who couldn't read or control her. Someone she could relax around and share her long life with; an oasis of peace and passion in this mad world. It was something every immortal wanted, but it was something Jeanne Louise had desperately yearned for most of her life.

By her teen years Jeanne Louise had given up on the dream of having loving parents of her own and had turned to fantasizing about someday having a life mate and her own children to shower with all the parental love she hadn't had growing up. She had spent countless hours imagining who her life mate might be, wondering if he would have fair hair or dark. Would he be her height or taller or even shorter? Would he be handsome and strong, science minded like her or more artistic? Would he be mortal or immortal?

And now she knew, or believed she did. If she was right, Paul was her life mate. She certainly wasn't disappointed when it came to his looks. The fact that he was obviously interested in science like herself was encouraging too . . . But the man had kidnapped her, which really wasn't a good way to start a courtship when you thought about it.

Jeanne Louise pushed that matter aside for other considerations. The main issue was that if she was right about his motives for taking her . . . well . . . put quite simply it would be a problem. Each immortal was allowed to turn only one in their lifetime. It was generally used for that most precious of creature, a life mate. Him. Not his daughter.

Of course, Jeanne Louise could turn him and he could then use his one turn to save his daughter. Which would still give him what he wanted. But what if she did that and Paul decided that he wasn't willing to be her life mate? While the fact that she couldn't read him suggested he was a possible life mate, it didn't guarantee he would be willing to be hers.

Paul would probably agree to anything right now to save his daughter, Jeanne Louise thought, even to spending an eternity with her. But she didn't want him that way. She had to know he truly wanted to be her life mate, and that he wasn't just agreeing out of desperation to save Livy. For that to happen, they needed to get to know each other. She needed to be sure they suited. She needed time, but Jeanne Louise very much suspected she wouldn't get it. Paul would put his daughter back to bed, find her the photo album, and perhaps feed her or sit with her for a bit, but eventually he would come back down here and tell her that his little Livy was dying and he needed her to save the child.

When he did that, Jeanne Louise would have to refuse, but without offering him even the hope of the alternative solution of her turning him and his turning Livy until she knew how he felt about her. Paul wouldn't be happy, which didn't give her much hope for her success in wooing him. He might even hate her for it. He certainly wouldn't like her for it.

Sighing, Jeanne Louise closed her eyes again. Her desire to escape had fled. Now she was a bundle of fear and hope—hope that she'd found her life mate, and fear that she wouldn't find a way to claim him.

"I'm thirsty."

"I'll get you a drink after I put you back to bed," Paul assured Livy, shifting her to one arm so that he could close the door to the basement with the other.

"I don't want to go back to bed, Daddy. I'm lonely there," she complained. "Can't I show Jeanne Louise pictures of Mommy?"

Paul didn't answer at first. He didn't take her directly up to bed though, but set her down in a chair at the kitchen table and busied himself getting her a drink. Livy hadn't felt much like doing anything the last week and had spent more and more time in bed. He'd expected her to mostly remain there while he worked at convincing Jeanne Louise to turn Livy and save her life. But really, it occurred to him now that she would be more likely to agree to do what he wanted if she spent time with the child and got to know her. No one could spend more than a few minutes with his Livy and not fall in love with her, he was sure. She was a lovely child, clever and sweet and so very precious. Everyone must see that.

Surely it couldn't hurt their cause for Jeanne Louise to get to know and love the child? It seemed like a smart plan, and Livy's interest and desire to spend time with Jeanne Louise could only help. But he was concerned about Livy. She'd been so weak and apathetic lately. This sudden desire to be up and about was unexpected, and a bit worrisome. He'd heard of cases where the dying had sudden bursts of energy and seemed to be feeling better just before the end and Paul feared he was running out of time.

"Jeanne Louise is pretty, Daddy," Livy announced suddenly as he poured her a glass of orange juice.

"Yes," he agreed absently, but it made him think of the woman presently chained up in what used to be his office in the basement. She wasn't what most people would classify as beautiful. Her face was a bit round, but her eyes were large and exotic and when she smiled her face was transformed. He'd noticed that the few times he'd seen her smile at Argeneau Enterprises. They were very rare occasions. He had seen her probably a thousand times in the cafeteria over the last few years, but suspected she'd never even noticed him. Mostly she seemed distracted, and frowned over notes as she ate. But every once in a while someone would join her, either one of her coworkers or one of her family members, and she'd smile in welcome, her face lighting up like a Christmas tree.

It was that smile that had always fascinated Paul. The way it transformed her from a plain, serious-looking woman to an unexpected beauty. It made him think she should smile more, that he'd like to see her smile more, *make* her smile more. But he'd never had any excuse to approach her. And in his heart he'd felt unfaithful for even wanting to. He hadn't been long a widower when he'd started at Argeneau Enterprises. Jerri had died just a little more than a month before that, hit by a drunk driver on her way home from work. It had left Paul alone, lonely and juggling work and being a single father. And then he'd finally felt he'd finished his grieving and had mastered being a single father, and had planned to take a vacation, the first he'd had in three years. It was supposed to be a tour of Europe for him and Livy during her summer break. He hadn't had a vacation the last couple years and had managed with some persuasion to get his supervisor to allow him a two-month chunk and . . .

And then Livy had gotten sick. She'd been having headaches the last month or so of school. He'd taken her to the doctor to check it out the week before their trip, just to be sure all was well. Paul hadn't expected anything really to be wrong. He'd thought perhaps she was dehydrated. That could cause headaches, and it was summer, hot and sweaty. The doctor had agreed that was probably the case and had run a battery of tests—blood work and scans. The Thursday before the trip, she'd asked him to take Livy for another scan. That had been slightly concerning, but she'd assured him she just wanted to double check. So Paul had bypassed sleep to take her in during the day. The next morning, the Friday before they were supposed to leave on their trip, his world had crashed down around him.

Paul had been starting his car in the parking garage of Argeneau Enterprises after his last night of work. He'd been whistling happily at the thought of showing Livy English castles and feeding her French food when his cell phone had rung. Recognizing the doctor's name on the screen of his Lexus, he'd hit answer as he'd backed out of his parking spot. The doctor had greeted him solemnly and announced she'd got the results back on all the tests and he should come to her office right away.

Paul had felt the cold clutch of real concern then. It was 7:30 in the morning. He'd hired Mrs. Stuart to watch over Livy while she slept, and had worked the night shift since Jerri's death so that he would be home to have breakfast with her and be available during the day if she needed him. Usually he slept while she was in school and was up by the time she got home in the early afternoon. But it also meant that if she was sick and had to stay home from school, he was there for her. Tired, but there.

The doctor knew his shift and had known he'd just be leaving work and could swing by her office on the way home. What had concerned him was that she wanted him to, that early. Ten minutes later he'd sat in her office, completely numb as she told him his daughter had a brain tumor. The position and size of it made removing it a very deadly proposition. She would most likely die in the operation. Chemo might shrink it, but wasn't likely to. It was one of the more aggressive types and had grown to twice its size between the first round of scans and tests and the second they'd done to verify it a week later.

Paul had listened to that with a blank mind, his brain unable, or unwilling, to take in the information. No doubt understanding that he was in shock, the doctor had told him to go home and to think about what he felt was best for Livy. If he chose the operation, they would book it at once. If he wanted to try chemo to shrink it first, that too would be booked right away. But she obviously hadn't held out much hope for either helping the child.

Paul had driven home, cancelled the flights and reservations for their trips and sat alone in the empty house all day, his brain whirling. Operation. She could die on the table. Chemo. Probably wouldn't work and would just make the child suffer. The end result either way seemed to be her dying before her sixth birthday. It was just a matter of whether she suffered with painful headaches and no treatment, suffered horribly with headaches and the misery of chemo on top of it, or died abruptly with the operation. None of the above had been palatable to Paul. He'd watched his wife die slowly after the car accident, one organ shutting down after another. He simply couldn't do it again with Livy. He refused to lose her.

Paul's thoughts had run around in panicked circles inside his head all day as he'd waited for Livy to come home from her last day of school. And then the answer had come to him, clear and simple. If Livy were immortal she would never get sick, never die.

Paul worked in drug development at Argeneau Enterprises. His job was to help come up with stronger and better tranquilizers to help Enforcers capture and bring in rogue immortals. To do his job properly, he'd had to be brought into the circle of those who knew about these incredible creatures— humans made immortal by bio-engineered nanos programmed to keep them at their peak condition. The nanos attacked anything that threatened their host: colds, flus, diseases . . . cancer. They also repaired injury and reversed the damage caused by aging. The nanos used blood to reproduce and propel themselves, as well as to make their repairs, more blood than a human body could produce, which meant the immortal had to take in blood from an outside source, mortals.

He'd been told that in Atlantis, where these nanos were apparently developed millennia ago, the recipients of the nanos had been given transfusions to meet this need for blood. But when Atlantis fell and the hosts, the only survivors of the catastrophe, had climbed over the mountains and joined the rest of the world, they'd found themselves in a much less developed world where blood transfusions and nanos weren't even yet dreamed of. The hosts had begun to wither and die without the transfusions, and the nanos in response had forced an evolution of sorts, giving them retractable fangs, better night vision, and more strength and speed to make them better predators, able to get the blood they needed.

They'd been forced to hunt and feed off their neighbors and friends to survive. At least until the development of blood banks. He'd been assured they now mostly drank bagged blood. It was less dangerous, less likely to make their presence known amongst the mortals, which was their paramount concern. If mortals knew about them, immortals would either be hunted down and killed out of fear, or captured and locked up for experimentation. Many mortals would be eager to gain the knowledge behind the nanos for themselves. At least, that was what immortals feared. Paul suspected that fear was justified.

Before being hired and given this secret, Paul had been put through rigorous psychological testing and several interviews meant to gauge how much of a threat he might be if he knew their secret. Once ascertaining that he could handle the information without using it against them or being unduly afraid of them, he'd been brought in for a briefing. Then he'd been given extensive counseling and testing to be sure he was handling everything he'd learned. Paul had understood their concerns, but he'd had no desire to blab to everyone about what he'd learned. First off, he'd most likely have been thought mad, and second, the whole thing had fascinated him. He'd wanted to know more, and had learned as much as he could the last several years working at Argeneau Enterprises.

There was much he didn't know, of course. Paul suspected they kept a lot of information from him about their kind. He would have liked to actually study the nanos themselves, but it wasn't necessary for his job so it wasn't allowed. He didn't need to actually study the nanos to develop new, stronger and better tranquilizers and test them on the immortals who volunteered to be guinea pigs.

Paul had tried telling them that he should really study the nanos to be sure he didn't create anything that might kill one of their people. But the response to that had been an amused, "No drug created would kill an immortal." Of course that was the only reason he now had Jeanne Louise locked up in his basement. If he had been given access to nanos at work, he never would have had to take her. Instead he would have tried stealing nanos from the lab. Paul would have preferred that. He wasn't normally the sort to run around kidnapping people to get them to do what he wanted, but he was desperate. This was his Livy. His little angel. The apple of his eye. She was the only reason for his continuing to live the last couple of years since her mother's death. He couldn't lose her too.

"Can I have more?"

Paul blinked, and glanced to see Livy holding out the now empty orange-juice glass. The sight made him smile. Her cheeks had a little color to them and she seemed happy and pain free for the moment. It was a stark contrast to the gray-faced little girl he'd found on returning home. But then she'd been fretting over what Mrs. Stuart had said about God not liking crybabies and not letting her see her mother in heaven. It seemed now as if she'd forgotten all of that. He was glad if she had, and hoped she didn't recall it again.

"Of course," Paul murmured and took her glass to pour more of the juice into it. As he handed it back he asked, "Do you think you could eat something now?"

Livy tilted her head and considered the question. Paul was sure she was about to say no as usual, but then she asked, "Can we have a picnic outside with Jeanne Louise? That would be fun. And I can show her pictures of Mommy."

Paul stilled at the suggestion, quickly considering his options. He wanted Livy to eat and this was the first time she'd shown any interest in food in a couple days. He also wanted Jeanne Louise to get to know Livy. Surely once she understood what a beautiful, sweet child she was, she couldn't refuse to help them. But it would be difficult to picnic with the woman chained up as she was, and he didn't dare unchain her. On top of that there was the concern that she would say something to Livy about the fact that she was there against her will.

"I'll tell you what," he said finally, moving to put the orange juice away. "I'll ask her if she'd like to picnic with us and if she would, we'll join her downstairs. Okay?"

"Okay," Livy said happily.

Nodding, he headed for the door to the basement, adding, "You just stay there and drink your orange juice. I'll be right back."

"Okay," Livy repeated as he opened the door and started down the stairs.

Pulling the door closed behind him, Paul moved slowly down the stairs, trying to think how best to convince Jeanne Louise to agree to a picnic and promise not to say anything about being kidnapped. The only thing he could come up with was begging. Paul wasn't too proud to beg for his daughter. He'd do that and a lot more for Livy, and suspected he would be doing a lot of it until the situation was resolved.

Grimacing, he approached his office, surprised to see that he'd forgotten to close the door when he'd carried Livy out earlier. The office was soundproof, but it only worked if the door was closed. It was one of the things he'd arranged over the last month when he'd decided on his plan. He'd moved his office out of this room because it was windowless, had had it soundproofed, then had moved the hospital bed he'd purchased while his wife, Jerri, had been ill into his office. He hadn't wanted her dying in a cold, sterile hospital. She'd spent the last two weeks of her life in that bed in their home with a nurse and himself tending to her and standing watch.

Paul had also bought chains and had begun taking a little blood from himself every day to build up a supply for Jeanne Louise while she was here. And while he'd done all that, he'd planned and re-planned when and how it was best to take her.

He could have kidnapped her and brought her here a lot earlier if he'd simply robbed a blood bank rather than build up a supply of his own blood, but Paul wasn't a thief and blood banks were already in short supply. His conscience hadn't been able to deal with stealing from a blood bank and risking someone dying because of it. It was all right, though. The added time had given him the opportunity to properly plan kidnapping her. He'd come up with several plans this last month, but the one he'd settled on had been the best.

Jeanne Louise appeared to be asleep when Paul stepped up to the open door, but her eyes opened almost at once and she peered at him solemnly and announced, "Yes, I'll join the picnic."

His eyes widened incredulously. "How did you—?"

"I heard Livy ask you," she interrupted gently. "We have exceptional hearing."

"Oh." Paul stared at her blankly. He'd known they were stronger and faster, but hadn't realized their hearing was improved as well. "What else do the nanos do for you?"

Jeanne Louise shrugged. Mortals working in R and D were briefed on immortals. He would know about the night vision, increased speed and strength, etc. What he wouldn't know about was that they were usually able to read the minds of and even control mortals. Those abilities had been necessary when they'd fed off the hoof, hunting humans and feeding off them. Slipping into their thoughts and keeping them in place while ensuring they didn't suffer any pain had been most useful. As had being able to make them think the small marks left behind were from an accident with open shears or something. Paul didn't need to know this though. To keep him from asking the questions she could see swirling in his eyes, she said, "You'll have to remove most of these chains. I can't eat like this. One around my ankle ought to be sufficient during the picnic. You can always put the others back on afterward."

Uncertainty immediately claimed Paul's expression and then he asked warily, "You're stronger. How do I know you can't just snap the one chain?"

"I can't just snap it like twine," she assured him. "It would take a little bit more effort than a quick jerk. You don't know that for sure, of course, and I could be lying. But if you keep your tranquilizer gun on you, it shouldn't be a problem, should it?" she pointed out quietly.

His eyes narrowed with a combination of confusion and suspicion. "Are you saying you won't try to escape?"

"I can do better than that. I promise you I won't try to escape. At least not until I've heard this proposition of yours," Jeanne Louise said solemnly.

Paul's eyes narrowed. "Why?"

Jeanne Louise hesitated. She simply couldn't tell him it was because he was a possible life mate for her and she hoped to claim him. In the end, she went with, "Because I like Livy."

It was the right thing to say and apparently thoroughly believable to him. He relaxed at once, a small smile curving his lips. "Everyone likes Livy. She's adorable and so smart and funny. She makes the world a brighter place."

Jeanne Louise stayed silent. The man loved his daughter. If she hadn't already figured that out, the way his eyes lit up and his face softened as he spoke of her would have done it.

"Right." He smiled, looking more relaxed than he had since she'd woken up to see him standing over her. "I'll make a picnic for us and then come down and get you. We can have it outside. It's a beautiful sunny day. Livy will like that and—" He blinked and paused, a frown suddenly tugging at his lips. "Oh. I forgot, you can't—"

"I can go out in daylight, I will just have to sit in the shade," she said quickly.

"Really?" Curiosity immediately filled his expression again. "Most immortals work at night. I thought you all avoided sunlight."

"We avoid it to avoid needing more blood, but we can go out in daylight," Jeanne Louise said solemnly.

Paul nodded and she could see a million questions swimming in his eyes, but in the end, he simply said, "You'll have to tell me more during our picnic. I'll go fix sandwiches and stuff for us. You like ham, cheese, and mayo right?"

Jeanne Louise blinked at the question. It was her favorite, but she had no idea how he knew that.

"It's what you usually order in the cafeteria on your first break," he explained and she relaxed. The man had obviously paid attention to the details while planning this kidnapping.

"Yes, I like ham, cheese, and mayonnaise," she agreed quietly.

Nodding, Paul turned to the door. "I'll be as quick as I can."

Jeanne Louise watched until he was out of sight and then laid back and closed her eyes again. This was good. A picnic outside. She suspected he wanted her to get to know and like Livy in the hopes that she'd be more agreeable to turning the girl, but it would also give them a chance to get to know each other better in a more natural setting. She would also be able to see if the other symptoms of life mates were there as well. Or perhaps not, she thought with a frown.

Not being able to read a mortal or immortal was only one sign of a life mate. A resurgence of appetite was another. A lot of immortals stopped bothering with food after the first hundred years or so, but Jeanne Louise was just 102 years old. She still ate, and mostly still enjoyed food, though she had noticed lately that it didn't seem as tasty as it had always been. Which was why she'd been so surprised that the food he'd offered when she'd woken up here had smelled and tasted doubly good. But he may just be a good cook. Cafeterias weren't known for tasty fare and that's where she usually had her breakfasts.

Other appetites awoke in an immortal when they found their life mate as well. Sex for instance, but that hadn't begun to wane yet for Jeanne Louise, so she wasn't sure she'd be able to tell anything at all there. In fact, she was presently casually dating a sweet, smart mortal who was very skilled in that area. So much so that she hardly ever took control of him to encourage him to do the things she liked. Something she disliked doing to begin with, but sometimes couldn't resist in the heat of the moment.

Truthfully, Jeanne Louise wasn't sure spending time with Paul would really help her figure out if he was her life mate. But it couldn't hurt either, she supposed, and wondered how long it would take him to get the picnic together and come back for her. It would be nice to get out of this bloody bed and get outside for some fresh air. By her guess it was midday or, perhaps, mid-afternoon. She doubted anyone would realize she was even missing yet and had to wonder how soon it would be noticed and what would happen then.

Jeanne Louise actually had a date tonight with her mortal that she would obviously be missing. But other than being annoyed and leaving nasty messages on her answering machine, he probably wouldn't do much. She kept her dates apart from the rest of her life, so it wasn't like he'd call her best friend, Mirabeau, or her brothers or father to find out why she hadn't shown up. As for anyone else discovering it . . .

She smiled wryly, knowing that it could be Sunday night, when she didn't show up for work, before her absence was noted. It wasn't that she led a solitary existence. Her father often called or visited on the weekends as did her brothers. At least her oldest brother, Nicholas, and his wife, Jo, often visited. Thomas visited much less though, since he was in England with his Inez. Although when he'd called last week, Thomas had said that Bastien was working on transferring Inez to the Toronto office so that they would be closer to family. Then there was her friend Mirabeau, her cousin Lissianna, her aunt Marguerite, and Rachel, her cousin Etienne's wife. She'd become a good friend since their marriage. Any one of the women might call.

However, they probably wouldn't worry about her not answering for a couple days, which might be a good thing. It would give her time to try to sort out if Paul was a life mate and what to do about it.

Three

"And that's Mommy and me at the family picnic. I was three."

Jeanne Louise smiled faintly at the picture Livy was showing her. The child had been an adorable little cherub at three. Her mother too had been a beauty. Tall, blond, with sky blue eyes, a beautiful smile, and the perfect body. It was enough to depress the hell out of Jeanne Louise. She was not tall, did not consider herself beautiful, and did not have the perfect body. At least not compared to her cousin Lissianna, who she did consider beautiful. Jeanne Louise's lips were a little thinner, her eyes large but almond shaped, and her face tended toward round rather than oval. She was also shorter and with less in the boob department. She didn't think she could compete with the perfection of Paul's first wife, especially when that perfection was a ghost whose beauty would therefore never wither in his memory.

"That's enough of the pictures for now, Livy," Paul said gently. "Set it aside and eat your sandwich, please."

"But I don't want it," Livy said unhappily. "It doesn't taste good."

"But it's tuna, your favorite," Paul said with a frown.

"I know, but it tastes funny," Livy said unhappily and then added a plaintive, "Everything tastes funny now."

Seeing the deepening concern on Paul's face, Jeanne Louise said lightly, "Maybe your taste is changing. Everyone's taste changes. Here, try this." She took half her own sandwich and set it before the girl. "It's ham and cheese. That's my favorite and your dad put on just the right amount of mayonnaise. Not too much, not too little. It's perfect."

When the child hesitated, Jeanne Louise slipped into her thoughts to encourage her and then stayed there, ensuring she took a bite, chewed, and actually enjoyed the bite. The child was all bone; she needed to eat to build up her strength. The turn was a rigorous attack on the body. Livy needed to be stronger to survive it . . . if she was turned.

"Good?" Jeanne Louise asked when Livy swallowed, smiled, and took another bite.

Livy nodded, too busy chewing to answer.

"Thank God," Paul murmured, the words a heartfelt sigh from his lips.

Jeanne Louise merely smiled at him, her concentration on ensuring Livy continued to enjoy and eat her sandwich. When the child finished the first half, Jeanne Louise wordlessly passed her the second half and continued to make her eat.

"Here."

Jeanne Louise glanced to Paul to see him holding out a second sandwich from the picnic basket he'd brought out earlier. It hadn't taken him long to put the picnic together. Then he'd returned to the room and cautiously unchained her and led her outside to a little gazebo in the center of the backyard. He'd used two chains to shackle one ankle to a post of the gazebo. Paul had then covered her with a light blanket to hide the metal tethers. After a hesitation, he'd then assured her he'd be right back and headed for the house.

Jeanne Louise hadn't needed to read his mind to know he'd been worried that she might escape while he was gone. But she hadn't even tried. She'd remained where she was, ignoring the way he kept glancing over his shoulder, and then peering out the kitchen window as he'd gathered the picnic basket and Livy before rushing back out.

The relief on his face when he got back to find her sitting sedately where he'd left her had nearly made her grin, but she'd controlled herself and turned her attention to Livy as the girl had begun showing her pictures of her dear departed mother.

"Thank you," Jeanne Louise said quietly as she accepted his offering. She quickly unwrapped the sandwich and took an absent bite as she concentrated on Livy. But the burst of flavor in her mouth made her blink and her efforts on Livy stutter slightly.

"Is something wrong?" Paul asked, pausing in unwrapping his own sandwich.

"No," she said quickly, returning her attention to Livy. "It's good."

She caught his smile out of the corner of her eye and knew he wanted to point out that she'd told Livy the sandwich was perfect without even trying it first, but he held his tongue. Probably afraid the girl would stop eating, Jeanne Louise thought wryly as she encouraged Livy to finish the last of her sandwich.

"I brought chips too," Paul announced, setting his own sandwich aside to retrieve two bags of chips from the picnic basket—barbecue and sour cream and onion. "I've seen you eat both kinds, but wasn't sure which was your favorite."

"Both are," Jeanne Louise admitted with a faint smile. "Sometimes I prefer barbecue and sometimes the other. It just depends on my mood."

"And which would you prefer today?" he asked, arching one eyebrow.

"Barbecue," she decided.

"And what mood does that mean you're in?" Paul asked with interest.

"In the mood for spicy?" Jeanne Louise suggested absently, her main concentration on Livy still.

"Hmmm," he murmured, and she heard the rustle as he opened the chips.

Livy finished her last bite and Jeanne Louise kept ahold of her thoughts for another moment to ensure the child's stomach wasn't rebelling at being so full, and that all was well, then released her to turn her attention to her own food. Her eyes widened when she saw the small mountain of potato chips on her plate next to the sandwich she'd unwrapped.

"Thank you," she murmured and picked up a chip to pop in her mouth. The explosion of flavor on her tongue this time made her eyes close. Dear God, she'd forgotten how good these were. Or perhaps they just hadn't tasted that good for a while. Her taste *had* been fading, Jeanne Louise realized. But it was definitely back. That thought made her open her eyes again and peer at Paul. He was definitely a possible mate for her then. She didn't know whether to be glad or dismayed. This was not going to be easy, any way she looked at it. The chances were better that everything would go sideways and she would lose Paul than that it would work out.

Realizing Paul was peering at her in question, she forced herself to chew and swallow the now soggy chip in her mouth and then picked up her sandwich.

"Ah ah ah," Paul said suddenly, and Jeanne Louise glanced to him to realize he was speaking to Livy. The girl had picked up her photo album again and was moving closer to Jeanne Louise with it. "Let Jeanne Louise eat first."

"But—" Livy began in protest.

"Why don't you go let Boomer out of the garage?" Paul interrupted. "I put him in there while Mrs. Stuart was here and forgot to let him out again when I got back. He's probably crazy for a run around the yard."

Livy was on her feet and skipping toward the house at once. Jeanne Louise watched her go with a smile and then glanced to Paul with a raised eyebrow. "Boomer?"

"Shih tzu," he said with a faint smile. "I bought him for Livy when Jer—her mother died. She was only three. Shortly after the last picture she showed you. Livy kept screeching 'boom boom' when she chased him around the night I brought him home, so I named him Boomer."

Jeanne Louise grinned at the words, and then gave a startled gasp as a small furry power ball lunged at her, startling and tumbling her backward on the gazebo floor. The fur ball followed, landing on her chest, front paws on her chin as it licked madly at her face with its little pink tongue.

"He likes you! I knew he would!" Livy squealed with delight and Jeanne Louise burst out laughing, and then quickly cut herself off and closed her mouth as the dog immediately turned his attention there.

"Boomer!" Paul said in a voice she suspected was supposed to be firm. However, the effect was somewhat ruined by his laughter.

Realizing it was up to her, she clasped the squirming little body in her hands and eased him gently down to her lap as she sat back up. Boomer wasn't having any of that, however, but kept trying to squirm out of her hold and up to lick her face again. She was vaguely aware of Paul standing and moving off, but he was back quickly and waving a small pink ball in front of the dog's face.

"Fetch," Paul said and then tossed the ball.

Jeanne Louise instinctively released the animal as he launched after it.

"Sorry about that," Paul said wryly, handing her a napkin. "He's an affectionate little thing."

Jeanne Louise chuckled at the words and quickly wiped her face, then glanced around for her sandwich, relieved to see that it still sat where she'd set it at her side, undisturbed by Boomer's arrival. She picked it up, her gaze seeking out Boomer and Livy to see that the girl was throwing the ball for the dog and cooing happily as he fetched it back to her.

"Livy hasn't been this lively for a while. She hasn't eaten much the last week or so either," Paul said quietly, watching his daughter play.

The young girl wasn't exactly jumping around, she was simply standing and throwing the ball, but Jeanne Louise wasn't surprised to hear this was active for the child. If Livy hadn't felt like eating than she wouldn't have had the energy to play at all. They had to get her to eat more.

"She likes you."

Jeanne Louise glanced to Paul at that comment and noted the way he was looking at her. Half intrigued and half calculating. It reminded her of the proposition he had for her.

Shrugging, she picked up half her sandwich and raised it to her mouth, saying, "I like her too," before taking a bite. It was the truth. She did like Livy. The child was sweet and loving and pretty as a doll, or would be once she was fattened up a bit and less worn looking.

"That's good," Paul said seriously, his eyes sliding back to his daughter as she threw the ball for Boomer again and giggled as the dog raced off across the yard after it. It was a large yard with a ten-foot privacy wall made of what appeared to be rose-colored brick all the way around it, which prevented her guessing where they were. She couldn't hear any sounds from beyond the wall that might have told her anything either. For all she knew they could be out in the country or smack-dab in the city.

"Why the wall?" Jeanne Louise asked rather than ask where they were.

"I like to sunbathe in the nude."

The answer caught her so by surprise, Jeanne Louise choked on the bite of sandwich she'd just taken and Paul burst out laughing and quickly thumped her back to help her out.

"Sorry, I couldn't resist," Paul said with a grin as she regained control of herself, and added, "We aren't far from the highway and the wall blocks the sound. Besides, Livy's little, and I didn't want to worry about her playing in the back yard with Boomer."

Jeanne Louise nodded, but avoided looking at him. She knew she was bright red. Besides, if she looked at him she suspected she'd imagine him naked. If she were honest with herself, she already was, which wasn't helping with her blushing, so she steadfastly peered at her plate and ate her sandwich, one bite at a time. It didn't help much with eradicating the image of him naked from her mind though. Damn the man.

"How long have you worked for Argeneau Enterprises?" Jeanne Louise asked as she finished the last of the sandwich. It seemed a nice, safe, non-naked subject.

"Two years and four months now," Paul answered, his gaze still on his daughter. "I started there a little more than a month after Livy's mother died."

Jeanne Louise nodded. "How did she die?"

"She was driving home from work the week before Christmas when a drunk driver blindsided her. Ran her into a telephone pole. She survived a couple weeks; almost to New Year's, but . . ." He let his breath out on a sigh and shrugged unhappily.

Jeanne Louise was silent for a minute, but then steered the conversation away from his beautiful wife by asking, "So Livy is almost six?"

"Six next month," Paul murmured.

He'd watched his wife die over two weeks, and now was getting to watch his beautiful daughter go as well, Jeanne Louise thought solemnly, and could understand the desperation that had led him to kidnap an immortal. Well, if she was right about his motive in kidnapping her, and she was very, very sure she was right, the only question that left was . . . "Why me?"

He glanced to her with surprise. "Why you what?"

"Why did you kidnap me?" Jeanne Louise explained. "There are a lot of immortals working at Argeneau Enterprises. Why me?"

He frowned, watching his daughter briefly, and then admitted, "I don't know. I just . . ." He shook his head helplessly and then glanced to her, looking rather perplexed. "You were the first person to come to mind when I . . ."

Jeanne Louise watched him for a minute, but he didn't finish that thought. She finished it for him in her mind, "when I decided I needed an immortal to save my daughter." He wasn't ready to admit that yet. No doubt he wanted to be sure she really, really liked Livy before he put his proposition to her. In his mind, it would increase his chances of her turning the girl. But then he had no clue what he would be asking of her. Or what he would lose if she did as he wished.

"I had noticed you at work several times," Paul said suddenly, his gaze on his daughter again. "We take breaks at the same time. We've shared lunch, snack breaks, and breakfast without sharing a table for the last almost two and a half years."

Jeanne Louise swallowed, but stayed silent. He had been in the cafeteria three times a day for two

years and four months and she'd never noticed him.
She'd probably walked right past him a thousand
times at Argeneau, never stopping to even glance
his way let alone try to read his mind. If she had . . .
dear God, her life mate had been that close to her
all this time, Jeanne Louise thought, with a combination of horror and dismay.

"You always look so prim and professional from
the ankles up, but you wear the damnedest shoes,"
Paul said suddenly with amusement.

Jeanne Louise blinked at his words and peered
down, but her feet were covered with the blanket hiding the shackles on her ankle. If it weren't,
she'd be looking at black, five-inch high-heeled
shoes with studs on the heels. Damnedest? They
were sexy as all get-out, as were all of the shoes
she bought. But she'd thought they were hidden
by the long pants she always wore. Jeanne Louise
supposed when she sat in the cafeteria with ankles
or legs crossed that her pant legs rode up and the
shoes showed. She'd never considered that. Had
never really thought anyone would even notice.
Apparently Paul had.

"Daddy, can Boomer and I watch that dragon
training movie?"

Jeanne Louise smiled at Livy as she approached
with Boomer on her heels, a frown curving her lips
as she noted the pallor to the girl's face. Slipping
into the girl's mind, she was immediately beset
with a pain that made her flinch and squeeze her
eyes closed. The child had a crushing headache.

Jeanne Louise took a moment to try to adjust to the pain, and then opened her eyes again and set about trying to ease it for the girl. If asked, she wouldn't have been able to explain how she did it, but she used the same technique she'd been taught to use when feeding off the hoof to keep her victims from feeling the pain of her teeth sinking into their necks.

"Do you have another headache, baby?" Paul asked, deep concern obvious in his voice.

"I . . ." Livy frowned, one small hand moving to her forehead as if feeling to see if it was still there, and then she said with surprise, "It was hurting a minute ago, but not now."

"Well . . ." Paul sounded nonplused, but Jeanne Louise didn't glance around, her concentration still on Livy as she continued to work to ease her pain. Unfortunately, being in her thoughts meant that Jeanne Louise was feeling the pain even if Livy now wasn't. It was an unbearable, pounding throb that reverberated through her skull. She didn't know how the child had borne it without weeping and wailing. She wanted to and she was an adult. Biting down on her lip to keep from moaning, she swallowed and tried to ignore the nausea growing in her stomach.

"Well," Paul said again, getting up now. "Perhaps relaxing with a movie is for the best. Yes, you and Boomer can watch a movie."

Jeanne Louise sensed him glancing her way, but was already dividing her attention between trying to keep Livy from suffering and trying to think of how to keep her from feeling it after she'd left her sight. There was no way she knew of. She had to be able to see the girl to continue to control her mind and keep her from feeling the pain.

"Jeanne Louise? Are you all right?"

"Fine," she said tightly.

"You've gone pale," Paul said sounding concerned again. "Do you need—?"

Blood, she supposed he was asking. And apparently he thought her fixation on Livy was because she saw the child as a big snack. At least that's what Jeanne Louise concluded when he suddenly stepped into her line of vision, blocking her view of the child.

Jeanne Louise shifted her eyes to his face, seeing the protective anger there and knew she was right. Paul thought she was eyeing Livy like a big juicy steak. Idiot, she thought, and then tried to see past him to Livy when the child suddenly sucked in a gasping breath. The pain had no doubt hit her full force now that Jeanne Louise wasn't controlling it, and it would have hit like a sledgehammer to the head, she knew.

Fortunately, Paul heard the sound too and moved to the child, allowing Jeanne Louise to see her again. She immediately slipped back into her thoughts and took control once more; quickly removing the pain again. Jeanne Louis ground her teeth as it began to pound at her own mind.

"What is it, honey?" Paul was asking.

"I— N-nothing," Livy said shakily, one hand on her forehead. "It's gone again."

Jeanne Louise saw Paul glance her way out of the corner of her eye, but ignored him. The seconds ticked by like hours as he peered at her and she knew he was trying to work out what was happening. Apparently, he didn't think it was anything good, because he suddenly turned, shifting his body so that his back was to her even as he moved Livy in front of him, blocking Jeanne Louise's view of the child once more and again breaking the connection.

She wasn't at all surprised to hear a moan from the child a bare heartbeat later.

"Livy?" Paul said with concern.

"My head," she groaned miserably.

Jeanne Louise immediately shifted sideways to get a glimpse of the girl again and focus on her thoughts. A second later Livy straightened her slumping body and blinked her eyes with something like confusion.

"It's gone again, Daddy," she whispered as if afraid speaking at all would bring it back.

"Gone?" Paul asked and then glanced over his shoulder toward Jeanne Louise to see that she too had shifted to see the girl.

She was aware of his staring at her, but concentrated on the girl while trying to sort out how best to ease the pain for both of them. Jeanne Louise had no desire to suffer any more than she wanted the child to.

"What are you doing?" Paul finally asked, uncertainty in his voice.

Jeanne Louise hesitated and then forced Livy into sleep. It was the only thing she could think to do at that point. Paul caught the child to his chest with concern as she slid limply against him. He then glanced to Jeanne Louise in question.

"She's sleeping," she said quietly. "She won't feel the pain now. The human body sends out endorphins while sleeping that will prevent her suffering."

"You made her sleep?" he asked uncertainly.

"It was the only thing I could think to do," Jeanne Louise said quietly.

"Will she stay asleep if you aren't with her?" Paul asked with a frown, easing his daughter into his arms.

"She should. If you jostle her and wake her up when you put her to bed, come get me and I'll put her to sleep again," she said simply.

Paul hesitated, but then nodded and stood to carry his daughter into the house. Boomer followed, jogging along at his side, his attention on the sleeping girl as much as Paul's was.

The moment he was gone, Jeanne Louise raised a hand to rub her own forehead. While in the child's mind, she'd suffered the pain as clearly as she knew Livy normally suffered it. That pain had been unbearable. She didn't know how the child handled it. She'd barely been able to stand it herself and she was not only a grown woman, but an immortal. The nanos would have been flushing endorphins into her system to try to ease her discomfort. She couldn't imagine having such repeated, crushing headaches over days, let alone weeks. Surely there was something they could give the girl?

Jeanne Louise lay back on the picnic blanket Paul had spread over the wooden floor of the gazebo. She closed her eyes and rubbed her forehead unhappily as the memory of the pain began to fade. She then turned her attention to what had to be done. She couldn't read Paul and food tasted amazing since she'd woken up chained to the bed. She was 90 percent sure that Paul was her life mate. She just needed that last bit of proof. The food she'd eaten since being here was ten, perhaps even a hundred times tastier than it had been a day ago. If it was the same way with sex with Paul . . .

Well, life mates were said to faint from the sheer passion that overwhelmed them during sex, and she could understand how that might be if sex was a hundred times more powerful too. She would have to find out, and quickly. Jeanne Louise's conscience simply wouldn't allow her to leave Livy to suffer as she was. And she couldn't turn her either. She had to step up her courting. She had to seduce the man and get that final proof that he was her life mate. And then she had to somehow make him love her and agree to spend eternity with her before explaining that she could turn only one, that it would be either Livy or he. But that if she turned him, he could then use his one turn to save his daughter.

If she succeeded at it, everything would be fine. They would be a family. She would have her life mate, and a daughter too. The thought made her smile faintly. It was like a dream come true. Jeanne Louise had not only always wanted a family of her own, she loved children. She'd been feeling a pining for one the last decade or so. But it had worsened with first the birth of Lissianna and Greg's little Lucy, and then with Uncle Lucian and Leigh's announcement that Leigh was pregnant again. While Leigh had lost their first child in the second month, she was now seven months along and mother and child were apparently well. Everyone was waiting eagerly for the child's birth.

Jeanne Louise didn't care that she hadn't given birth to Livy. She would accept her as her own and mother her as best she knew how. Which wasn't really well at all, she supposed. She hadn't a clue how to be a mother, other than what she'd seen with Lissianna and Greg.

Actually, Jeanne Louise realized suddenly, Livy was about the same age as Lucy. They were both beautiful little blondes too, she thought with a smile. They could go through training to feed together, would no doubt be in the same grade, might even end up the best of friends. The fantasy of a happy home life with Paul and Livy was building in her head when the scuff of a foot made her open her eyes. She blinked at the sight of Paul standing over her, his expression grim.

"You have some explaining to do," he said coldly and Jeanne Louise's fantasies of a happy future burst like a bubble.

Four

Jeanne Louise sat up slowly, her expression unperturbed, but her nerves suddenly jangling. He was worried, and his worry was coming out as anger. And he was worried because he didn't understand what she'd done.

"The nanos give us the ability to block a person's pain receptors or make them sleep. I presume it was considered necessary to aid in the hunt for blood," she said calmly before he could ask anything. "While biting them, they won't feel pain, and if we make them sleep, they don't feel the bite either. I did that for Livy to ease her pain."

"You blocked the pain, and then put her to sleep?" Paul asked slowly as if wanting to be sure he had it right.

Jeanne Louise nodded.

"How?" he asked quietly.

She hesitated. While Jeanne Louise knew she had to go into the person's mind to do it, she didn't know much more than that, really. It was sort of instinctual. It didn't matter though, she didn't think it would probably be good to admit that she could go into minds as she did. Finally she gave him a half truth. "I don't know exactly how it's done. It's sort of instinctual. But I have to be able to at least see her to do it. With some you have to actually be in physical contact to manage it."

Paul was silent for a minute, processing that, and then asked, "And her eating the whole sandwich?"

Jeanne Louise hesitated. She knew he was asking her if she'd had anything to do with that, but admitting she had would mean admitting to being able to control minds and she wasn't willing to do that. So, she simply said, "She's obviously ill. Perhaps her illness is affecting her taste buds somehow, like when you get a cold or flu. Nothing tastes the same as it normally does when you're sick. I'd try different foods with her."

Paul relaxed slowly, and nodded, apparently finding that a sensible explanation. Smiling wryly, he said, "I'll feed her ham and cheese sandwiches for every meal if it means she'll eat. She's lost so much weight so fast."

Jeanne Louise remained silent, but wished she could ease some of his concerns. The man had worry lines making grooves in his face and she suspected they probably hadn't been there before Livy got sick. She could ease that worry by suggesting she turn him, and he turn Livy, but then she'd risk spending the rest of her long life alone if he wasn't willing to be her life mate. It might seem selfish to a mortal for her to put her need for a life mate ahead of a child's life, but they were taught from birth to keep a certain emotional distance between themselves and mortals. Each of them would encounter hundreds of mortals they may like, care about, or even love to a degree, but they simply couldn't save them all. They could turn only one and the idea of having to spend centuries or even millennia alone . . . well, it was untenable.

Despite that, Jeanne Louise was tempted to make the offer anyway, but she forced it down and instead asked, "Is there nothing they can give her for the pain?"

Paul shook his head and ran one hand wearily around his neck. "They've given her the strongest dose they dare for her age and size, but it doesn't seem to do anything anymore. The next step is to keep her sedated in the hospital, but . . ."

But he didn't want her warehoused while she died. He wanted to save her, Jeanne Louise finished in her head when he fell silent.

"I guess I should take you back in. I don't want to leave her alone in case she wakes up," Paul said abruptly.

Jeanne Louise nodded and began to pack away the remains of their picnic, her gaze skittering to him when he knelt to help. Once everything was back in the basket and the blanket they'd sat on, as well as the one that had covered her legs, was folded, she stood and waited silently as he quickly unlocked her shackles from the gazebo post. She carried the blankets and he the basket and the end of her chains as they started to walk, and Jeanne Louise couldn't help feeling like a trained dog as they headed for the house. It stirred a slow anger in her, but she forced herself to take several deep breaths, and pushed the anger back down.

This situation was a difficult one, but getting angry wouldn't help at this point. It was another kind of passion she needed now.

"Don't you think you should keep me a little closer to Livy?" Jeanne Louise asked when they entered the house and he turned toward the door to the basement. When he paused to glance at her with a frown, she added, "If she wakes up in pain, I can help her."

Paul hesitated, uncertainty plucking at his brow and Jeanne Louise sighed with irritation. He was worrying about her escaping, of course. And until he learned to trust that she wouldn't, he would continue to think of her as a captive. She needed him to think of her as an ally if she was to woo him.

"I don't think—" he began regretfully.

"What if I promise not to try to leave the house?" she interrupted.

Paul looked torn. He obviously wanted to believe her, but in the end, just couldn't, and started to shake his head, his mouth opening to speak. However, he never spoke the refusal she expected. Jeanne Louise didn't let him. The moment his mouth opened, she dropped the blankets, caught the chain and tugged it from his hold with one hand. In the same moment, she snatched the tranquilizer gun from his back pocket with the other. She didn't even think about what she was doing then, but dropped the chain she'd pulled from him and used both hands to snap the barrel off the end of the tranquilizer gun with a satisfying snap.

Jeanne Louise let the two pieces drop to the floor and then stepped back from Paul, giving him space. She had no desire to scare him or make him feel threatened.

"Jesus, I knew you guys were faster, but . . . damn, you moved so fast you were a blur," Paul said with amazement.

Her voice calm, Jeanne Louise said, "I could have done that at any point over the last couple of hours. The only reason I'm still here now is because I choose to be."

"Jesus," Paul repeated, and then eyed her warily as he took a deep breath. Letting it out, he asked, "Then why are you still here?"

Jeanne Louise hesitated unsure how to answer that. The truth wouldn't do at all. He wasn't ready to hear that he might be her life mate, and she wasn't ready to tell him. First, she needed to be sure he was. And then she needed to see if he was willing to be that life mate, if he could see her as more than a possible way to save his daughter. Jeanne Louise, like every other immortal, had only one turn to use, and while her heart ached for Livy and she sympathized with Paul, she couldn't save every mortal who was terminally ill. She wouldn't give up her turn to just anyone, but had to use it wisely.

Aware that he was waiting for an answer, she finally shrugged and offered an evasive, "Consider it a test."

"A test," he muttered with a frown.

Jeanne Louise nodded.

"What kind of test?" he asked warily.

She bit her lip, but simply said, "You have your secrets and I have mine. Neither of us is ready to reveal them yet. In the meantime, I'm willing to help alleviate Livy's pain so that she can eat and rest and rebuild her strength. I presume you'd like that?"

Paul's eyes widened, but he nodded. "Yes, of course."

"Good. Then can you please remove the shackles from my ankle? They're beginning to chafe."

"Oh." Paul glanced around and then shook his head and reached in his pocket for the key as he knelt by her leg. He shifted her pant legs up and Jeanne Louise bent to hold them out of the way for him as he quickly undid both shackles and removed them.

"Thank you," she murmured, releasing her pant legs and letting them fall back into place as she straightened.

"My pleasure," he said wryly, gathering the chain and shackles and moving to set them on the kitchen table. He hesitated and then glanced toward the refrigerator. "Would you like some blood now?"

"Yes, please," Jeanne Louise responded, her lips twitching at how polite and stiff they both sounded. Good Lord. Nothing was ever easy, was it?

Nodding, Paul moved to the refrigerator and retrieved a jar of the dark crimson liquid.

Jeanne Louise's eyebrows rose when he undid the lid and handed it to her. "What—?"

"It's my blood," he explained quietly. "I used sterilized jars. I didn't have access to a blood bank or anything. I've been bleeding myself for nearly two months to get enough together for you." He glanced back to the refrigerator with a frown and then added, "I hope I have enough. I wasn't sure how much you'd need. They don't give us info like that. Only what we need to know."

"I'm sure you have enough," Jeanne Louise murmured and accepted the jar, then hesitated. She wasn't used to drinking out of a jar. Or a glass for that matter. She tended to just pop a bag to her fangs to avoid tasting it. Not that it was unpleasant to her, but she felt a bit self-conscious about drinking it in front of him.

Turning her back to him, she walked to the window as an excuse to keep her back to him as she quickly downed the beverage. She drank it as quickly as she could, very aware that he stood behind her, probably watching her drink his own blood. Dear Lord.

"More?" Paul asked when she finished and turned back.

Jeanne Louise shook her head and walked to the sink to quickly rinse the jar as if removing the last of the thick liquid would remove the memory of her drinking it from his mind. Watching her drink his blood would hardly paint her as an attractive female, she figured, and grimaced as she then set the jar in the sink. She then turned to peer at him.

"Right." Paul swung toward the door to the hall. "Upstairs."

She followed silently, not terribly surprised when he glanced over his shoulder to be sure she was following behind him.

"We can watch a movie or something if you like while she sleeps," he offered. "What kind of movies do you like?"

"Action adventure, comedies, and horror," Jeanne Louise answered easily and caught the smile on his face as he again turned forward.

"Me too," Paul admitted as he started up the stairs. "I have quite a collection of movies. We should be able to find something we both like in there."

"Sounds good," she murmured as they stepped onto the landing and headed up the hall. He led her past two doors, slowing at the second to glance in on a sleeping Livy, then continued on to an open door at the end of the hall. Jeanne Louise followed him inside and nearly stepped on his heels when he suddenly paused.

"Oh," he muttered, looking suddenly uncomfortable.

Jeanne Louise glanced around the room he'd led her to. It was twice the size of a normal bedroom, with a leather love seat, a wide stool, two end tables, and a 47-inch TV taking up one half of the room, while a king-sized sleigh bed and two end tables filled the other. It was the bed Paul was now staring at with something like dismay.

"I'm sorry," he muttered turning back to her. "I wasn't thinking. I suppose we'll have to watch a movie downstairs and—"

"This is closer to Livy," she said with a shrug and moved nonchalantly to the love seat as if she'd hardly noticed the bed. But it was impossible not to notice the bed. Dear God, it was huge, she thought, and glanced to him expectantly.

"Right," Paul muttered, his gaze sliding to the bed and then skittering away. Straightening his shoulders, he hurried to the cupboard holding the TV and knelt to open the double doors below it, revealing row after row of DVDs. Curious, Jeanne Louise got up again and moved to stand behind him and peer over the titles on display.

"Well, let's see, I have . . . pretty much everything," he said wryly, and then glanced over his shoulder and up at her to explain, "I buy the new releases pretty regularly."

"I suppose you don't get out much, what with Livy being sick," Jeanne Louise said with sympathy.

"No," Paul admitted, turning back to the DVDs. "But I didn't get out much before that either. Not since my wife . . ."

"Is that *Red*?" Jeanne Louise asked to change the subject when he fell silent.

"Yeah." He reached for the DVD.

"I heard it was pretty good," she said.

"It is. I really liked it," Paul said handing it to her to read the back. "Malkovich was amazing in it."

Jeanne Louise nodded and handed it back. "Would you mind seeing it again?"

"No, of course not. I've seen pretty much everything I have," he said closing the doors and straightening.

Leaving him to get the DVD started, Jeanne Louise moved back to the love seat and settled on it, her gaze skittering to the other half of the seat. It wasn't especially small, but it was a love seat, made to encourage closeness and cuddling. Well, she wanted to know about that final indicator, life-mate passion, Jeanne Louise reminded herself. The situation couldn't be better for it. She suspected though that she'd be the one making the first move. Paul didn't have a clue what they might be to each other, or what was in store. She did.

This was definitely a reversal of roles for her. Jeanne Louise wasn't usually the aggressor in these situations. She usually let the men make the moves and do the chasing. Mind you, she did occasionally give a mental push of encouragement to mortal men if she read they were interested and she was attracted to them herself. It saved time. One of the benefits of being immortal, Jeanne Louise supposed. Sadly, she couldn't use that on Paul. She couldn't even read him to see if he was interested. She was as ignorant and uncertain in this situation as a mortal woman would be . . . and she didn't think she particularly cared for it.

"There we go." Paul returned to the love seat, remote in hand. Jeanne Louise offered a smile as he settled beside her and pressed the button to start the movie, or at least the FBI warning at the beginning of it.

They fell into a slightly uncomfortable silence as they waited for the warning to finish rolling over the screen. Paul was staring at it as if the message was one he'd never seen before and needed to read. Jeanne Louise was staring at him, her gaze gliding over his short dark hair, before sliding to his face to take in the slightly weathered boy-next-door good looks.

By her guess, Paul was in his late thirties or early forties. She supposed he'd waited until his thirties to marry and have Livy. It made her wonder if they'd planned to have more children after Livy and fate had intervened, or if she had been all they'd wanted or could manage. Jeanne Louise briefly considered asking, but then decided against it. Bringing up the deceased wife didn't seem a smart thing to do when she planned to try to seduce him in the next hour or so.

Jeanne Louise grimaced slightly at the thought. It was something she was going to have to work up to. It wasn't like she could just throw herself on him now and plant one on him or something. Actually, having left the approach up to men all these years, she wasn't exactly sure what she was supposed to do here. Geez.

"There we go."

Jeanne Louise glanced to the screen at that satisfied mutter from Paul to see that the FBI warning was over and he'd fast forwarded through the movie trailers to the feature presentation. A digital clock face took up most of the screen. She took note of the time, and then smiled as the lead character sat up in bed.

Almost two hours later, Jeanne Louise sat back with a little sigh as the final credits rolled.

"Good?" Paul asked with a smile.

"Excellent, like you said," she responded with a grin.

Paul chuckled and stood to move to the DVD player, saying, "I have to check on Livy, but we could watch something else if you like. "

When he squatted in front of the DVD player, Jeanne Louise moved to join him, dropping to squat at his side as he opened the double doors again to reveal his collection. She glanced quickly over the row of movies, but her mind was on how she was supposed to make moves on him. She'd got kind of distracted with the movie and had lost the plot of what she was supposed to be doing here. The problem was, she didn't have a clue how to start it. Did she just lunge at the man and plant one on him? Was she supposed to say something smooth and seductive and then plant one on him?

Cripes, at that moment she couldn't even recall how the mortal she was presently dating had made his move. As she recalled, he'd just whispered something by her ear as they were dancing and when she'd glanced to him, he'd kissed her. It had seemed so natural at the time. Had he been standing there, holding her in his arms beforehand agonizing over how to do it as she was now? Jeanne Louise hadn't been in his thoughts at the time, so couldn't be sure.

"You're frowning. Is something wrong?"

"No," Jeanne Louise said quickly, and then movement out of the corner of her eye drew her attention. She glanced over to see Boomer entering the room. He padded to her side and pressed against her as she gave him a pet. Continuing to rub his fur, she turned back to the selection available and said, "I'll let you pick this time. I picked the last one."

"Hmm." Paul glanced over his collection as he replaced the *Red* DVD in its case and then shrugged. "I'll pick when I get back."

When he straightened, Jeanne Louise did as well and they both turned toward the door, but Boomer decided he should go as well and apparently he thought the fastest route was between her feet. Jeanne Louise gasped and shifted her step quickly to avoid stepping on the dog, then grabbed wildly for Paul's shoulder to keep from falling as she lost her balance. He paused at once and turned to catch her by both arms, instinctively drawing her against his chest to steady her.

"All right?" he asked with concern. "You didn't twist an ankle or anything, did you? I swear Boomer's gonna end up breaking my leg someday, he's always tripping me up."

"I'm fine," Jeanne Louise assured him with a wry smile as she lifted her head. The smile faded though when she realized just how close they were. His mouth was a bare inch away, close enough she could feel his breath on her lips, close enough to kiss. So she did. She simply leaned a little closer and pressed her lips to his before he could release her or move away.

He was definitely her life mate. Jeanne Louise knew that for sure when the gentle brush of her lips across his set off an explosion of sensation that rocketed through her body, shooting from her lips to every corner of her body.

Judging by the way Paul froze, she wasn't the only one who experienced it. In the next moment, what she should do next was no longer a problem. Paul used his hold on her arms to draw her closer still, and then slid his arms around her as his mouth began to move on hers. Jeanne Louise opened to him at once, her lips parting and her hands clutching at his shirt as his tongue thrust between her lips.

Jeanne Louise had been kissed by a lot of men in the almost 103 years she'd lived. Some had been incredibly skilled. But none had affected her as this one did. The next few moments were a rush of overwhelming sensation as his lips caressed, sucked, and nibbled at hers while his tongue played, and then his lips and tongue slid across her cheek to her neck to do the same there.

A long deep groan slid from Jeanne Louise's lips as his tongue found the hollow above her collarbone. Releasing the death grip she had on his shirt, she slid her fingers into his hair, and then tugged on the soft strands when his hands slid beneath the back of her shirt and up her back. When they stopped at the strap of her bra and then slid back down, nails scraping lightly, she thought her skin would pull itself right off her body to follow.

Dear God, no one in a hundred years had done that, and it felt good. Better than good. His mouth and hands on her, his pelvis pressing against hers . . . her body was reacting like a virgin's: stomach quivering and legs trembling. Even her lower lip was shaking, she realized, as wave after mounting wave of pleasure slid through her, and then she used the hold she had on his hair to drag his head up so she could claim his lips again.

Paul responded at once, his mouth covering hers, more demanding. His hands were kneading the skin of her back now, pressing her closer as they did, and then one hand slid around to find one of her breasts and Jeanne Louise rose up on her tiptoes with a gasp at the first touch. She then groaned into his mouth and pressed closer as he kneaded the soft flesh there through her blouse, her hips shifting and pressing her more tightly against the hardness growing between his legs. The action sent a sharp jolt of pleasure shimmering through her own body that had her shifting against him again.

Cursing, Paul gave up kissing her to pull back slightly as his hand released her breast to find the buttons of her shirt. He was impatient and she was sure he would pop a button or two in his efforts, would even have welcomed it if it would speed things along. But he managed to undo the first four or five buttons and then tugged the white blouse aside to reveal the pale pink bra she wore beneath her silk blouse. His head immediately lowered to allow his tongue to slide across the skin above her bra and then his fingers tugged the soft cup aside, freeing her breast. His lips immediately covered and latched on to her rosy nipple.

Now it was Jeanne Louise who was gasping out a curse and clutching at him as he suckled. The sensations battering her were almost too much to bear, and she groaned, shivered and moaned by turn, worrying that at this rate she'd faint before they got to actually having sex. Her legs were already shaking so badly she was having trouble staying on her feet. When Jeanne Louise sagged against him,

Paul helped her out by slipping one leg between both of hers. The pressure of his thigh against the very core of her was nearly her undoing.

Crying out, Jeanne Louise nipped at the skin of his shoulder, then turned her head and did the same to his neck, having just enough sense to keep her fangs in as she did. Paul nipped at her nipple in response, startling a yelp out of her, and then raised his head to claim her mouth again. His tongue thrust between her lips as his hand replaced his mouth at her breast, his fingers finding the erect nipple and tweaking it as he urged her backward.

She felt the wall press against her back. His body was pressing tight against her front, pinning her to that wall and Jeanne Louise was grateful for it. Her legs definitely weren't going to keep her upright much longer. Her hands had taken to clutching at his shoulders to help hold herself up, but now she moved them between them, running them over his chest, then finding the hem of the T-shirt he wore and pulling and pushing it up his stomach so her hands could slip beneath and run over the flesh there. She then slid them up to his chest, each finding a pec and kneading briefly before her fingers centered on his nipples and squeezed them.

The action brought a groan from Paul that reverberated between her lips, and then she groaned too as another wave of pleasure rolled through her. They were growing with each pass, building to the point where she felt sure they couldn't get stronger, and yet each wave was bigger still until she was sure she would drown under the foaming surf. It scared her, but it was also irresistible.

Jeanne Louise had never understood why the French called it the *petite mort*, or "small death." But she thought she might now, and wanted to experience it so badly in that moment that she thought she'd die without it. That goal her only thought, she raised her own leg now trapped between both of his and rubbed her upper thigh against his hardness. She was rewarded with another groan and another wave of passion rolling through her that just egged her on.

"Daddy?"

Jeanne Louise heard that soft call and froze. The fact that Paul didn't stop told her that he hadn't heard with his mortal hearing. She slid her hands back out from under his shirt with regret and caught his head between her hands to force him away. He peered at her blankly, blind with passion, and Jeanne Louise opened her mouth to explain, but Livy's call came again, a little louder.

"Daddy?"

Paul stiffened, the passion clearing at once and then he pulled away and hurried from the room.

Jeanne Louise sank back against the wall with a weak sigh. Damn. He'd snapped out of that in a hurry while she was still trembling and shaking like a cat who'd just had a brief dunking in a washing machine. The power of parenthood, she told herself, struggling not to be offended. The child was seriously ill, after all. Of course Paul would rush to her side rather than continue what he was doing. But damn, his head had cleared a hell of a lot quicker than hers.

Sighing, Jeanne Louise slipped her bra back into place, tugged her blouse shut, closed her eyes and took a couple of deep breaths. The good news was she now knew for sure that Paul was her life mate. She'd not only never experienced passion as heavy and hot as that in her life, but they'd also definitely been experiencing the "shared passion" everyone spoke about. The passion merging and running back and forth between them, growing stronger with each pass until she'd thought she'd die if it wasn't consummated.

And that was more good news, Jeanne Louise supposed, they'd been interrupted before she could experience the *petite mort* immortal style. Now she just had to see if Paul would be willing to be her life mate . . . and not just to save his daughter's life.

Grimacing, she took another steadying breath and then straightened, grateful when she was able to stand on her own. Her legs were still a little shaky, but some water on her face and wrists would help with that, she was sure. They would also hopefully bring an end to the tremble in her hands so she could manage doing up her buttons. With that thought in mind, Jeanne Louise glanced around and then spotted the door at the end of the room beside the bed. Moving to it, she opened it, half expecting to find herself in a walk-in closet. Instead the door opened into a large bathroom in cream and Indian brown.

Eyebrows rising, Jeanne Louise entered, her gaze sliding over another open door to her right, this one to an attached walk-in closet. She peaked inside briefly, then turned to survey the bathroom, taking in the marble counter with his and hers sinks, the toilet, the large tub, a shower big enough for two and then the door to what appeared to be a sauna. Walking to it, she opened the door and glanced curiously inside.

Yep, a sauna.

Jeanne Louise eased the door closed and moved to the sinks to turn on the cold water. She'd splash some water on her face and arms and then go see how Livy was doing. She hadn't sensed any pain in the girl's voice when Livy had called out, and suspected the headache was gone, but it had been a couple hours since lunch and if they could get her to eat again it would only be a good thing. She would control her and have her eat as often as possible to help her rebuild her strength for the turn.

Not that Jeanne Louise was entirely sure things were going to work out. Yes, Paul was her life mate, and yes, she was pretty sure that he'd been seconds from tearing her clothes off, throwing her on the bed, and taking her to the *petite mort*, but that didn't guarantee anything. The situation was a complicated one. It might all still crumble like a house of cards.

Sighing, Jeanne Louise turned off the taps and reached for the towel on the rack beside her to dry her face and hands. She then set it back and quickly did up her blouse before heading out in search of Paul and Livy.

Five

'I liked that horse,' Livy announced as her father stood and moved to the DVD player to eject the disc and put it away. "But I think I'd rather have a dragon like the black one, 'cause he was nice, wasn't he, Jeanie?"

"Yes, he was, Livy," Jeanne Louise agreed, smiling faintly. She had come out of the bathroom earlier to find Paul entering the bedroom with Livy in his arms. He'd settled the girl on the love seat, started the "dragon training" movie for her and then had asked Jeanne Louise if she'd mind sitting with Livy while he slipped away to fetch them some snacks.

She hadn't minded at all. She'd settled on the love seat next to the girl, and found herself getting wrapped up in the movie herself. It wasn't until Paul had returned with the drinks and popcorn that she'd pulled herself out of the movie at all, and then it was just enough to help Livy eat and drink and enjoy it.

They'd watched this second cartoon movie about Rapunzel afterward. That one had featured a rather intelligent and funny horse and they'd all laughed a great deal over the movie.

"I don't know," Paul said putting the DVD away. "I kind of liked the little salamander myself."

"Ewww," Livy said instinctively, then wrinkled her nose and said judiciously. "He was nice, but you can't pet a salamander, Daddy."

"Hmmm." Paul straightened and then turned and raised an eyebrow at his daughter. "Another movie or are you ready for dinner?"

"I think I'm hungry," Livy announced, sounding surprised, and then her eyes widened and her mouth formed an O.

"What?" Paul asked, smiling.

"Can we go to Chuck E. Cheese's, Daddy?" she asked, slipping off the love seat where she'd been cuddled between Jeanne Louise and Paul for more than five hours. She nearly stepped on Boomer as she went, but the dog was quick about getting out of her way and yipped excitedly in response to her own obvious excitement. "I like Chuck E. Cheese's. You'd like it too, Jeanne Louise. They have games and rides and—Oh it's so fun!" She whirled back to her dad excitedly, Boomer dancing around her feet. "Please! We haven't been there for a long time. Can we go?"

Paul stared at her, wide-eyed and obviously torn. Jeanne Louise could tell he wanted to say yes, but worry was making him hesitate. Whether it was worry for Livy or worry that Jeanne Louise might use it as an opportunity to leave, she didn't know.

"How long has she been cooped up in the house?" she asked quietly.

His gaze slid to her, silent and solemn.

"And you've probably spent most of your time here with her," Jeanne Louise commented. "I don't think an outing to Chuck E. Cheese's would be a bad thing. We could go, have pizza and then come back."

Paul relaxed, getting the silent message she was trying to give him. She would return afterward with them. He nodded, murmuring, "Thank you," and then glanced to Livy. "Chuck E. Cheese's it is then."

"Yay!" Livy did a little dance and then turned to grab Jeanne Louise's hand to try to pull her off the love seat. "Come on. Let's go before he changes his mind. You're going to love Chuck E. Cheese's. It's so fun. And the pizza's good too."

Chuckling, Jeanne Louise stood and allowed the still chattering child to tug her from the room and toward the stairs, aware that Paul was following with Boomer on his heels. They headed right out to the car, pausing just long enough to let Boomer loose in the backyard before going.

"I haven't seen her like this for quite a while," Paul said quietly, his eyes following his daughter as she played with several other children in the play section. He smiled wryly. "I guess it's only been weeks, but it feels like forever."

"It's good for her," Jeanne Louise said quietly, her concentration on the girl. A headache had begun to descend on Livy shortly after they'd arrived and she'd been working to mask it ever since.

"Yeah." She sensed his glancing her way and tried to appear normal, but knew she'd failed when he asked with concern, "Are you all right?"

Jeanne Louise gave a nod, not looking his way.

"You're pale and pinched. You're masking her pain again, aren't you?" he asked and she could hear the frown in his voice.

Sighing, she nodded reluctantly.

"How long?" Paul asked.

Jeanne Louise hesitated, but then admitted, "A headache started to develop shortly after we got here."

Paul cursed. "You mean you've been masking her pain for the last hour and a half?"

Jeanne Louise wrinkled her nose. Was that all it had been? It felt like three hours. First they'd played video games and such, then they'd eaten, then Livy had rushed off to play with the other children. An hour and a half? God.

"You should have said something," Paul said, sounding cross.

"She was having fun," Jeanne Louise said helplessly. "I suspect she hasn't done that for a while."

"No, she hasn't," he agreed solemnly. "Still . . ."

She heard him sigh, and then sensed him standing and moving away. A moment later she saw him approach Livy and speak to her, then urge her back toward the table.

"I know you were having fun, sweetheart. But we can come back another day. We have to go home now. It's getting late," Paul was saying as he led his daughter back to Jeanne Louise. Once at the table, he quickly pulled out his wallet to pay the bill, then lifted Livy up with one arm under her bottom and glanced to Jeanne Louise. "She can sleep on the way home."

She nodded with relief and made the child sleep. Livy sagged against her father, her head dropping to rest on his shoulder. Jeanne Louise stayed in her thoughts long enough to allow the girl's endorphins to do their work, and then slipped out. The immediate absence of pain was like a vacuum after suffering it for so long, and Jeanne Louise swayed in her seat. Paul immediately stepped closer and grasped her upper arm to steady her with his free hand.

"Are you all right?" he asked with concern.

Jeanne Louise took a deep breath and nodded, wincing when it made the dull ache that remained in her head increase a bit. She now had a headache of her own, probably from her constant tension while fighting Livy's pain, she supposed. The nanos would take care of it quickly enough, she told herself as she stood up. "I'm fine. Shall we?"

Paul walked her out, his hand on her arm the

entire way. Jeanne Louise didn't think it was because he feared her fleeing at this point, so supposed she must look as drained and pained as she felt. The fact that he was eyeing her with concern, as if expecting her to suddenly keel over at any moment, seemed to back that up.

Once at the car, Jeanne Louise opened the back door for him and slipped into Livy's mind to keep her from waking up as he settled her in the backseat and did up her seat belt. She was glad to slip back out a moment later as he straightened and closed the door.

Jeanne Louise started to open her own door then, but Paul stopped her by placing his hands on her shoulders and beginning to massage the tense muscles there. It brought a groan from her and she let her eyes close and her head loll as the tension slowly eased from her muscles.

"Thank you," she murmured after a moment, and then blinked her eyes open and peered at him with surprise when he released her neck to cup her face.

"No. Thank *you*," he said firmly, meeting her gaze. "I know it causes you pain to help her. And I do appreciate it. She would too if she knew." Paul closed his own eyes briefly, then let out a slow breath and opened them again to say, "Livy hasn't been this happy in a while. Thank you for that."

Jeanne Louise smiled weakly and raised her hands to cover and squeeze his, saying simply, "You're welcome."

He nodded, and then bent to press a kiss to her forehead before releasing her and opening the front passenger door for her. Jeanne Louise slid in and did up her seat belt as he walked around to the driver's side.

They were both silent on the ride back to the house. Jeanne Louise had no idea what Paul was thinking, but her own mind was taken up with thoughts of him. She'd earned his gratitude. It was a start, but she wasn't sure if it was a good start or not. She didn't want his gratitude. They couldn't be equal partners if he felt he owed her something. Jeanne Louise wanted him to want her, to want to be with her, to enjoy her company. Not to think of her as someone he owed a debt to. Unfortunately, the situation wasn't lending itself to that.

She was frowning over that when they turned onto his street. Jeanne Louise glanced along the row of houses and then sucked in a breath as she spotted two dark SUVs parked in front of Paul's house.

"Pull in here," she barked at once and Paul glanced at her with surprise.

"What?"

"Do it," Jeanne Louise hissed and wished for the first time that she could just slip into his thoughts and take control of him to make him do it. Fortunately, something of her urgency made him obey and he pulled into the driveway she'd indicated.

"What is it?" Paul asked, his gaze sliding to his neighbor's house as he braked the car in their driveway.

Jeanne Louise peered out the window past him to the SUVs. They looked empty. She bit her lip and then leaned in front of Paul to let her gaze inspect his yard and house. She watched silently for a moment and then straightened abruptly when she saw movement inside through the front window.

"Go back the way we came," she said firmly, settling back in her seat, her brain racing.

Paul hesitated, but then shifted into reverse and backed out of the driveway to head back up the road the way they'd come. When he reached the corner, he simply asked, "Which way?"

Jeanne Louise pulled herself from trying to figure out how they'd found her so quickly to consider the question. Finally, she sighed, "I don't know. Just take a right for now."

He turned right, and started up this new street, but glanced at her in question. "The SUVs?" Paul asked and when she hesitated over answering, he said, "I didn't notice them at first, but there were two of them. Black with black windows. I've seen them at Argeneau Enterprises."

"They're what the Enforcers drive, the equivalent of our police force," she explained quietly. "They must have figured out you have me and came looking for us."

Paul hesitated, but then said, "I was very careful."

Jeanne Louise considered that claim briefly and then queried, "You were in my car when I got in?"

He nodded.

"When did you get in?" she asked.

"About two minutes before you got in. I rode to Argeneau's in the trunk of Lester's car. A co-worker," Paul explained. "He didn't know. I waited in the trunk all night, then slid out and got in your car just before you got to it."

"They would have seen that on the parking garage cameras," Jeanne Louise pointed out.

"Yeah, but all that would do is lead them to Lester, and he had no idea I was in his trunk. He couldn't point them my way."

"Maybe they recognized you," she suggested.

"I was wearing all black and a balaclava. There was nothing to recognize," he assured her, and she recalled the dark shape rising in the rearview mirror. A mere silhouette of a person.

Jeanne Louise was silent for a minute and then asked, "What did you do with my car?"

"I'd parked my car at the back of a grocery store parking lot near Lester's apartment building. I drove your car back there, moved you to my car and left your car there, then brought you home."

"Did you check to see if there were security cameras in the parking lot?"

He hesitated. "I didn't see any. But even if there was one that I didn't see, I doubt they've found your car yet. It's a big busy grocery store and it hasn't even been twenty-four hours yet."

Jeanne Louise blew her breath out on a sigh. "If security saw you get in my car and me drive away with you, someone would have been sent to check on me. When I didn't show up at my place they would have started looking for me. There's a tracker in my car. Uncle Lucian made all of us put trackers in our cars."

"So they would have found your car pretty quick," Paul said with a grimace, and then shook his head. "Still, I did look to be sure there weren't any cameras in the parking lot. And I was wearing gloves when I drove your car, so no fingerprints. How could they have traced it back to me?"

She shook her head, and then asked, "Was I in the front seat or back of your vehicle? I mean, was I visible?"

"Front seat," he answered. "I strapped you into the front passenger seat. After spending the night in the trunk of a car I didn't want to put you there, and in the front seat it just looked like you were asleep. I figured a woman sleeping in the front seat would be less noteworthy than a woman passed out in the backseat."

Jeanne Louise nodded wearily. "That's probably how then. All they had to do was check any nearby traffic cameras for the time period when you would have reached and left the grocery store parking lot from Argeneaus. If there was even one that caught you driving by with me in the passenger seat they'd have gotten your license plate number from it." She shrugged. It was the only thing that made sense. His car had been caught on camera with her unconscious in the front seat. They'd checked the license plate and traced it back to Paul.

She supposed they had just been lucky that it had taken this long for them to be tracked down. Had the immortal Enforcers arrived at the house before they'd left for Chuck E. Cheese's, or even after they'd returned . . . Jeanne Louise grimaced at the thought. Had that happened, Paul would probably be locked up in a cell at the Enforcer house right now while her uncle decided what to do with him. She'd like to think Uncle Lucian would try to help her claim her life mate, but he was a bit of a stickler about certain things . . . like kidnapping an immortal with the intention of forcing them to turn a mortal. Yeah, that so wasn't going to go over well.

"I'm guessing we can't go home," Paul said quietly.

"Not unless you want to be taken into custody and locked up," she said on a sigh.

He nodded, his expression solemn. "So a hotel?"

Jeanne Louise sank back in her seat and rubbed her forehead wearily. The renewed tension had brought the fading headache back. It shouldn't. The nanos weren't eradicating it for her as they normally would. It didn't take a great deal of thinking to figure out why. She'd only had the one pint of blood in almost twenty-four hours, but the nanos had been working hard, first to remove the effects of the tranquilizer he'd given her, and then to ease her own pain as she'd suffered with Livy. She was probably in need of another good three pints of blood at that point. Low on the life-giving substance, the nanos were picking and choosing what to deal with and apparently a little tension headache wasn't on the top of their priority list.

"You're pale still. You need blood, don't you?" Paul asked quietly.

Jeanne Louise waved that away. There was no blood available at the moment. It would have to wait. Breathing out through her nose, she thought briefly, and then said, "I suggest heading out of town. They'll have hunters looking for your vehicle when we don't return to the house."

"Hunters?" he asked with a frown.

"Enforcers," she corrected herself, not wanting to explain about Rogue Hunters. That might lead to just how much trouble he was in. She didn't want to get into all that right now.

Paul was silent for a minute and then said solemnly, "We get volunteers to test the tranquilizers on. A couple of them have mentioned being hunters. Rogue Hunters, I think they said." She sensed him glancing her way. "Those are the Enforcers? The immortal version of cops you mentioned?"

Jeanne Louise nodded reluctantly.

"And they'll be looking for us because I kidnapped you?"

She sighed and explained, "Their main job is to take care of any immortals that go rogue and hurt mortals or do anything that might draw attention to our existence. But they also deal with mortals who find out about us and use that knowledge . . . inappropriately," she finished uncomfortably.

"Like by kidnapping one of you," Paul said quietly and then took a deep breath and asked, "I don't suppose the fact that you are actually staying willingly now would help my case much?"

"I'm afraid not. It won't negate the fact that I was originally taken against my will in the council's opinion. At least I don't think it would and we shouldn't take that chance. The repercussions for such a thing would probably be pretty steep," Jeanne Louise said quietly.

"How steep?" Paul asked, worry knitting his brow now.

Jeanne Louise hesitated. She wasn't sure just how the council would punish a mortal in this instance. It wouldn't be lightly though. It would have to be something that would make a statement and discourage all the other mortals who knew about them from getting such ideas. That being the case, death was a possibility, but it was more likely that they would do a three on one and wipe his mind, then dump him in a psychiatric facility somewhere to live out his days in a drugged, mindless haze. When she admitted as much to Paul, his jaw dropped with horror, but his first question was, "What about Livy? What would they do to her?"

"She wouldn't be punished for your actions," she assured him quickly.

"But what would they do with her?" he asked insistently.

Jeanne Louise shrugged helplessly. "They would probably place her with the family of a mortal who works for Argeneau Enterprises."

"Not for long," Paul said grimly.

Knowing he was thinking of her cancer and that he was probably right, Jeanne Louise didn't comment at first. However, when she realized he'd taken the on-ramp to the highway, she asked, "Have you thought of somewhere to go?"

"I have a cottage up north. It's a four or five hour drive, but—"

"That's no good. By now they probably know every piece of property you own and have people watching them," she interrupted and was aware of the sharp startled glance he sent her way.

"Seriously? They can get that kind of information this quickly?" he asked with disbelief.

"Paul, they can find out anything a mortal enforcement agency can find out, and probably quicker," Jeanne Louise said solemnly.

"How? Surely they don't have access to police databases and such," he protested.

"They can get access to anything they want," she said quietly.

"How?" Paul repeated.

Jeanne Louise just shook her head. "I'll explain later. Right now we need to think of somewhere to go that you don't own. We can't just keep driving around."

"Right," he muttered, his gaze on the highway ahead. After a moment, he suggested, "Well, we could take a hotel room somewhere and—"

"They can track your credit cards."

"Jesus," Paul muttered. "I only have twenty or thirty bucks on me."

"Did you leave my purse in my car?" she asked. She hadn't seen it since awaking in his basement.

"Yes," he admitted with a frown.

Jeanne Louise considered that briefly, and then asked, "How much gas do we have?"

Paul smiled faintly at the question. She suspected it was because she'd used the word *we*, making them a team. His gaze slid to the gas gauge and he said, "Half a tank."

"Then I suggest you hit a gas station somewhere between Chuck E. Cheese's and the house, and then hit an ATM in the area too. It won't tell them which way we might be headed in when we don't show up at the house."

"Good thinking," he murmured and shifted into the right lane to take the next off-ramp.

The next half hour was tense. Jeanne Louise spent the entire drive and then the time at the gas station expecting a dark SUV to pull in front of them and force them to a stop. She waited in the car while Paul rushed to use the ATM next, her eyes constantly searching the surrounding area for any sign of a dark SUV or vehicles belonging to her father and brothers. It was a relief when the passenger door opened and Paul slid back in. At least she was relieved until he said, "I just thought . . . Boomer's still at the house."

"They'll take care of him," Jeanne Louise said

reassuringly. "They'll take him back to the Enforcer house and look after him until we're found or this is resolved.

He nodded, but looked worried still, and then glanced to Livy, asleep in the back. "She won't be happy he isn't with us. That dog hasn't been out of her sight for more than a few hours since we got him. The only time they're apart is when she's at school. Or it was when she still went to school," he added wearily.

Jeanne Louise frowned now too. She didn't know what brought on the headaches with Livy, but getting upset might bring them on harder or more often. If that was the case, she didn't want the child upset. She was willingly taking on the girl's pain to spare her, and had every intention to continue to do so, but it wasn't pleasant and if some of that pain could be spared by getting the dog . . .

Shaking her head, she asked, "What's behind your house?"

"Other houses from the next street over. Why?" Paul asked curiously.

"We'll have to get Boomer. We'll have to park on the road behind yours. You can wait here with Livy while I fetch Boomer."

He frowned. "That's kind of risky, isn't it?"

"They'll be watching for your car. They won't bother about the dog in the backyard." *I hope*, Jeanne Louise added silently.

Paul hesitated, but then nodded. "Thanks," he murmured, starting the engine.

Jeanne Louise just nodded, trying to figure out in her mind how best to get the dog. She was trying to remember the setup of the backyard and figure out where it was best to hop the fence. Hopefully the animal was still in the backyard and they hadn't taken it into the house. And hopefully he'd come to her call. And hopefully no one would happen to spot her. Geez, Jeanne Louise couldn't believe she was taking this risk. But really, she'd do anything to minimize the pain Livy, and therefore she, suffered. Frankly, she was a big wuss when it came to pain.

"Keep the engine running," she said quietly, reaching for the door as Paul pulled to the side of the residential street behind his own.

"Maybe I should go," Paul said, putting his hand on her arm to stop her as she started to get out. "I don't know the people who live here and they might—"

"I'll handle the neighbors," Jeanne Louise assured him calmly, pulling her arm free. Getting out, she repeated, "I'll just be a minute. Be ready to leave the minute I get back in case I'm spotted and chased by one of the hunters."

She saw the worry increase on his face, but just closed the door and turned to start up the driveway of the house he'd stopped in front of. A high wooden fence ran around this house, starting at the garage and going around the backyard before coming back around and stopping at the side of the house. It was only six feet tall though compared to

Paul's taller wall and she could see the wall beyond it. She was approaching the gate rather than the house itself, but heard the front door open. Turning, she smiled at the man who stepped out to eye her suspiciously.

"Everything's fine, go back inside and watch the television," Jeanne Louise said, slipping into the man's mind to ensure he followed the order.

He nodded, smiled, then turned and walked back inside. Jeanne Louise didn't hesitate then, but continued to the fence. She tried the gate, not surprised to find it locked from the inside. Nothing was ever simple, she thought and glanced around to be sure no one was looking except for Paul, then leapt over the fence in one smooth move.

Jeanne Louise grunted as she landed on a concrete sidewalk inside the walled yard. The landing sent a jolt through her, but she ignored it and immediately jogged to the back fence. On the way here she'd debated different approaches. Hopping the fence, grabbing the dog and hopping back again would have been the easiest route. But while it was almost eight o'clock, it was summer, still bright daylight out. There was too much risk of being spotted by one of the hunters inside the house and pursued. There was also the risk of any one of the neighbors happening to see her hopping the fence. A slender woman in business clothes hopping a ten-foot wall as if it were knee high would draw attention. She'd had to come up with an alternate plan.

Grimacing, Jeanne Louise knelt in the rose

garden that ran along the back fence and began digging at the muddy earth. Apparently the garden had been watered not long before her arrival; the dirt she was digging was mud. Great, she thought, but continued to dig.

Much to her relief it didn't take long. While the wooden fence ran up the sides of the yard, they hadn't bothered with it across the back. Paul's wall offered all the privacy needed there and its retaining wall was only buried a few feet in the ground. With her increased speed and strength, she had a three-foot-wide and three-foot-deep hole dug pretty fast, even with just her hands to work with.

Once Jeanne Louise had dug what she considered to be far enough down, she lay down in the garden to work her arm inside the hole and started digging under the wall itself, scooping out the dirt quickly and impatiently. She had broken the surface on the other side before it occurred to her that she should have called for Boomer to be sure he was still in the backyard. With the next swipe of her hand, though, she heard an excited yip from the other side of the wall and felt one paw swipe at the back of her hand trying to catch it in passing. Boomer was in the backyard.

Jeanne Louise picked up speed then, afraid that Boomer's interest might draw the attention of someone in the house. It only took another moment before she'd dug out a space big enough for the animal to climb down through, which he did at once, wiggling eagerly under the wall and waddling up in the garden to leap at her face, tail wagging and tongue swiping at her cheeks.

"Good dog," Jeanne Louise breathed and stood quickly to hurry back across the yard, her ears straining for any sound from Paul's yard to warn her that someone had noticed something was amiss. When she hadn't heard anything by the time she reached the gate again, Jeanne Louise was sure her actions had gone unnoticed. Clasping the wiggling dog to her chest, she hopped the fence as she had on the approach, then jogged to the car and slid in.

Paul pulled away at once, his attention between the road, her, and the fence she'd just hopped, as if he half expected to see someone come running after them.

"I think we're good," she said, patting Boomer to try to get him to settle in her lap. The dog was desperately torn between trying to lick her face and trying to crawl into Paul's lap, but she held onto the cute little creature and just kept stroking him. "I don't think anyone noticed or followed."

Paul relaxed a little, his attention now only shifting from the road to her and occasionally the rearview mirror. He then cleared his throat, and asked, "Umm . . . Just how exactly did you get him?"

"I tunneled under your wall. I thought it was safer than hopping it and possibly being seen," she admitted.

"Ah," Paul murmured, and she glanced at him sharply, noting that his lips were twitching.

"Ah?" Jeanne Louise asked suspiciously. The man was trying not to laugh. "Ah what?"

He glanced to her, then away and cleared his throat, "That explains why you and Boomer look like you've been mud-wrestling."

Jeanne Louise glanced down at herself and the dog and sighed. Boomer's fur was matted with mud from wiggling under the wall. She was also mud-covered. Her hands and arms were the worst; they were coated with quickly drying mud, and the rest of her wasn't much better. Her white silk blouse was wet and muddy, probably ruined, and her dress pants were caked as well. She'd been first kneeling and then lying in the muddy garden after all.

"You can't be comfortable like that," Paul said quietly. "We'll have to stop and get you a change of clothes. Maybe we could rent a hotel room long enough for you to shower."

"A change of clothes will do," Jeanne Louise said quietly. "We shouldn't risk a motel until we're farther away from Toronto. In fact, I don't think you should stop for clothes here either. I can stand it for an hour or so."

"An hour away north or south?" he asked with a frown.

"Do you have any property in the south?" she asked. When he shook his head, she shrugged. "Then south."

"An hour southwest on the Highway 427 will take us to the Kitchener/Waterloo/Cambridge area," Paul announced.

"That's good enough," Jeanne Louise decided. There were a few immortals who she knew lived in the area, but then there were few places where there weren't at least one or two immortals anymore. They would just have to be careful.

Paul nodded and for the next few minutes they were silent as he concentrated on getting them to and onto Highway 427 headed southwest, and then they both relaxed a little. After a moment, he said, "Thank you for helping Livy."

Jeanne Louise noted the solemn gratitude on his face, and glanced away with a shrug. "She has to eat."

"Yes, and I appreciate your seeing to it that she does," he murmured. "I know it causes you pain to help her."

Jeanne Louise didn't comment, her gaze on Boomer as he finally gave up trying to lick her and curled into a ball on her lap to sleep.

"I'm sorry it took me so long to realize what was happening. I noticed that your face was pale and pinched while we were at Chuck E. Cheese's. But I wasn't sure what was happening. I thought maybe you just needed more blood," he said quietly. "And then I recalled that it got the same way when she was having her headache in the yard and it stopped." Paul paused for a minute, and then asked delicately, "To make her not feel it, you have to?"

Jeanne Louise sighed and shrugged her shoulders. "I have to be in her head and that's where the pain is. To mask it I have to stay there."

"You said it's instinctual, that you do the same

thing when biting people . . . so when you bite people you feel their pain too?"

"That pain isn't in their head. Usually it's in the neck," she murmured, and then frowned and said, "Although pain receptors are in the head." Jeanne Louise puzzled over that briefly and then admitted, "I don't know how it works, Paul. Like I said, it's instinct more than anything else."

"*Usually* it's in the neck?" Paul asked, sounding perplexed. "Are there other places you can bite?"

"Sure, anywhere the veins are strong and close to the surface. The crook of the elbow, the wrist, the genitals, the ankle . . ." She shrugged. "There are loads of places you can bite a person."

"The genitals?" Paul asked with disbelief.

Jeanne Louise grimaced, aware that she was suddenly blushing, but said, "Some used to swear it was the best place to bite. No one is likely to see the marks."

"Right," he muttered, and then fell silent for a while. She suspected he was thinking about her biting someone in the genitals. Men tended to have one-track minds, at least the men she'd read did.

"Do you want an aspirin or something?" Paul asked suddenly. "I think I have a bottle in the glove compartment. Or if you need something stronger, the bag in the backseat has Livy's meds, including some pretty powerful ones for pain." He frowned and added in a mutter, "Though they don't help her much."

"No, I'm okay," Jeanne Louise assured him. It

wasn't completely true. Her head still hurt, but mortal medicines weren't likely to help. The nanos would just see them as foreign substances to be removed from the body, which would use up more blood and no doubt increase her discomfort. She'd have to feed soon though if she wanted to be pain free, and she'd have to do it off the hoof. She would actually have to bite a mortal to feed, a practice that was forbidden except in emergencies where blood banks weren't accessible.

This counted as an emergency, Jeanne Louise decided and hoped the council would see it that way too. However, they might argue that all she had to do was make Paul take her to the Enforcer house or anywhere else where she could get blood.

"You know," Paul mused, "When I was a kid, my parents used to rent a cottage on Lake Huron, a little place this side of the Kettle Point Indian reserve. Ipperwash. I've often thought I should take Livy there."

"That's what? Two or three hours southwest of here?" Jeanne Louise asked.

"About that," he agreed.

Jeanne Louise considered it. The beach would be busy this time of year, crawling with mortals. It would make it difficult for the Enforcers to grab them without drawing attention if they tracked them down. It would also make it easier for her to feed with so many snack options available, and it was looking like she might be feeding off the hoof for a while. At least until she sorted out things with

Paul, had got him to agree to be her life mate, had turned him, had him turn Livy, and had returned to town to see what they could do to mitigate the trouble Paul was in.

She was hoping that if Paul was turned before he was caught that it might make a difference. The fact that he was her life mate and one of them should help. She hoped. It was the only reason she would even consider turning him on her own without drugs and IVs to aid in the endeavor. But she might not have to do without those items. A visit to the nearest hospital and a little mind control would get her anything she needed. Except for the specialized drugs developed in R and D, she acknowledged unhappily, but then decided she would worry about that when the time came.

"Sounds good," she said finally.

Six

'Jeanie?'

Jeanne Louise stirred slowly and opened her eyes to find Paul leaning over her. Blinking sleepily, she peered around, her hand automatically tightening on the bundle of fur in her lap as Boomer too began to stir. The car was stopped. They were parked in a big, busy Walmart parking lot. Obviously she'd dozed off and they'd reached the Kitchener/Waterloo area. Or maybe Cambridge. She wasn't sure which.

"I was going to let you sleep while I ran in to get you some clothes, but I don't know what size you wear," Paul explained, sitting back in his seat so that she could sit up.

"Oh." She smiled around a yawn and then shook her head. "I'll get them."

"Uh, well, it's maybe better if you don't. You

might draw some attention like that," he pointed out gently.

Jeanne Louise glanced down at herself and frowned as she noted the mud-streaked front of her clothes. She was dry now, at least, but the mud hadn't evaporated with the damp. She would definitely draw attention. Sighing with resignation, she nodded. "Size six most of the time, but sometimes an eight." When confusion entered his face, she chuckled. "Different manufacturers fit differently. Just go with six."

Nodding, Paul glanced in the backseat.

"I'll be here," she reassured him. "And I'm awake now."

"Thanks," he murmured, and then reached for the door handle and slid out, saying, "I'll be as quick as I can."

"Okay," Jeanne Louise said just before he closed the door. She watched him walk away from the car, and then glanced at the cars around them. He'd parked at the back of the lot, but still among the other cars rather than off alone. The parking lot was surprisingly busy for this hour. By her guess it must be nearly nine o'clock. Most Walmarts stayed open until eleven though.

A sleepy murmur from Livy drew her attention and Jeanne Louise shifted to glance in the back. The girl was still asleep, however. Her color was good, her cheeks actually a little rosy. Two meals and some time to be a child at Chuck E. Cheese's had done her good. She needed a couple more days of eating and having fun to rebuild her strength though before it would be safe to turn her.

Jeanne Louise settled back in her seat, her hand automatically holding Boomer in place as she did. When he gave her hand a wet swipe with his tongue, she smiled at the animal, and ruffled his ears. He was a good dog and had apparently slept the whole time she had, Jeanne Louise thought and then glanced after Paul, wishing she'd thought to tell him to get some dog food for the poor animal. They hadn't fed him before going out for supper. She supposed Paul had intended to when they got back, but instead they were driving around looking for somewhere to hide. And the dog still hadn't eaten.

Her attention was distracted from that thought by the sight of a family walking up the row of cars, bags in hand. Two young children were chattering away to a weary-looking mother and father as they were herded toward a small minivan across the aisle and a couple cars up. Jeanne Louise watched the parents stow the bags and kids in the van and then get in themselves, and grimaced as her fangs tried to slide out.

She was hungry, and not for food. Her belly was still happily full of pizza. It was blood her body wanted and the need was beginning to gnaw at her. She had to feed soon. That thought in mind, Jeanne Louise let her gaze slide over the people moving back and forth in the parking lot, some returning to cars, some leaving them to head into the store.

Most seemed to be in groups or at least pairs. In fact, several minutes passed before she spotted a man on his own. Her eyes narrowed on him, considering. He was young, perhaps in his early twenties with short preppy blond hair and an athletic build. Healthy-looking.

Jeanne Louise automatically reached for the door handle and then recalled Boomer in her lap. Pausing, she bit her lip and peered down at the dog. He was awake and lying nicely in her lap, but she couldn't guarantee that he wouldn't hop into the backseat and disturb Livy if she left him in the car.

Her gaze slid back to the young man. He was slowing as he approached the car across from Paul's, a small, sporty red coupe. Feeling her fangs slide down and out again, she forced them back once more, but then reached for the door and this time opened it.

Jeanne Louise took Boomer with her as she slid out of the front seat. Holding the dog to her chest with one hand, she eased the door carefully closed to keep from waking Livy and then turned to peer at the young man again.

He had opened the driver's door of his car and was about to slide behind the wheel. Jeanne Louise didn't speak, simply slipped into his thoughts and took control of him. It was as easy as poking a finger in soft butter. Unlike Paul, the man was as malleable as mud.

Smiling to herself, Jeanne Louise made him close his door and cross the aisle to her. His expression was blank when she brought him to a halt in front of her. She took a moment to search his thoughts and be sure he hadn't been drinking or taken any drugs, and when she found he was clean, and in fact a health nut, she relaxed and made him bend toward her as if about to kiss her. But at the last minute she made him turn his head.

To anyone watching it would look like they were merely embracing and she was nuzzling his neck, Jeanne Louise thought, as she braced her hand on his chest. She raised up on her toes, let her teeth slip out and—

"Jeanne Louise?"

She turned instinctively at that questioning voice, not thinking to retract her fangs until she saw the way Paul's entire expression froze. Cursing herself for not thinking to check the parking lot before making her move, Jeanne Louise quickly let her teeth slide back into place and removed her hand from the man she'd been about to bite. She stayed inside his head, though, sensible enough not to release him yet.

"Paul, I—"

"You were going to bite him," he hissed accusingly as he moved up to join them between his car and the sedan next to it.

Jeanne Louise didn't bother trying to deny it. She raised her head, straightened her shoulders, and said with simple dignity, "I need to feed, Paul."

His mouth thinned, and then he glanced sharply to her intended dinner. His eyebrows immediately drew together as he took in the blank expression on his face. "What have you done to him?"

Jeanne Louise grimaced. Now she'd have to explain things she hadn't wanted to explain. Buying herself some time, she said, "Hang on," then turned her full attention to the man again and sent him walking back to his car. She had him get in, and then took a moment to make sure he didn't recall his brief detour to her side, before releasing him.

They both watched silently as he started his engine, but the moment he drove away, Paul turned on her again, eyebrows raised. "Well?"

Jeanne Louise glanced around at the busy parking lot and suggested, "Maybe we should discuss this in the car."

"Oh, right. *Now* you're worried about the busy parking lot?" he asked dryly. "A minute ago you were playing Vampirella out here without a single worry about who saw, but *now* you want to talk in the car?"

"I wasn't playing Vampirella," she said with a sigh. "I didn't even get to bite him. You interrupted before I could."

"Well, good," Paul snapped. "Because you aren't going to be biting anyone while you're with me."

"I have to feed, Paul," Jeanne Louise said, trying to remain patient. "I need blood to survive."

"I thought you guys weren't allowed to feed off the hoof anymore?" he growled. "I thought you were restricted to bagged blood."

"We are," she said at once. "Except in cases of emergency and this is one. I can hardly stop by the Argeneau blood bank, or call in a delivery order, can I? You'd be taken into custody, and I can't—" She snapped her mouth closed and glanced over her shoulder at the sound of a door opening.

A small sigh slid from Jeanne Louise's lips when she saw the older gentleman getting into the van parked behind Paul's car. The way he was eyeing them told her he'd heard what they were talking about. While he looked a little confused, even having heard what he had without understanding it was bad enough so she slipped into the man's thoughts and rearranged them a bit, then turned to Paul. "We need to leave."

This time he didn't protest, but opened the car door with a jerk. He waited until she had folded herself inside with Boomer, and then dropped the huge bag of purchases he'd been holding by her feet and slammed the door. The sound, of course, stirred Livy from sleep and this time the headache wasn't gone. The child woke with a cry of pain and immediately started weeping miserably. It made Jeanne Louise glare at Paul when he opened the driver's door and slid in. Shoving the dog at him, she opened her door again and got out.

"Where are you going?" Paul growled.

Jeanne Louise ignored him and slammed the door closed, then opened the back door, and undid Livy's seat belt.

"It's okay, sweetie," she cooed, lifting her out

into her arms. She hugged her close, kissed her forehead, and then forced herself to slip into the girl's mind to help her with the pain. Excruciating agony immediately exploded inside her head and Jeanne Louise leaned heavily against the side of the car, clutching instinctively at the child to keep from dropping her as she tried to cope with it. It was so overwhelming this time that she didn't even notice Paul getting out of the car and coming around to join them.

"Put her to sleep," he ordered, taking the girl from her, but it took a moment for his words to make it through to her beleaguered brain. "Jeanie?"

She forced her eyes open, squinted at Livy and put her to sleep. It was an effort this time. The pain was really bad. She'd thought the first two headaches had been horrible, but this was unbearable. Jeanne Louise couldn't even think with her head hammering as it was and it took a moment for her to remember how to make the child sleep. She also had to wait longer this time before she was sure Livy's mind was flooding with endorphins to stop the pain receptors from receiving the pain, then she finally slipped free of the child's mind with relief.

Groaning, Jeanne Louise then pressed her hands to her forehead and turned to lean her cheek wearily on the roof of the car. She heard the front door open, and raised her head to peer around, then quickly slipped into the girl's thoughts to keep her from waking as Paul settled her in the front seat and buckled her in. It was a good thing she had because Boomer immediately decided that he should sit on Livy. His climbing on the girl would have woken her if Jeanne Louise hadn't slipped back into her thoughts.

Paul scooped up the dog, and then grabbed the bag of clothes as well. The moment he straightened and closed the door, she freed herself from Livy's mind and leaned on the roof of the car again.

"Come," Paul said quietly. He urged her out of the way, opened the back door and ushered her in. Jeanne Louise slipped into the backseat. She took the dog when he handed him to her, then the bag of clothes as well, and simply leaned her head back on the seat and closed her eyes. It was Paul who did up her seat belt for her. She didn't even have the energy to thank him.

Jeanne Louise was vaguely aware of his closing the door, quietly, she noted. Apparently he'd learned his lesson from the first door slamming. Then she heard the front driver's door open and the engine start. She merely clutched the dog and bag to her stomach and stayed where she was as he shifted into gear and steered them out of their parking spot.

Jeanne Louise didn't think she'd ever felt so exhausted and spent in her life. Her head was still throbbing, the earlier dull ache a fond memory, and without blood, she knew it wouldn't improve. She simply leaned back in the seat, trying to keep from vomiting from the pain as he drove.

Consumed by that effort as she was, Jeanne Louise couldn't have said how long he drove before the car stopped again. She didn't care either, and stayed where she was as Paul got out of the car. When the door beside her opened again, she didn't react until she felt Paul digging through the bag on her lap. Forcing her eyes open, she lifted her head a bit, just in time to see him retrieve a leash from the bag. He then shifted the bag off her lap to the car seat, before snapping the leash to Boomer's collar.

"Can you walk?" he asked in a hushed whisper.

Jeanne Louise grimaced, but nodded.

Paul lifted Boomer off her lap. Holding him under one arm, he unsnapped her seat belt, and then offered Jeanne Louise his hand to get out.

She scowled at him, still angry that he'd woken Livy and put both his daughter and herself through that agony. But then she accepted his offered hand and slid her feet out of the car.

Paul eased the door closed as soundlessly as possible once she stood beside him, then turned to usher her away from the vehicle.

Jeanne Louise reluctantly peered around, surprised to see he'd brought them to a park. He led her to a picnic table, saw her seated, then tied the end of the long leash to the picnic table leg and moved back to sit beside her.

"Bite me," he said grimly.

"Same to you," she muttered irritably.

Paul blinked, and then a surprised laugh slipped

from his lips. "No. I wasn't—I mean, really go ahead and bite me, Jeanie. You need to feed. Feed on me."

"Oh," Jeanne Louise said on a sigh, and then frowned at him. "First you were upset with me because I was going to bite someone. Now you want me to bite you?"

He grimaced and glanced away. "Yes, well . . . I shouldn't have reacted as I did. I guess I was a little jealous when I saw you cuddled up to that hunk in the parking lot. I suppose after that kiss earlier today I feel a little possessive." Paul shrugged uncomfortably, and then rushed on, "Besides, you shouldn't have to feed on others. You're only without blood because I kidnapped you. If you have to bite anyone it should be me. No one else should have to pay."

Jeanne Louise stared at him through the growing gloom. The sun had long set, darkness taking its place. She hadn't even noticed that when he'd led her from the car, which said just what kind of shape she was in. And her state of mind was helping her with sorting out what he'd just said. He was a little jealous when he saw her with the man? He felt possessive after their kiss earlier that day? And he was admitting it? Wow. She thought that was kind of important but in her present state wasn't sure if it was in a good way or bad.

"So, go ahead." Paul shifted a little closer, and turned his head to offer her his neck.

Jeanne Louise just stared at him. She couldn't

just bite him. She couldn't control his thoughts. She'd hurt him if she couldn't keep him from feeling the pain. She wasn't willing to hurt him. She wanted to bite him though. Not to hurt him, but to feed. The way he'd twisted his neck left his vein exposed and throbbing. She could almost smell the blood pounding through his veins. Groaning, Jeanne Louise turned away. "I can't."

Paul was silent for a minute, and then said, "You were controlling that guy in the parking lot."

"I told you, we can keep them from feeling pain so that—"

"You were controlling him, Jeanie," he interrupted grimly. "You weren't just keeping him from feeling pain. He didn't even seem to be there. It was like the lights were on but no one was home. He was walking, but he didn't seem conscious despite the fact that his eyes were open."

Jeanne Louise just nodded in defeat. There was no way to keep it from him now. "When we still hunted, it was a handy skill."

"So you *were* controlling him?"

She grimaced. "Yes, Paul, I was controlling him. I submerged his will and overrode it with my own. He won't even remember crossing the parking lot."

"Have you ever done that to me?" he asked quietly.

"No," she said wearily, watching Boomer chase his tail at the end of his chain.

Paul let that go and muttered, "I didn't know your kind could do that."

Jeanne Louise shrugged. "Knowing we can do that would make mortals nervous, so we generally don't tell."

"Hmm," he said, and then glanced at her sharply. "Jesus, you could have taken control of me and made me release you at any time." When she didn't comment, he asked, "Why didn't you?"

"Because I can't control you, Paul," she admitted wearily.

"You can't?" He frowned. "Why?"

Jeanne Louise shrugged and said vaguely, "It happens sometimes."

"But you can control Livy," he said. "That's what you're doing when you take the pain away and when you put her to sleep, right?"

"Yes," she admitted.

Paul nodded and then kicked his toe into the grass, before glancing at her and saying. "You're still terribly pale, Jeanie. You need blood."

"I can't bite you, Paul," she sighed and then added wryly, "Believe me, I wish I could. I do need blood."

"Well, then why can't you? You drank my blood at the house and it didn't seem to affect you adversely."

"It's not the blood itself," Jeanne Louise said on a short dry laugh, and then turned to peer at him. "I can't control you, Paul. I wouldn't be able to keep you from feeling the pain. It would hurt, and I won't hurt you."

"Ah, I see," he said with a nod of understanding, and then grimaced. "Well, perhaps it's what I deserve for kidnapping you in the first place." He peered at her solemnly and said, "I really don't want you having to feed off of others because of what I did. Hurt or not, I'd rather you bit me than feed on innocents around us."

"Paul," she began unhappily, but he interrupted.

"I'm serious, Jeanie. I would rather suffer the pain of your bite than have you bite others. So . . ." He tilted his head away from her, exposing his neck to her again. "Go on. Get it over with."

Jeanne Louise frowned at him, then shook her head and peered away, but her eyes quickly slid back. Damn, she was hungry. Her stomach felt like it was boiling with acid. And the muscles all over her body were beginning to cramp and ache as the nanos sucked blood from them to carry to the main organs. And if she didn't feed it would only get worse.

"Not here. The car," she said abruptly and stood to walk back toward his vehicle. Silence reigned behind her for a moment and then she heard Paul murmuring to Boomer to wait where he was and take care of business, he'd be back for him in a moment.

Jeanne Louise got into the backseat behind Livy. She left the door open for him, and slid along the seat, her mind racing over what she would have to do as she watched Paul approach. His steps slowed as he neared the car, some reluctance showing, but he straightened his shoulders and continued.

"The door," she murmured when he slid onto the seat next to her, one foot still outside on the ground.

Nodding grimly, Paul pulled his foot in and eased the door closed, and then tilted his head, offering his throat. Jeanne Louise rolled her eyes and immediately climbed to straddle his lap.

Paul jerked in surprise and grasped her arms. "What—?"

"Relax," she whispered, mindful of Livy asleep in the front seat. "I only know of one way to make it not hurt without controlling your mind."

"How's that?" he asked uncertainly.

By infusing him with pleasure. If he was experiencing the shared pleasure life mates enjoyed, he would be less likely to suffer the pain of her fangs sinking into his flesh. Jeanne Louise didn't tell him that, though. She simply leaned forward and kissed him.

After an initial stiffening, Paul relaxed under her caressing mouth and began to kiss her back. The moment he did the passion from earlier exploded between them. Jeanne Louise sighed her relief into his mouth and slipped her arms around his shoulders, her body instinctively pressing closer as her mouth opened to him. Paul accepted the invitation at once, his tongue thrusting out to caress hers even as his hands came up. One moved to her back, urging her closer still, while the other caught in her hair and tilted her head to a more comfortable angle.

Jeanne Louise moaned as his tongue lashed hers, and then gasped as the hand at her back slipped around to find her breast through her muddy blouse. His hand kneaded the tender flesh and then began to tug at her blouse, trying to draw it down to reveal her bra. Jeanne Louise helped, quickly undoing her buttons and then groaning as he jerked the cup of her bra aside so that he could touch the nipple unhindered.

When he broke their kiss to run his lips and tongue across her cheek to her ear, Jeanne Louise murmured eagerly and turned her head, offering it to him, then she tilted her head back, offering him her own throat as his mouth trailed down that. Paul didn't stop there. He found the hollow of her collarbone and sent shivers shimmying through her by nibbling there, then licked his way down her breast to her nipple.

Jeanne Louise rose up slightly on his lap as his mouth closed over the hardened nub, her hands clutching at the hair behind each of his ears to urge him on. Hunger was rushing through her, a blend of his passion and need, hers and her need for blood. Jeanne Louise was briefly torn by the conflicting desires, but when she tilted her head back on a moan and felt her fangs slide out to prick her tongue, she raised her head abruptly to peer down at him.

Paul's heart was beating in time to her own, his own need causing a hardness beneath her legs that was pushing against her with every shift of their bodies.

Jeanne Louise ground herself down on the hardness, bringing a groan from his mouth that reverberated around her breast and then he tore his mouth from the nub he'd been lavishing and raised his face.

The hand in her hair tugged her down as Paul sought her mouth again, but Jeanne Louise turned her head at the last moment and went for his throat. Her fangs sank into the soft flesh even as she again ground her pelvis against his hardness and Paul cried out, a sound muffled by her hand over his mouth. It was a cry of ecstasy not pain, but she couldn't risk Livy waking at this point, and Jeanne Louise kept his mouth covered as she fed, her pleasure in the act following the same connection as the shared pleasure and suffusing him.

Paul bucked beneath her, his hands catching her hips to hold her in place as he ground himself against her in frantic need. She ground right back, the passion and pleasure in feeding comingling and overwhelming them both. Jeanne Louise was so caught up in the moment that she might have overfed and harmed him had someone not pounded on the window next to them.

"For Christ's sake, get a room. This is a family park," someone barked, their voice muffled by the window.

Jeanne Louise raised her head on a furious snarl and turned to glare at whoever had interrupted her meal, but the person, an elderly man, had already continued on, shaking his head and muttering about perverts and the youth today.

She scowled after him, then glanced to Paul to see the dazed look on his face. Then Jeanne Louise twisted in his lap to peer over the front seat to Livy. Fortunately, the man's rude interruption hadn't woken the child.

Sighing, Jeanne Louise turned back to Paul and frowned at how pale he was. She'd taken too much blood. It wasn't a dangerous amount. Still, it was more than she should have and he'd need time to recover. Realizing her fangs were still out, she retracted them, then eased off Paul's lap and glanced out the window. It was dark enough she could barely see Boomer where he remained tethered to the picnic table. She felt better though. Her headache was a dull ache again rather than a hammering, and many of her cramps and aches were gone. Her stomach was also just roiling now rather than taking an acid bath. She would need more blood to be back to full throttle, but Paul couldn't spare it.

The thought made her glance to him. He was slumped on the backseat, his head back and eyes closed. Jeanne Louise suspected he'd fainted. Leaving him for now, she slid out of the car and started back to the picnic table to collect Boomer. She was just coming around the car when she noticed a man untying Boomer's leash from the table. Jeanne Louise put on immortal speed and rushed forward, making the man jump when she suddenly appeared at his side.

"Oh." He blinked with confusion and glanced around. "Is he yours? I was just checking on him."

Jeanne Louise's eyes narrowed. He was lying. He'd planned to take Boomer. He was one of those bastards who stole animals from backyards and playgrounds and sold them for animal experimentation. He'd been driving by with a van full of pets he'd stolen, but the sight of Boomer, seemingly unattended, had seemed too good to be true and he'd stopped to collect one more.

Taking control of the man, she made him hand over Boomer's leash, then had him lead the way to his van. It was only ten feet away. He'd just pulled over to the side of the road when he'd seen Boomer, Jeanne Louise read from his mind. She had him open the back doors of the van and found herself peering over two rows of cages inside. There were eight of them altogether, four lining each side of the back of the van, and each holding at least two animals apiece, some cats and some dogs.

Mouth tightening, Jeanne Louise made him pull out his cell phone and place an anonymous call to the police that a man with a van full of stolen goods was parked by the park. She then had to glance to the sign at the entrance to the park to be able to make him report which park.

After making him put his phone away, Jeanne Louise caught him by the front of the shirt and jerked him down so she could sink her teeth into his jugular. He groaned as her fangs slid into his skin, but this groan wasn't one of pleasure. She didn't bother masking the pain for him, though he wouldn't remember suffering it. She was still masking his memory.

This time Jeanne Louise deliberately took enough blood to put the man into a faint. She then turned with him and released his shirt so that he fell into the back of his van between the rows of cages. His feet were hanging out between the open doors, but she didn't bother about that and simply walked back to the car, leading Boomer.

When Jeanne Louise opened the back door of the car, Boomer hopped in and curled up next to Paul. She then eased the door closed and got in the driver's seat. She was feeling pretty good now. She would drive the rest of the way to Ipperwash and let Paul sleep and recover.

When Jeanne Louise pulled out of the parking lot a moment later, a police car was pulling up behind the van of stolen pets. The sight made her smile with satisfaction. There would be a lot of happy people getting their beloved pets back tonight. It totally negated any guilt she might have felt for biting the creep.

Seven

'I'm thirsty, Jeanie.'

"I bought some snacks when I checked us in, sweetie. I'll give you a drink as soon as I get you and Boomer into our motel room. Okay?"

Paul blinked his eyes open as a click followed that soft voice. The click had been the car door closing, he saw, as he raised his head and glanced around in time to see Jeanne Louise leading Livy and Boomer to an open door in a long, low white building in front of the car.

Giving his head a shake to clear it, Paul sat up and rubbed his hands wearily over his face. He was exhausted, and not sure why at first, and then he remembered being at the park, offering his neck to Jeanie and her leading him back to the car. He distinctly recalled her climbing onto his lap and . . .

"Jesus," Paul muttered under his breath as what

had followed ran through his head. They'd kissed twice now, and both times had been like nothing he'd ever experienced. It was as if his body exploded with desire when his lips met hers. He just went up in flames . . . and all his common sense apparently went out the window, because he'd been ready to strip her clothes off and take her right there in the backseat with Livy asleep in the front. The only thing that had stopped him was . . .

Well, Paul acknowledged, he didn't actually recall what had stopped him. He remembered their bodies grinding together, he remembered letting her nipple slip from his mouth so that he could claim her lips, and then . . . she hadn't let him kiss her. She'd turned her head and—

Paul raised a hand to his neck with a frown. He thought she might have bitten him, but he didn't remember feeling pain; just an overwhelming pleasure that had rushed through him in seemingly endless waves. And then he'd woken up to the sound of his daughter and Jeanne Louise speaking softly.

The door opening beside him drew his attention, and Paul glanced that way as Jeanne Louise bent to peer in at him.

"Are you okay?" she asked, eyeing him solemnly.

"You bit me?" It came out as a question, because he wasn't really sure. Her grimace told him he was right though.

"I got a little carried away and took more blood than I intended," Jeanne Louise said apologetically. "How do you feel?"

Paul considered the question. How did he feel? A little weak, a little tired, and horny as hell as he recalled the passion they'd shared. He was ready to go another round with her. If she was hungry, he was more than happy to feed her. In fact, his mind was drawing up their conversation about biting spots and how the genitals were a good spot because it left no marks. He'd volunteer to try out that one in a heartbeat, he thought dryly. But he could hardly tell her that, and could only think it was a good, Goddamned thing that she couldn't read his mind.

"Fine," Paul said finally, realizing she was still waiting for an answer.

Jeanne Louise hesitated, then leaned in to pick up the Walmart bag from where it now lay by his feet. She then backed out and gave him the room to get out.

Paul did at once, unbuckling his seat belt and unfolding himself from the backseat to straighten beside her. He held on to the door though, when the world did a slow spin around him. She'd definitely taken too much blood, he acknowledged. Perhaps he should hold off on offering himself up for another meal. At least until he'd eaten something.

"Do you need a hand?" Jeanne Louise asked worriedly.

"No," Paul murmured and cautiously released the door, then pushed it closed and glanced around. "Where are we?"

"Ipperwash. It's too late to look into cottages that might be for rent, and I saw this motel so I stopped." She glanced around too. "It will do for tonight. We can look into cottages tomorrow."

He nodded, and turned to walk slowly toward the open door Jeanne Louise had entered earlier with his daughter. The memory made him ask, "How is Livy?"

"Headache free at the moment, thank goodness," Jeanne Louise murmured following him to the door. "She's also hungry and thirsty. I gave her some juice and a chocolate bar to tide her over until morning."

"A chocolate bar?" Paul asked with a wince.

"It's all that they sell in the office," Jeanne Louise said apologetically, and then assured him, "I'll put her back to sleep once she's finished."

Paul relaxed and nodded.

"I got you some juice and a chocolate bar too," Jeanne Louise said as he reached the door to their room and peered around. It was your standard motel room done in neutral shades of brown on beige. There were two queen-sized beds and Livy was seated on the nearer one with Boomer curled up beside her. The girl was getting chocolate all over herself as she ate an Oh Henry! bar.

"There's dog food in with your clothes," Paul said, turning with the intention of taking the bag and feeding the poor mutt. It was well past Boomer's dinner hour.

"I'll get it," Jeanne Louise said, closing the door

behind them. "Go drink your juice and eat your chocolate."

Paul hesitated, but then left her to it and headed across the room to the bedside table where three or four chocolate bars and two bottles of juice sat. He grabbed a bottle of orange juice, opened it and drank it while watching Jeanne Louise dig out the dog food and the two small dog dishes he'd also thought to purchase.

Boomer was off the bed and at her side, tail wagging, the moment she opened the dog food. Jeanne Louise poured some into one of the dishes, then set the bag of food aside and carried the other dish into the attached bathroom to fill it with water. By the time she'd finished and placed the water beside the food dish for Boomer, Paul was done with his juice and reaching for a chocolate bar.

"Jeanie, can we go to the beach?" Livy asked as Jeanne Louise straightened.

"In the morning, pumpkin," Jeanne Louise said, her gaze skating over Paul before she took in Livy's chocolate-covered state. His daughter had finished her chocolate bar, but appeared to have more chocolate on her hands and face than she'd managed to eat. He smiled faintly and glanced back to Jeanne Louise in time to see the grin that claimed her face before she turned away to go back into the bathroom.

"Jeanie says we're in upper watch," Livy announced, smiling at him.

"Ipperwash," Paul corrected gently as he opened his chocolate bar.

"Yeah," Livy agreed. "And she says we're going to swim and collect shells, roast weenies over the fire and stuff too."

"Hmm," Paul murmured around his chocolate bar and nodded, but then frowned as he suddenly wondered how Jeanne Louise had rented the motel room. She didn't have her purse and his money was in his wallet in his back pocket. He could feel it.

"Here we go," Jeanne Louise said stepping out of the bathroom with a damp cloth and heading for Livy.

"Jeanie?" Paul asked after swallowing his bite of chocolate bar. "How did you rent the room?"

She stilled briefly in cleaning up Livy and then glanced to him. "The motel owner was willing to take cash. I told him you'd pay in the morning."

He arched an eyebrow at the guilty expression on her face. "And he agreed to that?"

"Of course," Jeanne Louise mumbled, avoiding looking at him by running the washcloth over Livy's now clean face again.

She'd controlled the motel owner to make him agree. Paul would bet money on that, but he let it go. He would pay the man in the morning. Everything was fine. Still, it was rather troublesome that her kind could make mere mortals do things they didn't necessarily want to do. He doubted there was a motel owner on the planet who would rent rooms on the promise of payment in the morning, not to mention a credit card in case of damage . . . unless made to do so by a passing vampire.

"There we go. Time for bed," Jeanne Louise murmured, tugging back the blankets and sheet on one side of the bed and patting it for Livy to move to it.

"But I just woke up," Livy protested.

"I know, hon. But it's bedtime and you want to be all rested and feeling good for the beach tomorrow, don't you?" she coaxed.

Livy considered that and then nodded, but rather than move, she said, "But I can't sleep in my clothes."

"There are pj's in the Walmart bag," Paul said, standing to go collect the bag from where Jeanne Louise had set it at the foot of the bed.

"I'll get it," Jeanne Louise said at once, hurrying to try to get to it first.

"I'm not an invalid, Jeanie. I can do it," Paul said with irritation as he snatched up the bag. He then grimaced and offered an apologetic expression before adding more gently, "I'll do it."

Jeanne Louise nodded and backed off, leaving him to dump the contents on the bed and sort through the clothes that spilled out. He'd bought the promised clothes for Jeanne Louise, as well as pajamas and a T-shirt and shorts for Livy, and another pair of jeans and a T-shirt for himself. He hadn't thought to buy either himself or Jeanne Louise pajamas though. He didn't normally wear

them and he just hadn't thought of it with Jeanne
Louise. He'd only bought them for Livy because
they'd seemed to jump out at him as he'd passed
the rack where they'd hung. They were pink with
white Dalmatians on them and he'd thought she'd
look adorable in them.

Sighing, Paul set his own clothes aside, along
with Livy's, put the clothes he'd got for Jeanne
Louise back inside, and then offered her the bag.
"Sorry. I didn't think to get you pajamas."

"That's okay," she murmured, accepting the bag.
"I can sleep in the T-shirt and my panties."

Paul blinked at the announcement. Not that
Jeanne Louise noticed, she'd turned away to set
the bag on the end of the bed Livy was in. Forcing
away the image she'd just put into his head, Paul
collected the pajamas and moved to the head of
the bed.

"On your feet, muffin," he ordered lightly.

Giggling, Livy stood up on the bed in front of
him and bounced around as he caught the hem
of her T-shirt and tugged it up and off over her
head. She continued to bounce around as he put
the pajama top on her, but he brought a halt to her
bouncing by catching her ankles and tugging them
out from under her when he was ready to trade her
shorts for the pajama bottoms. It was only after
he'd done it that it occurred to him that perhaps she
shouldn't be hopping or dropping about, that perhaps it would cause another headache to flare up.

Fortunately, it didn't, and Livy laughed uproariously as she bounced onto her behind on the bed. She then kicked her legs as he tugged her shorts off and put the pajama bottoms on. Boomer thought this was a fine game and immediately bounded onto the bed, barking excitedly.

Paul had to order the dog off the bed, but smiled as he finished tugging Livy's bottoms into place. Her eyes were bright, her cheeks rosy. If he hadn't seen the scans himself in the doctor's office, and been there for the headaches she'd been suffering for the last several weeks, he almost could have believed she was just your normal, healthy little girl. But she wasn't. She was dying. The thought made his smile fade and his voice was gruff as he murmured, "Under the blankets now."

"Okay," she said cheerfully, but stood up on the bed again, hugged his neck, and kissed his cheek before moving to the spot where Jeanne Louise had pulled down the covers. She dropped to her bottom, scooted her feet under the blankets, then grabbed them and pulled them up as she lay back. Livy then closed her eyes, and proceeded to make loud snoring sounds.

"Monkey," Paul said, managing a small smile.

Livy opened her eyes and grinned at him briefly, but just as quickly her eyes closed and her face slid into sleep. Helped along by Jeanne Louise, Paul knew. He didn't look to the woman, but continued to stare at his precious daughter and renewed his determination to save her life. He would convince Jeanne Louise to turn her. He had to.

"I'm going to take a shower," the woman in question said softly.

Paul nodded, but didn't glance around. He heard the rustle of the bag as she collected it from the end of the bed and a moment later there was a soft click as the door between the bedroom and bathroom closed.

Sighing, Paul bent to brush a wisp of hair away from his daughter's face. "Don't worry, baby," he whispered, running his finger along her cheek. "Daddy's here. He won't let you die."

Paul was peering out the window at the parking lot when Jeanne Louise came out of the bathroom. She'd washed her panties in the sink, wrung them out the best she could, then had laid them on the sink to dry a bit while she took a shower. Of course, they hadn't been dry by the time she'd finished and she'd had to don them wet, but they would dry on her body and at least they were clean.

Jeanne Louise had pulled on the T-shirt Paul had bought her then, a little dismayed to find he'd bought a small. It was tight, hugging her breasts like a second skin and barely reaching the top of her panties. She'd peered at herself in the mirror before leaving the bathroom and shook her head, but then had shrugged fatalistically. There was more of her covered like this than there would be if she were wearing a bathing suit.

On that thought, Jeanne Louise had dragged the new jeans out of the Walmart bag, stuffed her dirty clothes in and carried the bag and new jeans with her as she left the bathroom. She set the bag and jeans by the foot of Livy's bed and moved up to begin pulling back the blanket and sheets on her side.

"Jesus."

Jeanne Louise paused at that gasp and glanced to Paul. His eyes were wide and warm as they slid over her body. She felt like he was eating her alive from across the room. Forcing herself to keep moving, she finished pulling back the covers and climbed into the bed. By the time she had pulled the sheet and blankets back up he was at the bedside.

"You don't have to sleep with Livy. I was going to," Paul whispered, his gaze moving over the blankets she'd just pulled up as if he could still see her in his mind's eye. "She kicks in her sleep."

"It's fine," Jeanne Louise whispered back, turning onto her side. "It's a big bed. We'll be good."

Paul hesitated, but in the end had no choice but to leave her to it. He turned off the lights in the room, leaving just the bathroom light to illuminate his way.

"Cripes," Paul muttered leaning against the door after he closed it. He'd obviously bought Jeanne Louise the wrong size T-shirt. Or the perfect size depending on how you looked at it, he thought wryly. And he'd definitely been looking. The sight of her had taken his breath away when he'd turned and seen her walking up the side of the bed. And truthfully, he'd been hoping she'd suggest they share the other bed when he'd said Livy kicked in her sleep, and had been disappointed that she hadn't.

Giving his head a shake, Paul pushed himself away from the door and moved to turn on the shower. It would be a cold shower for him tonight. And then probably little to no sleep. He suspected he'd be lying awake all night, his body electrified by the knowledge that Jeanne Louise Argeneau lay half naked not two feet away in the next bed.

"Damn," he breathed, and began to strip off his clothes.

"Good morning, folks."

Jeanne Louise glanced briefly to the motel owner and murmured an absent "good morning," but her concentration was mostly on Livy as the girl ate her breakfast. The child had woken up fussy and difficult. She had a headache again. A low-grade one this time, thank goodness, but a headache just the same. Jeanne Louise was having to mask the dull ache and make the girl eat and enjoy her meal. It left her with little caring for what the motel owner wanted.

Fortunately, Paul was able to pick up the slack and greeted the man warmly. The two had met when Paul had stopped in the office to pay for their room on the way to the attached diner for breakfast.

"I called Jack, a friend of mine who owns some cottages on the beach. Mentioned you were looking to rent one," the man announced cheerfully. "Turns out Jack had a cancellation this week. Someone who had rented it from today to next Saturday. They only called this morning to cancel too, the dirty buggers, which is good news for you. He's willing to take cash and rent it to you."

Jeanne Louise smiled and nodded as Paul rose to shake the man's hand and thank him. The two men spoke about this and that, but she didn't pay much attention. Her concentration was still mostly on Livy until the motel owner left and Paul sat back down, saying, "If we can't go to the cottage until noon, we should probably find somewhere to buy more clothes. And maybe some groceries and such."

"Yes," she murmured.

Paul was silent for a moment and she could feel his eyes traveling over her face. He then asked quietly, "Is it bad?"

Jeanne Louise knew he was asking about the headache she was blocking Livy from feeling. She supposed it meant she was starting to show the wear and tear of doing so. Sighing, she admitted, "It was low grade when she woke up, but it's getting worse."

"Charlie says the best place to shop for swimsuits and such is London. It's about an hour away. She can sleep on the way," Paul said quietly.

Jeanne Louise nodded, knowing Charlie was the motel owner. She'd got his name when she'd dipped into his thoughts to convince him to let her rent the room and not pay until morning.

"All done, Livy honey?" Paul asked suddenly, drawing her attention to the fact that the girl was done eating.

"Yes, Daddy." Livy beamed a smile. "Can we go to the beach now?"

"Soon, muffin. But first we have to go buy bathing suits," Paul responded, pulling out enough money to pay for their breakfast and then rising to walk around and pick up Livy.

"I can walk, Daddy," the girl complained when he scooped her up.

"Yes, I know. But soon you'll be too big for me to carry so I may as well do it as much as I can now," he answered easily, and then glanced to Jeanne Louise and added, "Besides, soon you'll be sleeping."

"No, I won't. I'm not tired at all. I—" The sentence ended abruptly as Jeanne Louise ushered the girl off to sleep with a thought.

Sighing as she broke free of the child's mind, Jeanne Louise rubbed her head and stood up. She felt guilty for making the child sleep yet again, but surely sleep was better than suffering the agony she would be in if she were awake?

"Don't let me forget to pick up sunscreen," Paul said as they headed for the exit.

"Sunscreen," Jeanne Louise murmured.

"And mosquito repellent," Paul added.

"Mosquito repellent," she echoed dully.

"And towels, of course," Paul muttered with a frown. "I think maybe we should make a list before we go shopping."

"A list." Jeanne Louise sighed. They hadn't been awake much more than an hour, but she was already exhausted. A shopping trip wasn't in the least appealing, but they had little more than the clothes on their backs. It had to be done, she acknowledged, wincing as they stepped out into bright morning sunlight. She'd need to feed again soon if he kept walking her about in the sun, she thought. And then recalling the dog they'd left in the motel room during breakfast, she asked, "What about Boomer?"

"We can hardly take him shopping. He'll be fine in the room for a couple hours," he assured her, and then glanced toward the sky with a frown of concern and suggested, "Maybe you should wait here under the awning while I get Livy in the car. I'll drive back and pick you up. You probably shouldn't be out in direct sunlight anymore than necessary."

Jeanne Louise stopped at once with relief, but she kept her attention on Livy as he carried her to the car and set her inside, making sure the jostling didn't wake the child.

Once in the car, Jeanne Louise found a small notepad and a pen in the glove compartment and wrote down everything the two of them came up with as Paul drove.

"How's Livy's head?" Paul asked as he turned into the parking lot of a huge mall.

Jeanne Louise ripped off the list she'd made and slid it in her pocket as she turned to peer at the girl. She slid into her thoughts briefly, like dipping her toe in the tub to check the temperature, and relaxed when she felt it pain free.

"She's good right now," Jeanne Louise said with relief, and urged the child back awake much as she had put her to sleep.

Livy blinked her eyes open, almost instantly alert. "Are we there yet?"

"Yes," Jeanne Louise said on a laugh.

"It looks busy," Paul muttered, driving along the rows of parked cars.

"It's Saturday," she pointed out.

"Hmmm. I'm going to drop you two off here at the doors, find parking, and then catch up to you," he decided, heading toward the nearest mall entrance.

"I have to pee," Livy announced.

"Actually, so do I," Jeanne Louise acknowledged.

"Right," Paul chuckled. "Well, so do I. I'll meet you two at the bathroom closest to this entrance then," he said as he slowed to a stop in front of a set of doors.

Nodding, Jeanne Louise slid out, wincing at the harsh sunlight that immediately struck her. She closed her door, opened Livy's and quickly leaned in to unbuckle her seat belt and get her out.

"See you in a few minutes," she said, and then closed the door and hurried Livy to the mall entrance.

They stepped into air-conditioning that felt almost cold after the heat outside. Jeanne Louise let a little sigh slip from her lips now that the sun was no longer beating down on her. He'd let them off by the food court, a large area with tables in the middle and a variety of restaurant vendors circling it. Fortunately, it was past breakfast time and too early for lunch yet, so the food court was relatively slow, mostly empty tables with a few people chattering over coffee or cold drinks.

A quick glance around revealed the universal sign for washrooms to their left. Jeanne Louise caught Livy's hand and led her that way, weaving around one or two people who crossed their path. The bathroom wasn't busy and there were several stalls to choose from. Jeanne Louise ushered Livy into one in the middle of the row of stalls.

"Do you need me in there with you?" she asked uncertainly from the door.

"No, thank you. I'm a big girl," Livy said easily and slammed the door closed.

Something about the way she said it made Jeanne Louise grin. Shaking her head, she turned and paced to the sinks to lean against them while she waited. She'd barely rested her hips against the counter when a middle-aged brunette entered the room. Jeanne Louise returned the woman's smile, and inhaled to offer a greeting, but froze at the scent that wafted up her nose. Blood. The aroma was heavy in the air as the woman passed, though it was doubtful a mortal would notice. The scent made Jeanne

Louise's fangs ache. She was suddenly aware of how hungry she was, and not for food but for the tinny liquid presently filling the air in front of her. The woman either had an open wound on her somewhere or was having her period.

Jeanne Louise inhaled the heady scent again, her eyes now tracking the woman as she walked along the row of stalls. When the brunette chose the larger handicapped stall at the end, Jeanne Louise didn't even think, but pushed herself away from the counter. She followed her into the stall, sliding into the woman's mind to control her as she went. By the time she pushed the stall door closed behind them, the woman had paused and tilted her head to the side.

Jeanne Louise caught a glimpse of the woman's blank eyes staring at the ceramic tiles in front of them as she brushed her long hair out of the way, and then she concentrated on masking the woman's thoughts and pain as she sank her fangs into her throat.

Livy was standing uncertainly in the open door of her stall when Jeanne Louise slipped out of the end booth moments later.

"Oh, there you are," the girl said with a smile as she spotted her. "I was afraid you'd left."

"Never," Jeanne Louise said lightly, joining her at the sink and lifting her up so she could reach the soap and tap.

"I think Daddy likes you, Jeanie."

The announcement was so unexpected, Jeanne

Louise nearly dropped the kid. Keeping her grip as the girl busily washed her hands, she asked, "Oh? What makes you say that?"

"He smiles more with you around. And he doesn't seem so sad all the time anymore," Livy said simply. "He's been very sad as long as I can remember. I thought it was my fault, but Grandma says its because Mommy died. She says he misses her. But he doesn't seem to miss her so much with you around."

Jeanne Louise hesitated, but then asked, "Is that all right with you? If he likes me?"

" 'Course," she said with a grin. "I like you too. Besides, he'll need someone to make him smile when I go to heaven."

Her own smile freezing in place, Jeanne Louise peered at the child's innocent face and felt her heart squeeze.

"I'm done. You can put me down now," Livy announced, forcing her from her momentary stillness.

Jeanne Louise lowered the girl to the floor, quickly washed her own hands, and then snatched a couple of sheets of paper towel from the dispenser for the two of them. Once done, they tossed the paper towels and headed out of the washroom. It wasn't until they'd stepped out into the food court that she realized she'd been so distracted by her unexpected feeding that she'd forgotten to go to the bathroom.

Eight

'Are we going swimming when we get back?' Livy asked excitedly as Paul buckled her into her seat.

"As soon as we're at the cottage and get everything out of the car," Paul said, finishing his task and straightening to close the door. He glanced through the front passenger window as he did, frowning when he noted how pale and tight Jeanne Louise's expression was. His gaze slid back to his daughter. Livy was still awake and smiling. Frowning, he opened the passenger door and leaned in.

"Jeanie?" he said, worry crowding his thoughts as he noted that her complexion was actually gray, her teeth clenched, and the muscles of her jaw jumping. While she turned to peer at him, Paul would swear she didn't really see him. Her concentration was wholly internal on the pain she was suffering as she worked to keep his little girl from feeling it. The headaches were getting worse, taking more out of her each time, he acknowledged. They could bring an end to them if she'd just turn his daughter. But then he hadn't asked her to do that yet. Paul supposed he'd hoped she'd suggest it, and she still might. But if she didn't soon, he'd have to. The increasing speed and harshness of Livy's headaches made him suspect they were running out of time.

"Put her to sleep," he said quietly, and then had to repeat the suggestion more firmly because Jeanne Louise didn't seem to understand. Or perhaps she hadn't heard. Whatever the case, after he said it the second time some of the tension seemed to ease from her face and Paul peered into the backseat to see his sweet daughter was sleeping.

He sighed, some of his own tension easing as well. He didn't want his daughter to suffer, but felt no better knowing Jeanne Louise was doing so in her place.

Paul turned back to the woman to see that she was rubbing her head with her fingers, trying to massage away any lingering pain. He immediately raised his own fingers to her scalp to join her in the effort, moving his fingers in firm circles on her head.

"I'm sorry," he whispered as he worked.

Jeanne Louise mumbled wearily in response, though he wasn't sure what she said or if she'd even heard what he'd said.

Paul sighed and used his fingers on her head to draw her forward and kiss her forehead gently, and then he eased her back in her seat. "Sleep on the way back," he said softly as he did up her seat belt. "A nap will do you good."

Straightening, Paul stepped out of the way and closed the door, then walked around to the driver's side and got in to start the engine. Jeanne Louise's eyes were closed as he pulled out of the parking spot, so it came as something of a surprise when she suddenly sucked in her breath beside him with a hissing sound.

He'd just brought them to a halt at the lights at the parking lot exit. Paul glanced to her sharply at the sound, but couldn't at first tell what was wrong. Jeanne Louise's head was sideways on the headrest, turned toward the window. He started to reach toward her, to see if she was all right, and then his eyes slid past her to the vehicle next to them: A blue van with a dark-skinned woman at the wheel. The woman was staring straight at Jeanne Louise, her eyes flashing gold. He'd seen enough immortal eyes to recognize them and felt his own heart jump in his chest.

"Get us out of here," Jeanne Louise suddenly growled, swiveling her head away from the window to reveal a face stark with alarm.

Paul glanced from her to the woman and then turned to peer forward and hit the gas as the light turned green for them. He reacted instinctively, turning left onto the main road, cutting off oncoming traffic from the plaza across from them. He felt his heart thud again at the sound of wheels screeching in protest, and then flushed guiltily as he realized what he'd done. Fortunately, no one hit them and other than a couple of annoyed honks and no doubt some cursing that he couldn't hear, nothing happened. Paul glanced in the rearview mirror as he roared up the road, half afraid the van too might have turned against traffic and would be following them, but the van had been in the next lane over that was supposed to cross over into the plaza and it had done exactly that. That didn't mean it wouldn't now turn and come back out to follow them, though, he acknowledged.

"You have to get off this road *now*," Jeanne Louise said urgently, swiveling in her seat to peer out the rear window. He knew she had better eyesight than he did. For all he knew she could see the van and knew it was following. Paul didn't question her, but simply shifted into the right lane and took the first road right and then the very next left. He continued like that, taking turn after turn until Jeanne Louise slowly relaxed and eased back to sit in her seat. "I think we lost them."

Paul nodded, but continued taking turns a few more times before pulling over in a residential area to turn on his GPS and punch in the motel in Ipperwash. He was quite sure they'd lost the woman in the van, but in the process he'd got himself lost.

"Who was she?" Paul asked as he waited for the GPS to calculate the route back to the motel.

"My stepmother, Eshe," Jeanne Louise said wearily.

Her eyes were closed so she missed the horrified look he cast her. Dear God, of all the people to run into.

"Why didn't you tell me your parents lived in London?" he asked with dismay.

"They don't. They live in a small town about twenty minutes outside the city," she explained, and then grimaced and admitted, "And I wasn't really paying attention to where you said we were going shopping. My head hurt and—"

"Yes, of course, I'm sorry," Paul interrupted. The little scare hadn't done anything to ease the tension and pallor of her face. "It doesn't matter. We lost her. They might look for us here in London, but we won't be here. We'll just stay out of London and stick to Ipperwash."

"Yes," she agreed, leaning her head back and closing her eyes.

Jeanne Louise didn't say anything else, and Paul suspected she'd fallen asleep. It told him just how exhausted she was, because he couldn't have slept to save his soul at that point. They had got gas and hit the instant teller in Toronto so that the Enforcers wouldn't know which direction they'd headed and would be forced to spread their efforts over a large area. Now they would know and concentrate their search probably in London and the surrounding area. It was a lot less area to search than the entirety of Ontario. Ipperwash was only an hour away.

Of course, they might not expand the search to

the surrounding area, he told himself and then pursed his lips as he considered that if her people now knew they were in London, there was no reason for him not to use the credit card to get gas and save his dwindling cash. Hell, he could even hit an instant teller and load up on cash again.

Happy with that realization, Paul punched the "Point of Interest" button and then typed in the name "Canadian Tire." He found one far enough away from the mall they'd been at to be relatively safe and followed the directions that way.

"Well, what do you think?" Paul asked, dragging in the last of the bags from the car.

Jeanne Louise turned from checking the kitchen cupboards and smiled. "I think it's lovely."

"Yeah. A little grander than I expected," he admitted wryly, setting down his burden. "The cottage my parents brought me to was a three-room shack with a toilet in a room that I'm sure used to be a closet."

"Well, this definitely beats that," she said with amusement, peering around the large open kitchen/dining area and the larger living room beyond. There were two bedrooms up a hall behind these rooms, which faced out on the street side. There was also a curving staircase between the living room and dining room that led down into a basement with another sitting area and two more bedrooms. It was nice. Probably someone's home at one time before it was converted into a rental cottage.

The only complaint Jeanne Louise had was the endless windows everywhere. Fortunately, there were blinds she could close to escape from the relentless sun.

"Is Livy still in the car?" she asked, moving to the grocery bags first. The cupboards were filled with dishes, pots, and pans, but there was an empty cupboard for foodstuff and they'd definitely bought a lot of that in town, along with everything else.

"Yeah. Boomer's with her, and I figure it's better to let her sleep until we get this stuff stowed away. The minute she wakes up she'll want to get in the water." He glanced toward the car parked next to the screen door to the kitchen. Livy's door was open, allowing air in and letting them keep an eye on her and the dog resting on the seat beside her.

Jeanne Louise nodded and began pulling cold food out of the bags to put in the refrigerator. The nap on the way back had done her good. She felt almost back to normal. It had cleared her thinking too though, and now she was a bit worried about Eshe's spotting her in London. Not unduly so though. They might concentrate the search on London, but Ipperwash was an hour away. When they didn't find them in London they would probably look further south rather than try every single town east and west of it. She suspected they'd try Chatham and Windsor first, expecting them to choose large populated areas to hide in.

With both of them working, it didn't take long to

get the food stowed away. They then turned their attention to the clothes and towels they'd bought. The cottage supplied sheets and blankets and pillows, so they made the beds after that.

Paul suggested Jeanne Louise take the large main bedroom on the ground floor while Livy took the smaller one next to it. She refused at first until he pointed out that she would be close to Livy if the child needed her in the night. In case she woke up with a headache and needed help, Jeanne Louise realized, and gave in.

She expected Paul would take one of the bedrooms downstairs, but he announced he'd sleep on the couch in the living room in case Livy needed him.

Once they made the beds, their work was pretty much done and there was no reason not to wake Livy. Leaving Paul sorting through a bunch of stuff she didn't recognize, she went out to collect Livy. The girl was excited as all get-out when she realized they were actually at the cottage. She'd fallen asleep on the way back from town and had slept through their collecting Boomer and their things from the motel, as well as the drive here to meet the cottage owner.

While she was groggy when Jeanne Louise first roused her, the little girl was quickly awake and running the minute she set her down inside the cottage door. Boomer was hard on her heels, barking excitedly as she raced around the inside of the cottage looking in all the rooms, then attacked the small stack of clothes in the smaller room that was to be hers and began rifling through them in search of her bathing suit. She had her clothes off and was climbing into the pretty little blue one piece swimsuit she'd chosen as Jeanne Louise left the room.

She walked into the living room to find Paul in the process of blowing up a small raft. Her eyebrows rose as she glanced from it to the already inflated water wings beside him on the floor. "When did you get those? I don't remember seeing them anywhere."

Paul stopped blowing and blocked the opening with a finger as he explained, "At the gas station when I stopped for gas. They had some sort of promotional deal going on. Buy gas, get the raft half price kind of thing, so I picked it up. Then I saw the water wings and grabbed those too."

"Ah." Jeanne Louise smiled faintly and then glanced around with surprise as Livy charged into the room.

"Can we go in the water now, Daddy?" she asked eagerly, practically dancing on the spot with excitement.

"Just as soon as I finish blowing this up and change into my swim trunks," Paul said patiently and then returned to blowing.

Livy groaned, but otherwise didn't complain. She glanced to Jeanne Louise then though and said, "You'd better put your bathing suit on too, Jeanie. You'll want to swim too."

"Er . . . well . . ." Jeanne Louise shifted uncomfortably.

"There are a couple of lovely big trees out there to offer shade, and I bought a big umbrella for you too," Paul said quietly, pausing in his blowing again. "I know you can't actually swim until nightfall, but I thought that way you could at least sit outside with us."

Jeanne Louise sighed and turned to make her way to her room. She had allowed Paul and Livy to cajole her into buying a bathing suit, never really expecting to wear it. It wasn't often you saw an immortal on the beach unless they were in the middle of a stake and bake—not something any immortal wanted to happen since it was one of their more painful punishments. It was a death sentence that started with being staked out in the sun for hours, sometimes days. This forced the nanos to use up all the available blood to repair the damage caused by the heat and sun. When they ran out of blood in the veins, the nanos then attacked the muscles and finally the organs, drawing blood from them to try to keep the host alive. When the beheading that followed finally came, the victim was usually begging for it.

The bathing suit she'd bought was two scraps of black, a strapless top and tiny bottoms. Jeanne Louise pulled them on and then peered in the mirror critically. Dating mortals, she'd been shaving since women's shaving had started. She'd shaved during her bath before leaving for work Thursday night. It was now Saturday afternoon though, and for some reason her hair seemed to grow fast. Or perhaps all women had to shave every other day. Her legs looked okay, but running a hand across them revealed stubble.

Finding the razor and blades she'd thought to buy while in town, Jeanne Louise took them into the en suite bathroom and ran water in the sink, then found a wash cloth and a bar of soap. It wasn't easy, and Jeanne Louise found herself hopping awkwardly around a couple times, but it got the job done, she supposed as she tested her legs for smoothness and didn't find any stubble.

"Jeanie?" Paul's voice came through the door accompanied by a knock.

"Yeah?" she asked, straightening to peer toward the wood panel.

"Livy and I are heading down to the water. I'll take the umbrella and set it up. Got the beach towels too. Grab yourself a drink and come on out when you're ready to join us."

"Okay," Jeanne Louise called and then lifted her arms to check out the stubble of her armpits. She had a little more shaving to do.

"Jeanie! Look! I can swim!" Livy squealed, dog-paddling madly in front of Paul with Boomer right beside her. The words tore his attention from his daughter to Jeanne Louise as she came out of the cottage and hurried to the umbrella he'd set up for her. It was under the largest tree on the edge of the grass between the house and the beach. He'd laid out one of the towels for her there as well and she now dropped to sit on it as she smiled at Livy.

"Good girl!" she called. "Well done!"

"Aren't you coming out to swim?" Livy asked, giving up her paddling to float in the water between her wings.

"I will," Jeanne Louise assured her, and then added, "Later, when it's not so sunny. My skin doesn't like the sun. I have to stay in the shade until it goes away."

"Okay," Livy said happily and turned to dog-paddle toward her father again with Boomer on her heels.

Paul was aware of his daughter moving toward him, but didn't glance her way yet. He couldn't seem to tear his eyes off Jeanne Louise. The woman's skin was white marble, obviously never exposed to the sun. And her figure was perfect. Not the twiggy, completely fatless figure so popular in today's culture, but rounded and curvy where it should be. She actually had hips, and her breasts he knew had to be real, not bought and shoved under her skin by some guy in a surgical mask. She looked like an ancient roman statue that someone had slapped a swimsuit on.

Jeanne Louise looked damned good.

"Put me on your shoulders again so I can dive in, Daddy," Livy demanded, drawing his attention back to the girl.

Managing a smile, Paul turned her in the water so that her back was to him, then plucked her up and lifted her over his head, holding onto her until she balanced herself on his shoulders. When she clasped his hands with her smaller ones, he released his hold on her waist and let her balance herself holding onto his hands. Paul then glanced to the dog.

"Move Boomer," he ordered, but the dog was already dog-paddling himself out of the way.

Paul glanced to Jeanne Louise again as he waited for Livy to jump off his shoulders. She was watching them, a small smile on her lips and an unopened book in her lap. Paul smiled back and then shifted his attention to his daughter as she launched herself off his shoulders. He raised his hand in front of his face as she splashed into the water, deflecting the spray from hitting him there. Then he glanced to Jeanne Louise again, thinking she would probably have to feed soon.

"Again!" Livy demanded the moment she surfaced, and Paul chuckled at the girl and reached for her again. But he was thinking that he would have to ask Jeanne Louise about feeding again later. Perhaps after Livy was in bed. The thought of Jeanie crawling on his lap on the living room sofa, kissing and caressing him as he freed her breasts and claimed them with his hands and mouth . . . Well, the cold water wasn't doing much to keep his ardor down, Paul noted dryly as he lifted Livy to his shoulders again. His swimming trunks were bright red, and they were poking out in front like a sideways tent. It was a good thing the water reached halfway up his chest and Jeanne Louise couldn't see, he decided, as he helped Livy balance herself to jump off.

Jeanne Louise watched Paul, Livy, and Boomer in the water for a bit, and then relaxed back on her towel and opened the book she'd bought in town. It was one of her cousin Lucern's books. He wrote stories that were sold as paranormal romance, but were really the tales of the matings of their family members. She'd burst out with a delighted chuckle when she'd spotted it in the bookstore on the best sellers rack. Much as it annoyed Lucern that he was such a hit with readers, the rest of the family thought it was charming. Besides, it was always interesting to see their lives through his eyes. Or even to see themselves and how others saw them.

Jeanne Louise would never forget the description of herself that he'd written in the story of his brother Etienne and Rachel's finding each other. *A woman as beautiful in her way as Lissianna and Marguerite were, though she looked nothing like them. Her face was rounder, her lips a little thinner, her eyes more exotic and her hair was a midnight black.*

She'd never thought of herself as beautiful, especially compared to her aunt and cousin. When

Jeanne Louise took her measure against them she always felt she was lacking. And she'd certainly never thought of herself as being anywhere near exotic. She still didn't, but it made her think maybe she wasn't so bad after all.

Sighing, Jeanne Louise turned the book over to read the back. It was the tale of her father Armand and his life mate Eshe's coming together. She'd read it several times now and still cried in certain parts. Of course, she always skipped the love scenes. There was just something weird about reading about your family members having sex. As far as Jeanne Louise was concerned, none of them did. Any babies they produced were immaculate conception. Her family members were all Barbie and Ken dolls in her head, completely lacking sexual parts.

The thought made Jeanne Louise chuckle to herself with amusement. She was over a hundred years old, and she was a scientist, yet she was still uncomfortable with the concept of her loved ones making love. Go figure.

Shaking her head, she opened the book to the first page and started reading.

Despite having read it several times before, Jeanne Louise found herself caught up in the story. She was several chapters in when cold water splashing on her feet startled her out of it. Boomer had returned and was shaking himself by her feet, sprinkling water everywhere.

"Ah! I'm pooped," Livy announced dramatically as she arrived. She collapsed on the beach towel on Jeanne Louise's left with a weary sigh, and groaned when a wet Boomer launched himself on her, trying to lick her face.

"Is she all right?" Paul asked, arriving at her feet now, worry on his face.

Jeanne Louise was just slipping out of Livy's thoughts and nodded reassuringly. "She's just tired, Paul. Lots of sunshine, fresh air, and swimming will do that to a kid."

"Right." He relaxed and smiled slightly, then settled on the beach towel on her right. He lay back on it with hands folded under his head, and legs crossed at the ankles. His eyes closed on a weary little sigh of his own. It seemed Livy wasn't the only one tired out by the day's fun, Jeanne Louise thought, her gaze sliding over his damp body in the wet trunks.

Damn, the man was well put together. Nicely shaped legs, narrow hips, a flat stomach and naturally wide shoulders with well-defined muscle everywhere. Not muscle bound like a body builder or anything, but the body of a natural athlete. Jeanne Louise suspected if he hadn't gone into science, he could have played a professional sport of one kind or another.

"I'm hungry," Livy announced suddenly and Jeanne Louise glanced her way to see her staring up at the tree branches above them. Boomer was curled up at her side, watching the child moving her fingers around in a jabbing motion toward the leaves overhead as if counting them or something.

"Hmm," Paul murmured, eyes still closed. "Hamburgers on the barbecue or weenies over a fire on the beach?"

"Weenies!" Livy squealed, making Boomer bark excitedly.

"Go find some long branches to use to cook them then, and gather firewood," Paul said, not opening his eyes.

Livy was on her feet and rushing along the beach in search of what he'd requested at once. Boomer followed, tail wagging.

"That ought to keep her busy for five minutes," Jeanne Louise said with amusement.

"Yeah." Paul smiled wryly and opened his eyes. "Just long enough for us to deal with feeding you."

Jeanne Louise's eyes widened with surprise at the words and he grimaced.

"Not with the feeding itself, of course. I meant, I haven't forgotten you need to feed and I wanted to reassure you that we'll see to it later. Just as soon as Livy goes to bed." Paul paused and then when she remained silent and wide-eyed, asked, "All right? Can you last that long?"

Jeanne Louise stared at him for a moment. Her gaze then dropped to his bare chest and his lap before rushing back up to his face. Tongue now stuck to the roof of her mouth, she merely nodded.

"Good." Paul leaned forward and kissed her forehead, then got up to follow his daughter and help gather wood for a fire and branches to cook the weenies on. Boomer trailed him, wagging his tail.

Jeanne Louise stared after him, her eyes gliding over every inch of tan male skin that his red trunks revealed. Damn, he was feeding her later. That was definitely something to look forward to.

Nine

Jeanne Louise turned onto her back in the water and stared at the darkening sky. It was still light out, but the sun was setting, the sky awash in umber and purple. It wouldn't be long before those colors too were gone and full night fell. In the meantime, she'd decided to catch that swim she'd been yearning for all day, but hadn't dared take while the sun was out.

Breathing out a pleased little sigh as the water slid over and around her body, Jeanne Louise turned her head in the water and glanced toward the cottage. The lights were on in the kitchen and living room. While it was still bright enough to see out here, inside, shadows were already filling the spaces.

They'd had their weenie roast, and then roasted marshmallows as well. Paul had built the fire at the very edge of the beach where the shade from the tree had offered Jeanne Louise some cover so that she could participate. Afterward, they'd gone in to watch one of the huge selection of movies that belonged to the cottage. Most of them were older movies, with only one or two current ones, but they hadn't minded. Livy had begun to doze off toward the end of the movie so Paul had decided it was time to put her to bed.

Leaving him to it, Jeanne Louise had come outside, taken one look at the water under the darkening sky and had decided it was time for her swim.

The clack of the screen door closing drew her attention to the house and Jeanne Louise smiled when she saw Paul walking down toward the sand. Shifting to her feet, she started to walk out of the water. Paul met her at the water's edge, unfolding a beach towel she hadn't first noticed he held.

"Thank you," Jeanne Louise murmured as he wrapped the towel around her shoulders. "Did you manage to get Livy off to sleep?"

"Out like a light with Boomer curled at her feet," he said with a smile. "And not one headache since arriving at the cottage."

"Maybe the fresh air is good for her," she suggested, clutching both ends of the towel under her chin.

"Maybe," Paul agreed, stepping back. He stared at her for a minute and then said abruptly, "You're probably hungry."

Jeanne Louise stilled. He wasn't talking about

food. And he was right. She *was* hungry. The gal in the public washroom at the mall had barely been a snack. The problem was she was worried about getting overexcited and taking too much blood from him.

"Howdy, neighbors."

When Paul glanced toward that call, Jeanne Louise did as well, a smile automatically lifting her lips in response to the grin on the face of the tall, lean middle-aged man approaching them.

"I'm Russell Jackson," he announced, holding out his hand as he got nearer.

Paul took it first, shaking in greeting. "Paul Williams," he introduced himself, using the name Jeanne Louise had used to register them at the motel. She could hardly use their real name when they were on the run, and Williams had seemed better than Smith. Turning to gesture to Jeanne Louise, he added, "And this is my wife, Jeanie."

She glanced at him with surprise, but recovered quickly and managed a smile as the man then turned to offer her his hand as well.

"Pleasure," Russell said as he released her hand. "We're renting the cottage next door. Been here a week. Have one more before we head back home to work," he said with a grimace that suggested he'd rather stay on vacation.

"Nice here?" Paul asked.

Russell nodded. "Beautiful. The weather's been good, the cottage is gorgeous and so far the others staying around here have been great."

"Good to hear," Paul murmured.

"Well, we all get to know each other and sort of hang around together. At least we did last week. All but two families were only here for a week. The Corbys on the other side of you and us." He gestured to the cedar building on the right of their cottage. "My family and I are in the one on your other side," Russell added, gesturing back the way he'd come.

"Are the Corbys as friendly as you?" Jeanne Louise asked with a smile.

"Yep. Good people," he assured her. "They have a couple boys eight and ten, and my wife and I have a daughter who's six and a son who's nine. The four of them have been playing together and having a whale of a time while we adults relax and visit. Both families went to the provincial park today, took the kids for a little nature walk while the leaving renters cleared out. Stopped for dinner on the way back and just got in. That's why no one came to greet you sooner," he admitted and then asked, "You got kids?"

"A daughter," Paul said with a nod. "Livy. She's five."

"Oh, my Kirsten will be happy about that. A girl to play with instead of all the boys," he said with a chuckle.

"I'm sure Livy would love to meet her tomorrow," Jeanne Louise said when Paul hesitated. "She's sleeping now though."

"Yeah, my wife's putting the kids to bed right now

too. All the fresh air and play knocks 'em right out," Russell said with a grin that suggested that wasn't a bad thing. "After we get the kids down though, we adults were thinking to build a fire and relax with a couple drinks. Are you two up for that?"

"Yes," Jeanne Louise said when Paul glanced her way uncertainly.

"Good, good." Russell glanced back to his cottage and then toward the Corbys', and Jeanne Louise read what he was thinking. A fire in front of the cottage she and Paul were in would be best, made it equidistant from both the Jacksons' cottage and the Corbys' so that everyone could keep an ear out for their kids.

"We could have the fire here in front of our cottage if you like? Couldn't we, honey?" Jeanne Louise suggested for Russell when she read his hesitation to be so forward.

Paul nodded at once. Not only was it equidistant to the other cottages, but it kept them close to hear Livy, she knew.

"That's a fine idea," Russell said, grinning. "I'll just go tell John. Corby," he added since he hadn't given them his first name before this. "I'll go tell him and then head back to the cottage to tell the wife and pack some drinks and snacks in a cooler. We'll meet you back here in . . . say . . . half an hour?" he suggested.

"Sounds good," Paul said at once.

Nodding, Russell moved off toward the Corbys' cottage.

"We'd best go inside and see to the feeding now then," Paul said quietly, taking her arm to usher her to the cottage.

"That's all right, Paul. It can wait until after we come back in," Jeanie said at once, but didn't pull free. If they were going to sit around a bonfire with other couples, she wanted to put on one of the T-shirts and pairs of shorts she'd picked up while in town.

"Are you sure?" Paul asked as he opened the cottage screen door and held it for her.

"Positive," Jeanne Louise answered as she moved past him to enter the kitchen, and she was. As hungry as she was and as carried away as she got when he kissed and caressed her, she'd rather wait and see if she couldn't manage a snack on one of their neighbors first to ease the worst of her hunger. The last thing she wanted was to accidentally kill Paul. Pushing that unpleasant thought away, she headed for her room saying, "I'm going to change."

"Okay. I'll get some drinks and snacks together for us," Paul said, moving to the refrigerator.

Jeanne Louise was quick about changing and was back in the kitchen to help Paul before he finished gathering what they needed. She then helped him carry it down to the beach. While Paul started a bonfire, she gathered six of the eight lawn chairs that belonged to the cottages and set them up around it.

"Look at that. You build one hell of a fire, Paul," Russell greeted as he approached out of the darkness with a cooler in hand and a petite brunette on his heels. The woman had a plate of cheese in one hand and a couple bags of chips in the other. "This is my wife, Cecily. Cecily, Paul and Jeanie Williams."

"Hi," Jeanne Louise said and hurried forward to take the chips as one of the bags started to slip from the brunette's clutches.

"Thank you," Cecily said with a grin. "And hello."

Jeanne Louise chuckled and followed her to the two chairs Russell set the cooler between.

"I have some sausage cut up and crackers inside still," Cecily announced as she set the cheese plate on the cooler. "I won't be a minute."

"Do you need a hand?" Jeanne Louise offered.

"Actually, yes, if you don't mind," Cecily said with a smile. "I need to grab some glasses too."

"I don't mind at all," Jeanne Louise assured her, setting the bags of chips down by the cooler and following her back to the cottage the Jacksons had rented.

"I was relieved when Russell said you two had a little girl about our daughter's age. Not that the boys haven't been including our daughter, Kirsten, in their play, but I know she'll have more fun with another little girl to play with," Cecily said as they approached the cottage.

"I'm sure Livy will be happy to have a friend too," Jeanne Louise assured her, eyeing the woman's long hair and thinking it would hide the marks from her bite. At least it would hide them from Paul. She'd have to put it in the woman's head that they were mosquito bites to explain them away to her husband, though, in case he saw them. The punctures wouldn't be that big, but they would be there.

"Here we are," Cecily said, leading her into the cottage. It was set up much the same as the one they were in, and it was decorated just as attractively, Jeanne Louise noted, and then glanced to Cecily, slid into her thoughts, and moved up behind her for a quick bite. It was always best to bite same sex donors from behind. Most people's memory was visual. If they saw nothing but blank wall during the biting it made it less likely that seeing something or someone would bring back the memory of being bitten.

Jeanne Louise was careful not to take too much blood. It was easy to do when you weren't overexcited and in the throes of passion. She then helped Cecily collect the remaining items she'd wanted and carry them back out to the fire.

The Corbys had arrived by the time they reached the bonfire. Russell introduced John Corby and his wife, Sharon, to Jeanne Louise and then the group all settled around the fire and began to get acquainted.

The two couples were quite nice, the conversation friendly and amusing, and Jeanne Louise was actually enjoying herself when a sudden shriek from the cottage behind them made her stiffen. She was on her feet in a flash and nearly forgot and used her immortal speed to rush to Livy, but caught herself at the last minute and forced herself to move at mortal fast instead. It was hard though—she wanted to hurry. Jeanne Louise didn't know what had woken the child, but she was obviously having another one of her headaches.

She didn't realize Paul had followed her until he reached past her to open the cottage door for her.

"Thanks," Jeanne Louise murmured as she stepped inside. She immediately gave up on mortal speed for immortal now that she was in the house and not visible to the others.

Livy was lying on the floor beside her bed, heart-wrenching sobs shaking her whole body. Boomer was licking her face and whining with concern. Jeanne Louise slipped into her thoughts as she entered the room, but there was no headache this time.

"Oh, sweetie, what is it?" she asked, bending to pick up the girl.

"I fell out of bed," Livy wailed, wrapping her arms around Jeanne Louise's neck and holding on for dear life.

"Ah, poor muffin," Jeanne Louise cooed, hugging and rocking the girl. "Did you hurt yourself?"

"My elbow," Livy cried pulling back to point at the broken skin on the end of her elbow. She'd either banged it on the bedside table or the floor as she'd fallen, Jeanne Louise supposed, but could have wept with relief. No headache, just your average "child falls out of bed" moment.

"I didn't think to buy a first-aid kit," Paul said, joining them beside the bed.

Jeanne Louise glanced at him, noting that he looked relieved to find his daughter just had a normal child moment too.

"I'll go see if the Jacksons or Corbys have some antiseptic and a bandage they can spare," he added and turned from the room.

"Okay." Jeanne Louise said and continued to rock Livy until her tears eased, and then sat on the bed with her in her lap to wait.

"Hello?"

Jeanne Louise glanced toward the door at the sound of that female call. She recognized Sharon Corby's voice. "Back here."

"Paul said you needed a Band-Aid and some antiseptic," Sharon said appearing in the doorway a moment later with both in hand. "He wanted to come back, but I told him we women could handle it," she said lightly, and then her gaze slid to Livy and she asked sympathetically, "Did someone fall out of bed?"

Livy sniffed and nodded, then held up her elbow for her to see and Sharon moved forward at once, "oohing" and "oh dearing" and generally making a fuss as she spread some salve on the wound and then covered it with a bandage.

"Better?" Jeanne Louise asked as Sharon straightened from her nursing duties. When Livy nodded, she smiled faintly, kissed her cheek and stood up with her. Turning, she set her in bed, pulled the sheet up to cover her and kissed her forehead affectionately. "You go back to sleep, sweetie. You have lots of playing to do tomorrow."

"Yes, Mommy," Livy said sleepily, her eyes blinking closed, and Jeanie positively froze at the title, her heart stopping.

"Wow, she dropped right off to sleep, poor thing," Sharon whispered with amusement.

Jeanne Louise straightened slowly, telling herself Livy had just been confused because she was so tired. It didn't mean anything that she'd called her Mommy. She shouldn't be feeling like she wanted to grab the girl up and hug and kiss her like crazy.

"All that weeping and wailing must have worn her out."

Managing a smile, Jeanne Louise turned to the woman. One more snack before feeding off Paul later tonight could only be a good thing, she thought, eyeing the woman's short hair with pursed lips. The marks would be visible on the neck. Her gaze slid down to the woman's wrist and the large clunky watch she wore. The band would hide marks on her wrist though, Jeanne Louise decided.

"Thank you so much for your help," she murmured, slipping into the woman's mind as she moved forward. Jeanne Louise made her turn and walk out into the hall, and then took her hand and had her peer up the hall as she eased the watch band aside and raised Sharon's wrist to her mouth.

Moments later, the two women walked outside, Jeanne Louise chuckling softly as Sharon commented that she wished she'd had a girl along with her boys and told her some of the antics her sons had got up to over the years. She was sure a girl would be less troublesome, or at least would need fewer trips to the emergency room for stitches.

"Livy okay?" Paul asked as they reached the bonfire.

"She's fine," Jeanne Louise assured him as she settled in her chair next to his. "She went right back to sleep as soon as she was bandaged up."

"Good." He smiled softly, then reached out and took her hand to give it a squeeze of thanks.

Jeanne Louise smiled back, and relaxed in her chair, but then was almost afraid to breathe in case he realized he hadn't let go of her hand. She liked his holding her hand. It felt right. It was a bit distracting though. Especially since he was absently rubbing his thumb over the back of her hand, sending shivers up her arm. With him doing that Jeanne Louise found herself having trouble following the conversation going on around the fire now, and was relieved when Cecily gave a large yawn after an hour passed and announced that she was ready to call it a night.

"Already?" Sharon asked with regret and then glanced at her watch, her eyebrows rising. "Goodness, is it midnight already? I guess time does fly when you're having fun."

"Yeah, and the kids will be up with the dawn," Cecily said, standing and beginning to collect the remainder of the things she and Russell had brought.

"Yes," Sharon said on a sigh, getting to her feet now as well. "Come on, John, your boys will be knocking on the bedroom door at dawn demanding you take them fishing as promised."

John Corby groaned. "I forgot about that."

"Well, I can guarantee that the kids haven't," Russell said with a chuckle as he stood as well and picked up his cooler. He glanced to Paul. "Do you and Livy want to come along, Paul? There's room for two more in the boat and Jeanne Louise can go shopping in London with the girls. That's what they have planned for the morning."

Jeanne Louise stiffened at the offer, but needn't have worried. Paul chuckled, but shook his head. "Thanks for the offer, Russell, but I get seasick, and Livy takes after her old man. Besides I promised the girls a trip to the ice cream shop tomorrow morning."

"All right then," Russell said easily, turning away. "Maybe we'll see you tomorrow afternoon. It's 'loll on the beach and watch the kids swim' time in the afternoons."

"Sounds good," Paul said. "Night."

A chorus of good nights followed as the other two couples moved away from the fire, headed for their own cottages.

"Do you really get seasick?" Jeanne Louise asked curiously.

"Fortunately, yes," Paul admitted wryly.

"Why fortunately?" Jeanne Louise asked with surprise.

"Because I'm a terrible liar and would have had trouble coming up with an excuse to avoid it otherwise."

"Not keen on fishing?" she asked with amusement.

"Jeanie, I'm a science geek," he said dryly, as if she may have forgotten it. "Give me blood, cell cultures, and petri dishes to play with and I'm happy. But worms and hooks and scaly, slimy fish are just gross."

She burst out laughing at the claim, and then glanced around with a sigh. "I guess I should gather our stuff together and head in too. Livy will probably be up early."

"Yeah," Paul said with regret, and then stood up, using his hold on her hand to pull her up as well. She wasn't expecting that, and came up with a gasp and sort of stumbled against him. Paul immediately closed his arms around her, one of her hands still in his as he caught her close, the action unintentionally making her arch against him, her hips grinding into his.

They both froze briefly at the contact, and then Jeanne Louise leaned her head back to peer up at him.

"You need to feed yet." The reminder was a bare growl of sound on the night breeze. If Paul had been immortal, she was sure his eyes would be glowing, and knew hers probably were.

Jeanne Louise just stood still for a moment,

allowing the heat to build in her, and then she reached up with her free hand, slid it around his neck and drew his head down until she could reach his lips. The kiss was at first tentative and questing, but then Paul released her hand to cup her face and deepened the kiss, his mouth becoming demanding, his tongue slipping out to lash her.

It made her groan, and Jeanne Louise slipped her arms around his waist, fingers scraping hungrily up his back, and then dropping to slip beneath his T-shirt and touch the flesh it covered. Paul moaned at the contact, and then urged her head back to allow his mouth to travel over her chin and down her throat. He then released her face and let his hands travel, sliding them over her shoulders and down her arms in a tantalizingly light caress. Then he reached for the hem of her T-shirt.

Jeanne Louise glanced down, and then instinctively raised her arms as he tugged the T-shirt up and off over her head as if undressing a child. The shirt was floating to the ground and Paul's hands had found and cupped her breasts through the strapless swimsuit top that remained before she could even lower her arms.

Moaning at the caress, Jeanne Louise grabbed his shoulders and rose up on her tiptoes in response, her upper body arching up and away while her pelvis pressed tighter against him.

When he released one breast and reached around behind her, she began pressing kisses to his throat, and licking at his salty skin. She felt him work at the clasp of her bathing suit top, and then the scrap of black cloth slipped away, leaving her bare to his attention. Jeanne Louise gasped and nipped at his neck as his hands fondled and kneaded the firm globes now revealed.

She heard Paul murmur her name and leaned back to peer at him, only to have him cover her mouth with his. His kiss was hungry, his kneading of her breasts becoming almost painful, and then he broke their kiss to begin trailing his mouth down her throat again as his fingers found her nipples and tweaked teasingly.

Jeanne Louise cupped his head and moaned, her upper body leaning back to give him better access as his mouth continued toward the slope of one breast. His tongue laved her along the way and then curled around her erect nipple as his mouth closed over it. That made her gasp and clutch at his hair and then she gasped again as his hands dropped to find her bottom and urge her tighter against him.

When one hand then slid down the back of her shorts to clasp her behind, Jeanne Louise groaned and rubbed herself against the hardness between his legs. Paul groaned in response and retrieved his hand to catch the waistband of her tight jean shorts and push them down, trying to force them over her hips without undoing them. They weren't going, of course, and he growled with frustration against her breast, then gave up trying to push them down and instead cupped her between her legs through the heavy cloth, nearly lifting her off the ground as he did.

Jeanne Louise cried out and clutched at his shoulders, then gasped in surprise when she felt his other hand at her waist and the snap of her jeans suddenly gave way. In the next moment, his hand slipped from between her legs and her jean shorts slid over her hips and slid down her thighs.

"Paul," she breathed, the vague thought that they should take this inside dancing at the edge of her mind, but not fully taking root before he was pushing down the scrap of her bathing suit bottoms and replacing the material with his fingers, sliding them between her legs to cup her again, but this time without the cloth to hinder him.

Gasping, Jeanne Louise tugged viciously at his head, pulling his mouth from her breast to claim it in a kiss that was hard, hot, and somewhat frantic as his fingers slid between her folds and began to play over her slick skin. When her legs, already trembling, began to give out, Paul dropped to his knees in the sand with her, his kiss and caresses unrelenting as he sent wave after wave of heat and passion surging through them both.

"Christ," he growled suddenly, tearing his mouth from hers to press heated kisses to her cheek and neck as he muttered, "I touch you and I go up in flames."

"Yes," Jeanne Louise gasped, though she wasn't so much answering or agreeing as urging him on as she released her hold on his shoulders to reach for the snap and zipper of his jeans. She undid both and pushed the material down until his eager erection popped out, hard and hot, surging with delicious blood.

Jeanne Louise actually considered trying out the genital biting she'd heard so much about, but worried it might cause him some discomfort after the fact, and instead suddenly pushed him backward. In her eagerness, she used a little more force than she'd intended and Paul fell back, landing hard on his back in the sand with a grunt. She didn't give him a chance to recover. Feeling barren without his hands on her, Jeanne Louise crawled up his body until she could kiss him, and then lowered herself to rub against his hardness.

Paul kissed back on a groan, his hands moving to clasp her breasts and fondle as she rubbed herself over him again and again. But then he reached for her hips, holding her still as he shifted himself beneath her, and then he was urging her down, his hardness pressing into her.

Jeanne Louise broke their kiss and threw her head back to stare blindly at the stars as her moist heat closed tightly around him, clenching and squeezing him from tip to base and trebling their combined pleasure. She then lowered her head again to peer down at him and raised herself until he nearly slid out, before dropping to take him in again.

Paul met her gaze, his jaw clenched against the waves rushing through him. When he raised his hand to her face, she turned into it and then opened her mouth to allow one finger to slip between her lips. She immediately drew the digit into her mouth and began to suck on it as she moved, so caught up in the combination of things she was doing that she was completely caught by surprise when Paul suddenly snatched his finger free of her lips, caught her by the waist and rolled them both.

In the next moment, Jeanne Louise was on her back in the sand with him over her. Paul paused briefly, his erection sunk deep in her, but when she reached up and drew his head down for a kiss, he began to move, driving them both over the edge and into the void.

Ten

Paul woke up with the thought that he was lying on the lumpiest bed in existence. When he regained full consciousness and opened his eyes to see that it was Jeanne Louise he was lying on, he did a quick push up, removing his crushing weight from her chest. He peered down at her then, worried that he'd suffocated her or something, but when he saw her breasts rising and falling as she breathed, he relaxed a little. He also eased himself to the side and sat up to peer around.

The fire had died down to embers and the lights were out in the Jacksons' and Corbys' cottages, but the moon and stars were reflecting off the smooth surface of the lake, giving some illumination. Actually, the water looked incredibly inviting under the moonlight, and Paul found himself thinking he should take a swim.

His gaze slid back to Jeanne Louise. While he was mostly dressed, she was completely nude, splayed on her back in the sand like an angel fallen from the heavens. Paul's eyes slid over her pale limbs and torso, recalling the feel of her body sliding against his, and closing wet and warm around him and immediately hardened at the memory.

He hadn't expected what had happened. Well, okay, perhaps in his heart of hearts Paul had been hoping for it. But he'd honestly expected she'd kiss and caress him a bit and then bite his neck. Task over. Instead, passion had exploded over them like a shower of sparks. It had filled his mind until all he could think of was finding the release that fast and furious passion had promised.

It had definitely lived up to the promise, he thought. In fact, it had been so powerful that Paul didn't think he'd fallen asleep after they were done. Much as it made him squirm to admit it, he actually suspected that he'd just sort of passed out as it rode over him. He'd never experienced anything like it. Had never known a woman like Jeanne Louise. Around her he felt . . . hope, he realized. And happiness. And desire like nothing he'd ever enjoyed, even with his wife Jerri.

The acknowledgment brought a wave of guilt over him, and Paul turned his gaze to the water once more. He'd loved Jerri with all his heart. He'd thought he'd never find anyone who could fill his heart as she had. But Jeanne Louise . . . He glanced to her again, his eyes caressing her face, carefree in sleep. Jeanne Louise filled his heart, his mind, and seemed to even fill his body. He felt like she slid into his skin when they kissed, like she was there with him as he rode the waves of pleasure. It was not something he'd ever even imagined experiencing. Truly, he'd thought that he'd had his grand love affair, that no one could compare to Jerri, and that all that was left was to raise Livy.

When he'd thought of his future after Jerri died, Paul had seen himself alone from now on, a single father, seeing his daughter happily on her way in life, raising her, sending her off to college, walking her up the aisle, greeting his grandchildren . . . and maybe then, after his job was done, he'd thought he might enjoy a senior fling with a nice neighbor widow who understood that he could never love like he'd loved his wife again.

Instead, Paul was starting to envision a different future, one with Jeanne Louise in it . . . and it was distracting him from his purpose in kidnapping Jeanne Louise. Rather than trying to convince her to turn his daughter and save her life, he was hungrily stripping her clothes off and merging his body with hers in the cool sand under a bright moon. Not just his body. It had almost felt as if their souls had been intertwined here under the stars and he wasn't sure he'd got all of it back.

While he should be sated and clearheaded after the vigorous session, Paul wanted her again. He was hard and aching, fighting the urge to lean down and kiss her and start the madness all over again.

And again. And again. In truth, Paul thought he could happily just stay here on the beach, his body entwined and inside Jeanne Louise's forever.

He'd lost the plot of his plan, Paul realized unhappily, and while he had, his daughter continued to suffer her headaches and move closer to death.

But he wasn't the only one who'd got caught up in things to the point of losing track of what they were supposed to be doing. Jeanne Louise hadn't even fed this time, which had been the reason behind the start of what had exploded into uncontrolled ardor. Which meant they'd be doing this again.

The thought had the member between Paul's legs standing up like a flagpole. Sighing, he glanced to the smooth surface of the lake and pushed himself to his feet. His pants immediately started to slip down his hips. Paul let them drop to the sand, and stepped out of the warm cloth. He removed his T-shirt next, dropping it to lie beside the jeans.

His gaze then slid to Jeanne Louise again, lying still and perfect in the sand, and then he turned and jogged toward the water.

Jeanne Louise sighed sleepily and shifted onto her side with a little shiver, one hand searching blindly for her missing sheets. She must have kicked them off in her sleep, she thought unhappily, but frowned when rather than soft bedding her fingers encountered grains of sand. Eyes opening, she stared at the expanse of beach spread out before her and then sat up abruptly as memory returned as to how she'd got there.

Paul wasn't beside her, as she'd expected, though his clothes were. Following that clue, Jeanne Louise turned to peer toward the lake, relaxing when she saw him swimming away from shore. He'd woken before her, she realized. Well, if he'd fainted, she thought next. She knew she had, but—her gaze slid to the dying fire, and then Jeanne Louise reached for his clothes, relaxing when she felt the warmth still clinging to them. He hadn't taken them off long ago and by her guess at least an hour or two had passed since their neighbors had left and they'd fallen into each other's arms like a couple of horny teenagers. He'd fainted too.

Her gaze slid to the lake again and she briefly considered joining him in it. Just the memory of what they'd done was bringing back her desire almost full blown and making her want to touch and kiss him again, but then reason reared its ugly, but sensible, head. If she followed her instincts and joined Paul in the water, they wouldn't make it out before they were doing the same thing all over again. And if that happened and they fainted in the lake, she might survive, the nanos reviving her when she washed ashore, but Paul would drown. That was not something she wanted to risk.

Grimacing, Jeanne Louise gathered her swimsuit, shorts, and T-shirt and got up to head to the cottage. Removing herself from temptation seemed the safest route.

When she entered the cottage, she immediately headed for the master bedroom, stopping to look in on Livy on the way. The girl was sleeping soundly, but Boomer raised his head and wagged his tail. Jeanne Louise smiled. The dog was as devoted to the girl as her father was, she thought, as her gaze slid to Livy's sweet sleeping face. The two days' worth of meals the girl had been enjoying were beginning to show already. At least, Livy didn't appear quite as thin and pale as she'd been when Jeanne Louise had first seen her. That was good.

Leaving her undisturbed, Jeanne Louise continued up the hall into her own bedroom and then into the bathroom. The sight of herself in the mirror there made her pause. She was covered with sand from head to toe. The fine grains sticking to her body like fleas on a dog.

Jeanne Louise grimaced and quickly dropped her dirty clothes on the floor. She then turned on the shower. Leaving it to warm up, she slipped back into her room to grab one of the two nightgowns she'd bought at the mall. Jeanne Louise didn't normally wear them, but she'd thought it for the best since she might have to be up to rush to Livy's side in the night if the child needed her. Taking the rose-colored, knee-length nightie back into the bathroom, she laid it on the counter, then reached into the shower to test the water temperature. Finding it warm enough, Jeanne Louise stepped into the small stall and closed the door.

Never one to dawdle, she was quick about her

shower. Ten minutes later she was out. Jeanne Louise quickly wrapped her hair in a small towel, and then used a larger one to dry her body before donning her nightie. She followed that up with towel drying her hair and brushing it back from her face. She was going to leave it like that, but the idea of crawling into bed with wet hair made her grimace. When a quick search of the cupboard under the sink produced a hair dryer, Jeanne Louise quickly used it and the brush to dry her hair, curling it under as she did.

Satisfied that she wouldn't be sleeping on a damp pillow, or waking up with her hair standing up all over the place from sleeping on it wet, Jeanne Louise put the dryer and brush away and then headed back into her room. She contemplated the bed briefly, and then decided she'd best check to make sure Paul was still all right in the lake. Mortals had been known to suffer cramps and drown. Besides she was kind of thirsty and a glass of water sounded good. She'd grab a drink and look out to check on Paul.

Slipping from her room, Jeanne Louise glanced in on Livy again and then moved out through the living room to the kitchen. A quick glance out the large living room picture windows didn't reveal much, but she just peered out in passing. In the kitchen, she grabbed a glass from the cupboard and then moved to the sink and turned on the tap. Leaving it to run for a moment, Jeanne Louise then looked out the window above it to scan the beach and lake, frowning when she didn't see evidence of Paul. There was no one in the lake that she could see. Her gaze shifted to the remains of the bonfire and she'd just realized that his clothes were missing too when the door opened behind her.

Relaxing, Jeanne Louise turned her attention to slipping her glass under the running water, asking, "Good swim?"

"Lovely," Paul answered, easing the door closed to keep it from clacking and waking Livy. She heard him set something on the table and cross to stand behind her as she turned off the water, but was still startled when his arms slid around her waist from behind.

"You're still wet," Jeanne Louise protested on a laugh as he pulled her back against his chest and brushed her hair aside to press a kiss to the side of her neck.

"Mmmm, I didn't have a towel," he murmured against her throat. "And you forgot to feed."

Jeanne Louise clutched her glass and glanced over her shoulder at him, then gasped as one of his hands slid up to find a breast through her cotton nightgown. She gasped again as his other hand slid down to cup her between her legs and press her back against him. Not only had Paul not had a towel to dry off, he hadn't bothered dressing, Jeanne Louise realized as she felt his body press against her through the thin material.

"Paul," she whispered, and couldn't have said what she'd meant by it. Whether it had been a plea, a caution, or a reprimand. It didn't matter. Paul lowered his head to kiss her, and Jeanne Louise just didn't care. She cared even less when his hand slid up to slip inside the top of her nightgown to find and caress first one breast and then the other. The touch drew a moan from her throat, and Jeanne Louise arched into his touch as she kissed him back.

When Paul broke the kiss to trail his mouth to her ear, she sighed and tilted her head. The cold splash of water on her hand as the glass tilted in her hand reminded her that she still held it and Jeanne Louise immediately set it on the counter. Paul's hand at her breasts had tugged the nightie down now to fully reveal them, and he was fondling and toying with first one and then the other with the one hand. With the other he was tugging her nightie up.

Jeanne Louise covered the hand at her breast with her own. With the other she reached back to catch him by the neck. She then turned her own face back to him for another kiss. Paul gave in to the demand, covering her mouth and blocking the gasped groan that followed when his hand finally slid under the nightgown and between her legs.

When his fingers found the core of her, Paul broke their kiss to whisper, "God, you're hot and wet for me already."

Jeanne Louise merely removed the hand that had been encouraging him at her breasts and reached behind to find the hardness prodding her, evidence that he was in a similar state. Closing her fingers around him, Jeanne Louise squeezed and then groaned again as the passion sliding through her increased.

Cursing, Paul urged her back a bit from the sink with the hand between her legs. He then used the other to wrench her nightie up and out of the way. In the next moment, Jeanne Louise was grabbing for the countertop as he slid into her.

Paul released a long groan by her ear as he entered her, the hand between her legs never stopping its caresses, while the one that had pulled her night gown up now clasped her upper thigh, pulling her back into him as he pushed forward.

Jeanne Louise closed her eyes briefly at the rush of sensation pounding through her, and then moaned as he withdrew and slid back in. The tension was building in her, amplified by his, and Jeanne Louise was sure she was about to explode, when Paul suddenly froze. She blinked her eyes open, catching their reflection in the window, and seeing the frown on Paul's face.

Before she could ask what was wrong, he'd pulled himself out of her, caught her wrist and was dragging her from the kitchen. Jeanne Louise followed unprotesting as it occurred to her that it would have been a painful landing on the kitchen's hardwood floor at the end.

Paul led her to the master bedroom and straight to the bed, before pausing and turning to face her. He reached for the hem of her nightgown, no doubt intending to remove it, but Jeanne Louise took him by surprise and pushed him back on the bed. He bounced on the soft surface, eyes wide, and then grinned.

"Like to be on top, do you?" he asked with amusement, pulling himself further up the bed so that his legs no longer dangled off the edge.

Jeanne Louise simply grabbed the hem of her nightgown and drew it up, to quickly strip it off. Tossing it to the floor, she then moved along the side of the bed until she was even with his hips, then she reached out and caught his erection in hand.

Paul stiffened, but just watched her.

"Move closer to the edge," she whispered, afraid of waking Livy in the next room.

Paul's eyebrows rose, but he slid to the side until there was no room between himself and the edge of the bed.

Jeanne Louise smiled and immediately swung her left leg over him to rest on the bed by his other hip, leaving her right one still planted on the floor. She then used her hold on his shaft to direct him into her.

Paul groaned as Jeanne Louise lowered herself onto him, his hands reaching for her. One found her breast and began to play and fondle there, but the other slid between them, finding the core of her excitement and caressing that. Jeanne Louise left the hand between her legs, but she claimed the one at her breast, clasping it and bringing it to her mouth to kiss as she raised and lowered herself on him again. Then she licked between his fingers briefly, before kissing and nibbling her way across his palm to his wrist as she raised and lowered herself again, finding the foot on the floor made the action easier.

Meeting his eyes over his arm, Jeanne Louise raised herself up once more, but this time as she slid back down his length, she allowed her fangs to slide out and sink into his flesh. Paul grunted, his body arching and going stiff in the bed, and then he thrust his hips up, his hardness ramming into her as every muscle spasmed under the rush of pleasure that followed.

Jeanne Louise was aware of his cry of pleasure, of his body shuddering beneath hers with release. But her own body was caught up in the waves too, vibrating like a plucked guitar string as she sucked at his wrist and ground down on him, unable to stop either motion until the final tidal wave of pleasure rushed over her, crashing against her mind with a violence that left her stunned and sinking into darkness.

A far off keening woke Jeanne Louise. Opening her eyes, she stared blankly at the chest she was splayed on, and then became aware of the sobbing and wailing coming from the next room. Livy. She stiffened briefly, and then eased herself up and off of Paul, managing the task without waking him. Once on her feet, Jeanne Louise caught up her nightgown and tugged it on over her head as she headed for the girl's room. However, the child wasn't in there when she entered.

Frowning, Jeanne Louise turned and followed the sobs and wails to the living room and found the girl curled around Boomer on the sofa, clutching him desperately as she cried her heart out.

"What is it sweetie? Another headache?" Jeanne Louise asked, moving quickly toward her.

Livy lifted her head from Boomer's furry back at once. Her eyes widened, and then she wailed, "I thought you and Daddy were dead!"

"What?" Jeanne Louise asked with amazement, sinking to sit on the sofa next to her and wincing when she dipped into the child's head and felt the pain raging there.

"I h-heard a scr-scream," Livy explained. "It woke me up and my head hurt and I came to find you and Daddy and you were both asleep, but I c-couldn't wake you u-up," she sobbed miserably. "I thought you were dead."

"No, of course we aren't, sweetie," Jeanne Louise murmured, quickly working to mask the pain in the child's head. "Your daddy's fine too. We were just sleeping."

"Then why didn't you wake up when I shook you and screamed?" Livy asked, her sobs lessening as Jeanne Louise took the pain away and onto herself.

"We probably just had too much wine by the bonfire," Jeanne Louise lied. Good Lord, they must have been well and truly out of it if the girl's shouts and shaking them hadn't woken either of them. And good Lord, they'd both been naked and . . . well, basically in a rather compromising position. Not that Livy seemed to have noticed. Thank God.

"A scream woke you up?" Jeanne Louise asked suddenly, slow to pick up on that with the pain now pounding in her head.

Sniffling, Livy nodded. "Both Daddy and you screamed."

"Hmm, well we must have had a bad dream," Jeanne Louise muttered, knowing it had been their cries of passion that had woken the child. They would have to ensure they weren't in the next room in future when indulging in . . . er . . . Jeanne Louise let the thought go. She just couldn't think clearly anymore. This headache was worse still than the last. They were becoming more and more unbearable.

Deciding the girl had been comforted enough, Jeanne Louise put the child to sleep. Livy slumped on Boomer and Jeanie stayed in her mind for several more minutes to ensure all would be well. Then she leaned back on the sofa beside the pair and waited for her own pain to abate.

Jeanne Louise tried to think about their situation as she waited, trying to sort out if it was time to explain about life mates to Paul and that he was hers, but hard as it was to think at the moment, she didn't get far. Grimacing, she let the matter go and got to her feet. The moment she picked up Livy, Boomer was up and off the couch, ready to follow as Jeanne Louise carried his little girl to bed. When she set the girl in the bed and covered her up, the dog leapt up onto the bed to curl at her feet. Jeanne Louise gave the loyal dog a pet, kissed Livy's cheek, and then slipped out of the room.

Paul was still sound asleep when Jeanne Louise returned to the master bedroom. She hesitated, wondering if she should sleep on the couch so as not to disturb him, but then climbed carefully into bed beside him, easing under the covers. Once there she paused and eyed him. Paul was crashed out on top of the blanket next to her and would no doubt get cold in the night. After a brief internal debate, Jeanne Louise gently shook his shoulder.

"Paul?"

"Hmmm?" he murmured sleepily, turning his head toward her voice, but not opening his eyes.

"Do you want to get under the covers?" she suggested.

When Paul mumbled in his sleep, but didn't seem to fully wake, Jeanne Louise shrugged to herself and left him as he was. She lay down in the bed, but found herself peering at him. Her life mate. Damn. The thought still made her shake her head and marvel. Most immortals waited centuries, even millennia to find their life mates. Few were fortunate enough to find them so young. And at just over a century Jeanne Louise was definitely considered young by most of her kind . . . a baby really. Yet there he was . . . her life mate. The one man she couldn't read or control, and the one man she could think freely around and not guard her thoughts.

Paul was her oasis in a chaotic world where Jeanne Louise usually had to be on guard . . . and she was terrified of losing him.

The thought made Jeanne Louise turn on her side away from him and huddle under the blankets. Things were going well enough, but it was still tricky. She thought he liked her for herself, but who could say with men? He might just like her for sex and what she could do for Livy.

Jeanne Louise stilled and listened as Paul began to shift around in the bed beside her. He'd woken up after all, she realized, when the blankets lifted behind her, and had to wonder if the cool night air on his naked skin had finished what she'd started. Then his body slid up behind her, his front pressing to her back as he slid an arm around her to draw her back against him. Once he had her positioned where he wanted her, his hand slid lazily to cup one breast as he kissed her neck. Jeanne Louise released a little sigh as her body responded, but she was concerned about having fed off him and asked, "How do you feel?"

"Honestly?" Paul asked in a murmur by her ear.

"Yes," Jeanne Louise said with amusement.

"Like I want to make love to you again, but I'm too tired," he admitted wryly, and she chuckled at the admission.

"That's all right. Sleep," Jeanne Louise said sliding her hand over his arm and down to cover his hand on her breast. "There's always tomorrow."

"Tomorrow, huh?" Paul asked with amusement, nuzzling her ear. "Are you going to break out into song, Annie?"

Jeanne Louise's eyes widened in the darkness. "Well, Mr. Jones. It seems you have a vein of sarcasm hidden in your sweetness."

Paul chuckled at the words and pressed a kiss to the side of her head. "Just a little one, Ms. Argeneau. I shall try to refrain from tapping it."

"Don't bother on my account," she said easily. "It makes you interesting."

"You vampires," he tsked, tugging her tighter against him. "You always go for the veins."

"Hmm," Jeanne Louise murmured. "Speaking of veins, did I hurt you?"

"Not at all," Paul assured her, and then asked, "Are you going to try a different vein each time?"

"Hoping I'll eventually go for a genital bite?" she asked with amusement.

"Absolutely," he said unabashed, and Jeanne Louise chuckled softly at the enthusiasm in his voice.

"Maybe next time," she said lightly, and then murmured, "Good night, Paul."

"Good night, John boy," Paul responded, and then grunted when she smacked his hand in punishment.

"Someone watched way too much television growing up," Jeanne Louise said dryly.

"*Someone* still does," he admitted, and allowed his hand to drift away from her breasts and down between her legs. "Maybe you can help me find something more interesting to do in future."

Jeanne Louise's eyes opened sharply as he began to caress her lazily. "I thought you were tired?"

"I'm waking up," Paul said, and shifted his hips against her bottom, proving just how awake he was.

Jeanne Louise groaned as she felt his hardness prod her, and reached back to clasp his erection in hand as she cautioned, "Okay, but we have to be quiet. We woke up Livy last time."

"We did?" he asked, stilling. "Was she okay?"

"Headache," she admitted. "And it scared her when she couldn't wake us up."

"She was in here? She saw us?" Paul asked with alarm, his hands halting abruptly.

Jeanne Louise sighed and shifted onto her back in front of him. "It's all right," she said reassuringly. "I soothed her, took away her headache, and put her back to bed."

Paul remained still for a minute and then let his breath out on a sigh. "Thank you," he murmured, his eyes full of sincerity as they met hers, but filling with something else entirely when they dropped down to see that the blanket was around her waist, leaving her breasts on offer. Sliding his hand up to clasp the nearer one, Paul breathed, "Damn, I think I love your breasts."

"You love my breasts?" Jeanne Louise asked dryly.

"And other parts," he murmured distractedly,

lowering his mouth to claim the nipple of the breast he held.

Jeanne Louise bit her lip as Paul began to suckle, sending shockwaves of pleasure through her, then sighed and relaxed, murmuring, "It's a start."

Eleven

'What shall we do now?'

Jeanne Louise smiled at Paul's question as they wandered out of the antiques section. But before she could respond, Livy shrieked, "Ice cream!"

She glanced at the girl, chuckling at the way the child was hopping about and clapping her hands.

They had headed to Grand Bend first thing that morning. Or first thing on Livy waking them, she acknowledged with a wry smile. Certainly Jeanne Louise hadn't been ready to wake yet, and doubted Paul had been either after the two of them had spent most of the night getting acquainted with each other's bodies, passing out and getting reacquainted again. They'd been like a couple of junkies, jonesing on each other and reaching repeatedly for that next fix the moment they woke up after each session.

After taking turns in the shower, they'd piled Livy in the car and had headed to Grand Bend and the Pinery Antique Market. Paul had read about it in a stack of brochures and fliers left on the table by the cottage owner. In the market one could find a Sunday breakfast, live entertainment, and ice cream made from real cream, along with antiques and various other things one wouldn't expect.

They'd had breakfast first, then toured the vendors, and the entire time Livy had been on about the ice cream Paul had promised she would get on this outing. It didn't matter that she'd just had a large breakfast, she'd wanted ice cream from the minute they'd arrived. The girl's appetite was definitely benefiting from the lack of pain and the fact that Jeanne Louise ensured Livy thought she enjoyed what she ate.

"All right, all right," Paul said with amusement. "Ice cream it is. And then we should probably head back to the cottage for some swimming."

"Ohhh," Livy's eyes were wide and happy. "Swimming."

"Yes, and probably playing," he added. "The people in the cottage next to ours have a little girl close to your age. Her name's Kirsten. So you might have someone to play with while we're here if the two of you like each other."

"Yay!" Livy squealed and danced in circles.

Paul shook his head at her excitement and then caught her hand in his, slipped his other hand around Jeanne Louise's waist and herded them both to the ice cream stand. Jeanne Louise ordered a combo cone with a scoop of rocky road and black cherry. Livy immediately asked for the same and Paul ordered pistachio. Once their cones were in hand, they walked slowly back toward the parking lot, licking madly at the quickly melting ice cream.

It was nearly noon and extremely hot. Jeanne Louise was very aware of the sun beating down, but didn't want to spoil the moment by reminding Paul that she shouldn't be out in it. It was as if he'd completely forgotten that she was immortal, like they were a typical mortal family, enjoying a sunny Sunday outing . . . and she liked it. Jeanne Louise had never really thought she envied mortals being able to enjoy simple pleasures like this, but in that moment she did. She was happy, relaxed and sated from their night together.

Not that Jeanne Louise didn't still want the man presently walking along beside her listening to his daughter's happy chatter. She would have happily lured him into the nearest public washroom, the backseat of the car, or any private spot they could find if they didn't have to keep an eye on Livy. She definitely wanted the man still and was eager for the day to end and night to descend so they could put Livy to bed and enjoy each other again. But, in the meantime, she felt content.

"Jeanie?"

Paul's tense voice made it through her thoughts and drew her attention. Seeing the tension in his expression, she followed his gaze to a dark SUV parked a row over from Paul's car. Her eyes narrowed and she moved to the side to get a look at the license plate and felt her heart drop. It was an Argeneau SUV. They all had specialty license plates and this one was no exception. Her eyes shot to the windows, but the vehicle was empty.

"Get to the car," she said grimly, dropping her cone to the ground to leave her hands free.

Paul immediately scooped up Livy and hurried toward the car. Jeanne Louise didn't follow at once, but instead turned in a slow circle, looking for the driver of the vehicle. When a full turn and scan didn't reveal anyone to her, she hurried after Paul and Livy. He was buckling the little girl into the back when she arrived at the car. Jeanne Louise opened the front passenger door, but didn't immediately get in. She took the opportunity to scan their surroundings again, checking eyes and faces of anyone she saw. Again, though, she didn't spot an immortal anywhere. Not that she knew every hunter working for her uncle, but the eyes tended to be a giveaway, as did their pale skin at this time of year. And most immortals would be wearing long sleeves and slacks rather than shorts to protect them from the sun as much as possible. But everyone she saw was in shorts and T-shirts or some other short-sleeved or completely sleeveless top.

Paul slammed the back door, and she glanced his way as he rushed around to the driver's side. Jeanne Louise gave up scanning people and folded herself into the front seat as he got in. But she continued to scan anyone and everyone she saw as he started the engine and began to back out of the parking spot. She didn't relax until they were on the road and had put some distance between their vehicle and the market.

"I don't think we were followed," Paul said quietly as she shifted to face forward in her seat.

"No," Jeanne Louise agreed on a sigh. "I guess we got lucky. Although I don't know how they missed recognizing your car and license," she added with bewilderment. "We really should have dumped the car. And I should have thought of that."

"Oh . . . er . . . no need for that," he said, looking suddenly uncomfortable.

She peered at him curiously. "Oh?"

Paul nodded, cleared his throat and then admitted, "I bought a black magic marker while we were in town yesterday, and when I was unloading the car, I used it to change the two sixes on my license to eights."

Jeanne Louise's eyes widened. "Really?"

He nodded wryly, and shrugged. "It seemed a good idea. I didn't think they'd search out this far from London, but there was a slight possibility, so I just thought . . ." Paul shrugged helplessly.

Jeanne Louise relaxed a little more at this disclosure, but she was looking at him with admiration and murmured, "Aren't you clever."

"I'm not just another pretty face, you know," he said with a grin.

"No, you certainly aren't," she agreed solemnly.

Paul glanced at her sharply, and then reached over with one hand to squeeze hers. It made Jeanne Louise realize that his hands were as empty as hers.

"Where did your ice cream go?"

"I dropped it in the parking lot," he admitted and then added, "Like you did." He shrugged and added, "It seemed sensible to have my hands free."

"Yes," she said and squeezed his fingers with her own as she glanced in the backseat. Livy was the only one still with a cone, which explained the silence. The girl was still madly licking at her cone . . . and without being controlled and made to think it was good, Jeanne realized, eyes widening. She'd given up making the girl think it tasted good as she'd concentrated on looking for any immortals in the area. But the girl certainly seemed to be enjoying it anyway.

"Damn shame though," Paul said suddenly, regret in his voice. "That was good ice cream."

Jeanne Louise chuckled at the words as she settled back in her seat. But he was right. It had been darned good ice cream, she acknowledged and then suggested, "Maybe we should stop at a store and pick up some Häagen-Dazs or Ben and Jerry's."

"Definitely," he agreed. "We can celebrate our lucky escape with it."

"It was lucky," Jeanne Louise said solemnly. "I didn't expect them to check this far from London."

"Neither did I," Paul admitted, his smile fading. "Maybe we should stick close to the cottage for the next day or two. It's rented under the name Williams and the license has been changed, so as long as we aren't seen we should be good."

"Yes," Jeanne Louise agreed. It just seemed the sensible thing to do. They'd got lucky this time, but it didn't mean they would again.

In the end, they decided to bypass the stop for ice cream. If Enforcers were searching the area, it just seemed a better idea to get back to the cottage and not risk running into one of them.

While Cecily Jackson and Sharon Corby were still on their shopping excursion with Kirsten, their husbands and sons were back from their fishing and descended on them as they got out of the car. Paul was forced to feign enthusiasm as they were shown the morning's catch and regaled with tales of how this one was a fighter, and that one was an even harder fighter, and the other was the biggest fish ever.

Jeanne Louise stood beside him with what he suspected was silent amusement as he tried not to grimace at the smelly fish that were dangled before him. Livy on the other hand was free to say "gross" and "p-ewww" and then rush off to let Boomer out. Paul envied her that. He would have liked to echo her comments and flee the stench, but knew it would be considered terribly unmanly of him. Instead, he spent several minutes offering congratulations to the men before their wives' return distracted them. The triumphant fishermen then rushed off to regale the womenfolk with their stories of success, assuring Paul and Jeanne Louise that they'd hit the beach right after lunch as they went.

Relieved to be free of the chore of admiring the scaly vertebrates, Paul whistled for Boomer and ushered Jeanne Louise and Livy into the cottage. He groaned when Jeanne Louise said she'd make lunch. Having dead fish shoved under his nose had rather stolen his appetite. But Livy responded eagerly enough. The child seemed to be hungry all the time now and he wasn't sure if that was Jeanne Louise or the girl's natural appetite returning now that she was no longer in constant pain.

By the time lunch was ready, however, Paul found himself hungry and enjoyed the bacon, lettuce, and tomato wraps she served up. They then gathered what they would need together and headed down to the beach.

Paul had been worried about Jeanne Louise's need to stay out of the sun, but both Cecily and Sharon were seated in the shade when they went out to join everyone on the beach. Jeanne Louise settled happily with them while Paul and Livy headed straight for the water with Boomer charging ahead and straight into the waves.

Russell waited at the water's edge with Kirsten. They introduced the two girls who played shy for all of five minutes before wading into the water together, splashing each other and giggling as little girls do. Paul watched with a smile, his heart actually aching a little to see his daughter so happy. It was a vast difference from the pale, thin, sickly girl who had been sleeping in Livy's pretty pink room the last couple of weeks. It was like night and day, and he knew he owed it all to Jeanne Louise.

The woman hadn't turned his child yet, but she'd taken away her pain and that had given Livy the chance to be a normal little girl again.

They spent the afternoon with their neighbors, and then had a communal barbecue with everyone contributing food. The men congregated around the large gas barbecue that belonged to Paul and Jeanne Louise's cottage while the women moved between the cottages making potato salad and macaroni salad and gathering chips and drinks.

Once they'd eaten and cleared away the remains of the meal, the children rushed off with Boomer to play while the adults all settled around another bonfire to talk and keep an eye on them. It was nice. Paul hadn't enjoyed evenings like this since Jerri's death. He'd been invited to join neighborhood barbecues and such, but had felt like a fifth wheel and refused. He didn't feel like a fifth wheel with Jeanne Louise at his side.

"Those look like rain clouds."

Paul followed John Corby's glance toward a grouping of large, dark clouds in the distance and nodded, solemnly. They were almost black against the dimming sky as the sun headed for the horizon. Grimacing, he said, "Looks like we're in for one heck of a storm."

"Hmmm," Russell commented. "And they're moving pretty quick."

"Well they did say that we were in for a doozy of a storm tonight," Sharon said with amusement. "High winds, buckets of rain. The whole works."

"Did they?" John Corby asked his wife with surprise.

"Yeah, Cecily and I heard it on the radio on the way back from London this morning," Sharon said and then shook her head with exasperation. "I told you that when we got back from shopping."

"I didn't hear you," John said with a frown, his gaze sliding to their dock and cottage with concern.

"You never hear me," Sharon said dryly.

"Well, you need to speak up, woman," he teased absently, and then sighed and got up. "If we're in for a storm, I guess I'd best make sure the boat's secured and have the boys help me gather up anything we don't want blowing away."

"Sounds like a plan," Russell commented, getting up as well and taking his wife's hand to tug her out of her chair. "Thanks for the fire, Paul. Jeanie. A pleasure. We'll do it again tomorrow if you're up to it."

"We'd like that," Paul said easily, glancing to Jeanne Louise as she stood and folded her lawn chair in preparation of taking it up to the cottage. He got up, put out the fire, and then helped her gather the chairs as the other two couples took their things and headed away. They stowed the chairs in their usual spot, and then picked up their own bits strewn about that they didn't want blown away, towels that had been hung on the line to dry,

Livy's sand pail and shovel, the raft and her water wings . . .

After one last look over the yard to be sure they hadn't missed anything, Paul whistled for Boomer, who was romping on the shoreline. He then glanced up the side of the cottage to where Livy and Kirsten stood hunched over, poking at something with a stick in the front yard. "I guess its bath and bedtime for small fry."

"I'll take Boomer in, feed him, and run the bath while you get her if you like," Jeanne Louise offered, smiling as she peered toward the two girls.

"Thanks." Paul nodded and squinted his eyes. "What the hell are they poking at?"

"A dead bird," Jeanne Louise answered, narrowing her eyes. "They're prodding, not poking. They're sure it's sleeping and are trying to wake it up."

"Oh God," Paul muttered and started toward the pair, Jeanne Louise's soft laughter behind him. He stepped around the cottage just as Cecily appeared in the yard next door and knew she had come in search of her daughter as well. He smiled her way, then glanced back to the two girls and called, "Livy, honey, leave that poor bird alone and say good night to Kirsten. It's time for a bath and bed."

Livy turned startled eyes his way, then glanced around and frowned. "But it's still light out."

"I know, but it's late, muffin. Besides it looks like it's going to rain," Paul said patiently. "Come on. A bath and bed."

"You too, Kirsten," Cecily called. "Say good night to Livy."

"Okay," Kirsten said with a put-upon sigh. She then turned to Livy and hugged her. "We'll play again tomorrow. Okay?"

"Okay," Livy said with a smile, hugging her back. The pair then parted to rush toward their respective parents.

Paul held out his hand, smiling when Livy grabbed it. She skipped along at his side as he led her back around the cottage to the kitchen door. As promised, Jeanne Louise had a bath ready and waiting and agreed easily when Livy announced she wanted her to give her her bath that night.

Paul felt a pinch of hurt that she'd choose Jeanne Louise over him, but he was also glad. His daughter liked Jeanie, and it was obvious the immortal liked her too. He thought that could only be a good thing, and as he leaned in the door watching the two females laugh and splash water, Paul allowed himself a brief fantasy of their being a family . . . of Jeanne Louise staying with them, and Livy getting better and growing up . . . of a future. It was a beautiful daydream that had him smiling widely.

Paul and Jeanne Louise both put Livy to bed after her bath, tucking her in, and each of them kissing and hugging her good night . . . which just seemed to further his fantasy. Paul felt warm and safe and content as he caught Jeanne Louise's hand to lead her from the room. Once in the living room, he paused and turned to her, then cupped her cheeks in his hands and simply stared at her face. She was so precious, this woman. Somehow she had become as important to him as Livy. He'd give his life for her, just as he would Livy. Each of the two females possessed a piece of his soul.

Paul wanted to express all that, to tell Jeanne Louise how he felt, but he didn't have a clue how to say it, and in the end simply bent and pressed a kiss to her forehead, each eyelid, her nose and then finally her lips.

When he lifted his head, Jeanne Louise opened the eyes she'd closed as he'd kissed them. They were glowing softly in the dim light, a vibrant silver blue. She smiled softly and said, "I love you too."

"I do love you," Paul said at once, relief sliding through him as he acknowledged what he was feeling, what all his feelings meant. He hadn't known what to say, but in the end it was so simple. He loved her. She'd understood that and she loved him too. Thank God, Paul thought, and then he kissed her again, but this time it was no gentle caress, it was hot, and passionate and demanding. He wanted all of her, body, heart, and soul.

Jeanne Louise moaned and arched against him as they kissed, her hands clasping his shoulders. But when he tore his mouth from hers to seek other pastures, she whispered, "Not here."

Pausing, Paul raised his head to peer at her in question, and then glanced to the side when Jeanne Louise nodded that way with her head. He found himself looking out the picture window along the side of the living room and straight into the Jacksons' kitchen. Russell, Cecily, and their oldest son sat at the kitchen table playing some sort of board game. Even as he looked, Russell glanced over, spotted them and smiled and waved.

Paul automatically smiled and waved back, then caught Jeanne Louise's hand and turned to lead her to the stairs to the lower level. They could have just gone to the master bedroom, but he was mindful of having woken Livy the night before with their cries the first time. They'd tried to be quiet the subsequent times after that, using pillows, the blankets, and even each other's bodies to muffle the sounds of their pleasure, but suspected this time even that wouldn't help. He felt full to bursting with emotion, and he was ravenous for Jeanne Louise. Paul was hoping that the bit of distance combined with the flooring would help muffle whatever sounds they made.

Jeanne Louise was silent as Paul led her downstairs. She knew he would soon ask her to turn Livy and that the time had come for her to tell him about life mates and her having only one turn. But after. Admitting the feelings that had grown so quickly in her over the past several days, and hearing him speak his own aloud made her want to hold him, be held by him and welcome him into her body. She wanted to make love with him and knew it would be all the sweeter because she now knew his feelings for her.

Paul led her through the small TV room at the foot of the stairs, past the first bedroom and on to the last one. The one farthest from Livy's room, she noted and thought that could only be a good thing. He led her straight to the bed before stopping and then turned and began to remove her clothes, brushing her hands away when she tried to touch him or his own clothes.

Jeanne Louise let him have his way, standing still as he removed her clothes one item at a time, his hands sliding over her body as he worked, offering brief, teasing caresses. When Paul had her naked, he urged her onto the bed, then turned his attention to his own clothes, stripping them away much more swiftly and with less care as he stared at her where she reclined on the bed. His shirt went first, muscles rippling as he pulled it off over his head, and then he removed his jeans and boxers together.

Paul stepped out of them to climb onto the bed beside her and settled on his side next to her. When Jeanne Louise reached for him, he caught her hands and pinned them on either side of her head as he leaned down to kiss her. She could have freed herself easily, but didn't, merely kissing back and arching her body until her breasts rubbed against his chest.

They both groaned as the contact sent pleasure rippling through them, and were panting when he finally broke the kiss.

"You need to feed," he whispered, pressing kisses to her cheek and ear.

Jeanne Louise nodded and smiled slowly. She'd fed again on both Cecily and Sharon while they'd prepared the salads for dinner, but needed more.

"What's that smile about?" Paul asked with amusement when he lifted his head and caught sight of it.

"I was just thinking I know exactly which vein I want to tap this time," Jeanne Louise murmured, and his eyes widened.

"Oh," he asked with interest, nipping at her lip. "And which one would that be?"

"If you'd care to trade places with me I'll show you," she promised.

Paul raised his head, peered at her briefly and then chuckled and shook his head. "You do like to be on top, Miss Argeneau."

"Do you mind?" she asked, arching an eyebrow.

Paul grinned. "Not at all. But this time you'll have to wait. I intend to have my way with you first."

"Your way with me, huh?" Jeanne Louise said with a husky chuckle that died when he released one of her hands to slide his own over her body, cresting one breast before letting his fingers dance down across her stomach toward the apex of her thighs. By the time his fingers slid between her legs they were both breathing heavily.

"Why is it when I touch you I feel pleasure?" Paul asked, his voice almost a groan.

"It's called shared pleasure," Jeanne Louise gasped out, as he began to shift himself down her body, his mouth following the trail his hand had taken just seconds ago. "You feel mine and I feel yo— Oh God," she groaned as he dipped his head between her legs, his fingers and mouth now working together and making her forget what she was saying . . . along with everything else.

Jeanne Louise was vaguely aware that Paul was groaning along with her as he worked. But it was just a peripheral awareness. Her concentration was on the fire burning in her belly, and the tension building in her body. God, he was good at that, Jeanne Louise thought wildly, digging her heels into the bed and dragging a pillow over to cover her mouth as she became aware that she was starting to get a little noisy. But then he was experiencing her pleasure along with her, was feeling exactly what felt best, and knew right when to increase the pressure or tempo.

She stopped thinking after that and became nothing but sensation, her body singing to the tune he was playing until the tension finally exploded in a rush of pleasure that had her screaming wildly into the pillow. Jeanne Louise was so caught up in it that she didn't even hear Paul shout out with her. She felt it though, a reverberation against her skin that simply seemed to add to what she was experiencing.

Paul woke up to find himself lying flat on his back on the bed with Jeanne Louise leaning over him, kissing and nibbling her way down his throat to his chest. When he reached for her, gliding his fingers into her hair, she lifted her head and smiled at him.

"Time to feed," she whispered with a naughty smile that made the blood rush south. She then brushed his hand away and continued what she'd been doing, now paying attention to first one nipple and then the other before continuing downward. It seemed it was her turn, and Jeanne Louise was going for the vein she'd mentioned earlier.

Obviously not the neck or arms, Paul thought wryly as she traced a path across his stomach. He moaned and shifted under her teasing, his hands fisting in her hair as she nipped at his skin. But as Jeanne Louise moved lower, he caught her hair up in his fingers so that it no longer curtained her face and he could watch her nibble her way to and along his hip bone.

By the time she turned her attention to his shaft it was already completely erect with anticipation. When Jeanne Louise caught it in hand and ran her tongue its length from the base up until she could curl it around the tip, Paul groaned and closed his eyes. When she then took him in her warm, wet mouth, he had to release her hair for fear of pulling it out.

Christ, this wasn't the first time a woman had done that to him, but it had never felt that damned good before, Paul thought. But then no other woman had enjoyed the aid of that shared plea-sure business she'd mentioned. He had no doubt it was guiding her just as it had him, that feeling his pleasure with him, Jeanne Louise was able to tell exactly what felt best and where and how to caress him to the best effect.

Shared pleasure was definitely the bomb, Paul decided, and his last semi-sensible thought was to thank God for it and for whatever scientist had created nanos that allowed for it.

Twelve

Jeanne Louise stirred sleepily and opened her eyes.
She was in bed in the downstairs bedroom . . .
alone. Paul had slipped away. He'd also covered
her first, she realized as she sat up and the blankets
dropped to her waist.

She glanced toward the door, wondering where
he'd gone and then smiled when she heard the
sound of soft footfalls coming down the stairs
in the other room. Paul appeared in the door a
moment later, naked as a baby and bearing a tray
with two plates of food and glasses on it. He smiled
when he saw her sitting up.

"You're awake." Paul set the tray on the bedside
table, and then leaned down to give her a quick
kiss. As he straightened, he said, "I checked on
Livy, made us sandwiches, locked the doors and
turned out the lights."

Jeanne Louise nodded, but asked with interest, "Sandwiches?"

He chuckled at the question, and crawled onto the bed next to her, arranged and fluffed both of their pillows for them to lean back on, then pulled the sheets over to cover himself before picking up the tray again. Paul settled it on his lap and smiled at her. "Hungry?"

"Mmm." She nodded, her gaze moving over the sandwiches. "What are they?"

"Ham, mayo, and cheese."

"My favorite," Jeanne Louise said with a grin.

"We aim to please here at casa Jones, ma'am," he drawled teasingly.

"And you definitely do that," she assured him, leaning to press a kiss to his cheek. When she then sighed and kissed the corner of his mouth, Paul urged her back.

"None of that now, you insatiable wench. This man needs sustenance to continue pleasing you."

Jeanne Louise chuckled and accepted the plate he held out. She was feeling rather hungry, and they both fell silent as they started to eat. Hungry as she was, Jeanne Louise practically inhaled her sandwich. Even so, Paul was faster. The moment she finished hers, he took her plate and set it on his own on the tray. He then handed her one of the glasses of what turned out to be iced tea.

"Jeanie," he said reluctantly as she sipped at the sweet, icy liquid. "We need to talk about Livy."

"You want me to turn her," Jeanne Louise said softly.

Paul froze briefly, then lowered his head and took a deep breath. His expression was apologetic and pleading when he raised his eyes to meet hers again. "I'm sorry to ask you. I mean . . . when I first kidnapped you, I thought that was all I cared about. You were a way to save Livy. But I think even then I . . ." He closed his eyes and then opened them again and admitted, "I could have taken someone else, but I wanted it to be you."

"You could have taken someone else?" she asked, peering at him uncertainly.

Paul smiled wryly and admitted, "There's a pretty little redhead named Bev in my department who has made it clear she'd be interested in a . . . er . . . friendship." He ended with a pained grimace.

Jeanne Louise arched her eyebrows at the term. He meant this Bev wanted to be his lover. The idea caused jealousy to flare up in her briefly before she stamped it down. Obviously he hadn't accepted the offer. Besides there was nothing to be jealous of, she was his life mate. So Jeanne Louise simply waited silently for him to continue.

"It would have been the easiest thing in the world to call her and tell her I'd decided I'd like that," Paul pointed out. "I could have invited her over to the house for dinner, shot her with the tranquilizer when she came through the door and—" He shrugged. "It would have been the safest and simplest way to get my hands on an immortal. No muss, no fuss, no worry about cameras or security."

Jeanne Louise stared at him silently, knowing

that he was right. That would have been much simpler, not to mention easier than sneaking around, breaking into his friend's car to get into the parking garage, and then hiding out in his trunk all night waiting for her to get done her shift. Which begged the question—"Why didn't you?"

"I almost did," Paul admitted with a grimace. "And then I ran into Marguerite while I was shopping for chain—"

"Marguerite," Jeanne Louise interrupted sharply. "Marguerite Argeneau-Notte? My aunt?"

"Yes."

"How the devil do you know my aunt?" she asked with amazement.

Paul smiled faintly. "We met my first day at Argeneau Enterprises. Bastien was giving me a tour and we'd just come from your lab." Paul paused to smile at her wryly. "You hardly paid me any attention, by the way. Didn't even lift your head when Bastien introduced us, just mumbled a greeting and kept on peering into your microscope at whatever you were examining."

Jeanne Louise stared at him nonplussed. She'd actually met him? Apparently. Well, sort of.

"Anyway, Marguerite came up the hall in search of Bastien as we left your lab," Paul continued. "She was supposed to have lunch with him or something. He introduced us and she said she'd love to help out, and perhaps she could drive home volunteers after we've tested the tranquilizer on them. So on those rare occasions when we have a volunteer who can't arrange a ride of their own, she comes and collects them and takes them home." Paul smiled and said simply, "We've kind of become friends."

"Friends," Jeanne Louise said faintly, and then shook her head. This was her aunt he was talking about. "And she encouraged you to kidnap me?"

"Well, not in so many words," he said on a laugh. "She didn't know I planned to kidnap anyone. But I went looking for sterilized jars, and bumped into her in the canning section at Canadian Tire—"

"You bumped into Aunt Marguerite in the canning section of Canadian Tire?" she asked dryly. Marguerite didn't can anything. She didn't even cook as far as Jeanne Louise knew.

"Yes, and she asked how I was and how Livy was. Of course, I didn't tell her that Livy was sick."

He didn't have to, Jeanne Louise thought dryly, Marguerite would have plucked it from his mind without even trying. It would have been right there on the surface, the one fact probably filling his thoughts at the time. The main thought that had filled his thoughts since he'd got the news, she was sure. Jeanne Louise didn't say as much though.

"Anyway, then she said the oddest thing," he said, and murmured with bewilderment, "She said it just out of the blue."

"What was that?" Jeanne Louise asked warily.

"That it was always best to go with your heart. That sometimes it wasn't the easiest route, but it was always the right one," Paul said solemnly.

She considered that briefly and then asked, "And kidnapping me was 'going with your heart'?"

"I wanted you," he said simply. "I noticed you that first day during the tour and—despite still grieving over Jerri—found myself looking for you. I varied my break times to figure out when you took yours until I had your routine down. I even took note of what you ate and drank," Paul admitted wryly. "At first, I didn't know why you fascinated me. Your hair is black and I've always preferred blondes, and then too in the beginning it was just a little more than a month after my wife died and I felt guilty as hell for even looking at you." He grimaced, but went on, "But I just . . . every day I looked forward to taking my break so that I could just see you. It made me feel . . . I don't know. At peace, sort of. Maybe happy." Smiling crookedly, Paul added, "And then I began to notice your shoes and it became something of a game to see which ones you were wearing each day and I'd try to guess what mood that meant you were in."

He set his drink on the end table and then scooted down in bed, lying on his back and staring at the ceiling as he confessed, "While it would have been easier to get Bev to the house, I wanted it to be you. I wanted you to meet Livy and like her and . . . to like me. I think I was hoping in my heart of hearts that something like this would happen. That we'd have this connection and passion."

"And we do," Jeanne Louise said softly, thinking that she would have to have a talk with her aunt when this was all resolved. The woman had to have read Paul's thoughts and known what he was up to. She hadn't intervened except to give him the nudge he needed to decide on taking her rather than the easier route of taking Bev. The woman was incredible, she thought dryly and then set her own drink on the end table on her side of the bed and lay down as well. She then rolled onto her side and propped her head on her upraised hand to peer down into his face.

Paul glanced to her, and then raised an eyebrow in question. "You don't seem happy to know this."

"I am," Jeanne Louise assured him, and she *was* happy to know that he had been interested in her for more than turning Livy before taking her. That he'd chosen her because he'd been attracted to her for more than two years. But that didn't change the facts, and now she had some explaining of her own to do. "Paul, immortals have laws just like mortals do."

He blinked at what appeared to be a change of subject, but simply waited for her to continue.

"We aren't allowed to feed on a mortal unto death. That's to protect mortals, but it also protects our people," she admitted and pointed out, "It would cause a frufaraw if bodies started popping up drained of blood with bite marks on them. It might lead to the discovery that our people exist."

Paul nodded, and asked, "What happens to an immortal who breaks that law?"

"Death," Jeanne Louise admitted, and then added, "We're kind of strict with our laws."

He grunted at that, and asked, "And your other laws?"

"We are also restricted to bagged blood. It too helps protect us from discovery, and breaking that law—except in an emergency—could very well mean death too."

"I'm sensing a pattern here," Paul muttered.

Jeanne Louise smiled slightly, but continued. "Basically, immortals are never to do anything that might draw attention to the existence of our kind. Doing so is punishable by death in every case," She said solemnly, and then added, "But there are also two laws that were put in place to keep us from growing too quickly as a population and outgrowing our food source."

Paul wasn't a stupid man. Jeanne Louise knew that, so wasn't surprised when his expression suddenly turned worried, but she continued, "One of those rules is that we are allowed only to have one child every hundred years. Breaking that law means death."

"And the other?" he asked tensely.

Jeanne Louise took a breath, and then told him, "Each immortal is allowed to turn only one mortal in our life time." She paused and then added, "Again, breaking that law is punishable by death."

"And you've turned yours," Paul guessed dully.

"No," she admitted, and then before he could say anything, added, "I, like most immortals, was saving that for my life mate when I found him, in case he was mortal."

"Life mate?" he asked uncertainly.

"That one person we cannot read or control, who could be a true mate to us. The one who re-invigorates our appetite for food and sex and who merges with us so totally during lovemaking that our passion is shared and overwhelms us both."

"The shared pleasure?" he asked.

She nodded.

Paul blinked several times as his brain digested that and then he breathed, "You can't read or control me."

Jeanne Louise nodded solemnly. "You are my life mate, Paul."

"Your life mate." He said the words slowly as if tasting them, and then asked, "How long—I mean, does this shared pleasure and stuff fade off, or . . . ?"

"No. Immortals mate for life," she assured him. "They are truly mated till death do they part."

"And I'm yours?" Paul asked with wonder. Joy spread on his face, but his voice was solemn and sincere when he said, "I'd like that. To be with you until death."

She smiled back, relief pouring through her. It was going to work out. He wanted to be her life mate. He would be a true life mate, and not simply do it to save Livy. This was what she'd hoped for, what she'd needed to be sure of before she could reveal the way to save Livy and have him too. Closing her eyes briefly, she savored the moment and then opened her eyes and said, "I want that too.

I want to turn you and spend the rest of my very long life with you as my mate."

He started to smile, but just as quickly frowned instead. "But if you turn me, you can't turn Livy."

"No, but you could," she pointed out with a wide grin, and then cautioned, "But it means if I died, you wouldn't be able to turn any future life mate you might encounter who was mortal." Jeanne Louise really didn't think that would matter to him. That he would put Livy above such a consideration, but felt Paul should have all the facts before he made his decision.

As expected, he waved her words away as unimportant. "You aren't going to die, I won't let you. Besides, no one could replace you for me," he added solemnly.

Jeanne Louise didn't point out that he'd probably felt that way about his mortal wife Jerri at one time. She simply leaned down and kissed him, relieved that things had worked out after all. Well, at least things with him. There was still the fact that he'd kidnapped her to get her to turn and save his daughter. They would have to deal with that and the council, and especially her uncle, who headed up the council and could be pretty unforgiving about things like that. The man had beheaded his own twin brother whom he'd loved dearly when the man had broken one of their laws.

The thought made Jeanne Louise frown and worry her lip. She'd been so worried about how to woo Paul and get him to want her for herself that she hadn't even started to consider the other troubles ahead of them.

"So," Paul said quietly, "You could turn me, and I could then turn Livy?"

Jeanne Louise nodded.

"And we could be a family. You, Livy and me," he said.

"Yes, we could," she said softly and was as pleased at the thought as he appeared to be. Jeanne Louise already loved the little girl as her own. She would enjoy helping to raise her.

Realizing that Paul had been quiet for a while, she glanced to him and frowned when she saw him pinching his arm. "What are you doing?"

"Trying to wake myself up," he said dryly. "This has to be a dream. You're giving me everything I want and life just never goes that smoothly."

Jeanne Louise bit her lip, and then said, "I didn't say it was going to go smoothly."

Paul stopped pinching himself and met her gaze solemnly. "Tell me."

"The turn is very painful, Paul. It's an ordeal and sometimes the turnee dies. It's rare, but it has happened in cases where the turnee is ill or otherwise weakened."

"Like Livy," he said on a sigh.

"Yes. So we might want to hold off on turning her for a bit, until we get her stronger."

"Which means you'll be suffering her headaches for her," Paul said grimly, and then stilled and asked, "Can I do that for her after you turn me?"

Jeanne Louise knew he felt a lot of guilt over her suffering in Livy's stead, so was almost sorry to tell him, "Probably not. You need to be trained in stuff like that. You won't come out of the turn with the knowledge and skills of an immortal who's been trained in it."

"Right," he said unhappily.

Jeanne Louise hesitated to add to his unhappiness and worries, but he had to know, so she added, "And that's not our only problem. There's the little matter of your kidnapping an immortal with the intention of convincing them to turn Livy."

Paul grimaced. "I suppose that's not going to go over well, is it?"

"It could be a problem," she admitted, and then added, "But hopefully the fact that I stayed willingly and that you're my life mate will be taken into account."

Jeanne Louise could tell from the worry on his expression that he didn't think that was likely. Since it was a worry on her own mind, she decided they'd done enough talking and it was time for some distraction . . . for both of them. To that end, she leaned down and kissed him.

Paul lay still and unmoving under the gentle caress at first, his mind obviously preoccupied with the possible problems ahead of them. But after a moment he began to kiss her back. She was just starting to think she'd succeeded in distracting him when he suddenly caught her arms and forced her back to break the kiss.

Catching sight of her disappointed expression, he said, "I just—you said we're only allowed one child every hundred years. Do we have to wait until Livy is one hundred before we have a child? Should we be using protection?" he asked, and then added huskily, "I don't want to risk you being put to death for—"

"No," Jeanne Louise interrupted. She didn't take the time to explain that an immortal woman could only get pregnant and carry the child to term if she deliberately overfed on blood to keep the nanos busy enough not to expel the child as a parasite, but simply said, "Livy will be counted as your turn, not a child born of an immortal."

"Right." He relaxed and even managed a smile. "So it's okay to start on a little sister for her right away?"

"I'd like that," Jeanne Louise admitted quietly, though she knew it wasn't possible. She simply didn't have access to the blood needed to get pregnant.

Before Paul could respond, the sound of something skittering across the floor upstairs made them both stiffen and glance toward the door. It sounded like a toy or something else small had been sent sliding across the hardwood, as if it had been batted about or accidentally kicked.

"It's probably Boomer," Paul murmured. Turning back to her he pressed a kiss to her forehead, and said, "I'll check and call if it's Livy and you're needed."

Jeanne Louise nodded and sat up as he rolled off the bed. "I'll dress just in case."

"There's no need," Paul said, but paused as he glanced back to see that the blankets had slid to her waist leaving her bare from the waist up. Moving back to the bed, he kissed her again, this time on the lips. They were both breathless when he ended the kiss.

"On second thought, you go ahead and dress," Paul whispered, covering one breast with his hand and squeezing gently. "Then I can undress you again when I come back down."

Jeanne Louise chuckled at the words, and removed her arms from around his neck to allow him to straighten. She watched him put on his jeans, her eyes eating up every inch of him before he pulled them up. Despite all the difficulties and problems, they'd managed to work it out. She could hardly believe it. She hadn't thought it possible. But it gave her hope that they could overcome the problems with the council too. They had to.

"Back in a minute," Paul promised, heading out of the room.

Paul left the bedroom door open and used the light spilling from the room behind him to navigate his way to the stairs and start up them. Moonlight was shimmering through the windows as he reached the main floor, making it easier to see. He stepped off the stairs and turned to move toward the hall to the bedrooms, but froze as a dark shape appeared before him. It took a moment for his mind to process that it was a man in front of him with glowing eyes. And then the immortal bared his teeth, flashing some pretty nasty, pointy looking fangs as he growled, "Where is she?"

Paul took a wary step back, and then gave a choked gasp as the man suddenly caught him by one hand at the throat and lifted him off the floor to bear him backward into the kitchen. In the next moment, his back hit what he thought was the refrigerator. At least he was sure it was the door handle of the refrigerator that slammed painfully into his arm as he hit.

"It wasn't very smart to let your daughter play out front, mortal. I was driving by and saw her, then I saw you." He tightened his hand around his throat, snarling, "We know you have Jeanne Louise, and if you've hurt her, you'll regret it the rest of your very short and miserable days. Now where is she?"

Unable to speak, Paul tried to shake his head that he hadn't hurt Jeanne Louise, but even that was impossible with the man's grip on his throat. In the next moment he felt a strange ruffling in his head and realized the fellow didn't need him to speak, he was looking for the answers in his head himself.

Paul couldn't breathe and darkness was starting to blur the corners of his sight. To stave off the panic trying to claim him, he told himself that he'd be released as soon as the immortal realized Jeanne Louise was here willingly, and that then he would be able to breathe again. But movement over the man's shoulder caught his attention and he desperately blinked away the darkness trying to crowd in on him and stared with horror as he recognized Livy's small figure standing by the stairs. As dark as it was he could tell that her eyes were wide, her mouth gaping with terror.

His attacker must have caught some sound, or perhaps her scent, because the immortal suddenly swiveled his head, spearing the child with a look, his fangs still protruding and flashing white in the darkness. Livy's eyes widened further, her face paling and then she shrieked in terror, and whirled to make a run for it. But Boomer was there. The small dog gave a squeal of pain as her foot came down on him, and then lunged away and scampered out of sight as Livy was pitched off balance and to the side. The sound of her small body tumbling down that curved stairway, and the way her cry was cut off so abruptly would haunt Paul for a long time.

Jeanne Louise had got as far as pulling her panties and T-shirt back on when she heard Livy scream. Dropping the jeans she'd just picked up, she charged out of the bedroom just in time to see the child's small body tumbling down the stairs in a blur of arms and legs.

Crying out, she rushed forward, reaching the bottom of the stairs as Livy came to a halt there. The child landed on her back; arms and legs splayed and head to one side, her nightgown twisted around her little knees. Jeanne Louise dropped to kneel beside her to search for a pulse, her head lifting, eyes going hard as she spotted Justin Bricker coming down the stairs at speed.

"Did you do this?" she growled accusingly just before Paul appeared at the top of the stairs and started down as well.

"It was an accident," the Enforcer said, sounding horrified. "She saw me and screamed and turned to run and—"

"And you didn't take control of her and stop her," Jeanne Louise snapped.

"I tried. I couldn't," Bricker said, guilt and confusion in his voice.

Jeanne Louise scowled, then glanced to Paul as he reached the bottom of the stairs and found his way blocked by Justin. The immortal didn't move, but kept him from reaching either of the females, ignoring his frantic efforts to push him aside.

"Is she—?" Paul cut off the question, unable even to say the word *dead*.

"She's alive," Jeanne Louise said as she found a pulse. She didn't add "barely," but feared that was the case. Livy's pulse was weak and thready. Furious and afraid for the child, she started to slip her hands under the girl to pick her up, but froze as she felt the open gash on the back of her head.

"Christ," Justin muttered, and Jeanne Louise silently echoed the word. Lifting her even that much had revealed that the carpet where the girl had landed was soaked with blood.

"Oh God," Paul moaned and Jeanne Louise peered at him. He was no longer trying to get past Justin. In fact, he was swaying where he stood, his expression tortured. She felt her eyes fill with tears as she took in his pain. It was a pain she was suffering herself. Jeanne Louise had come to love the child dying before her, and she could no more stand by and watch it happen without doing anything to stop it than she could have if it were Paul lying there on the floor.

She sent the man she loved a look of apology, then turned her gaze to Justin and glared at him with all the rage she was feeling as she gave up her future and did the only thing she could. Jeanne Louise bit violently into her wrist, ripping away a flap of skin. She then pressed the gushing wound to Livy's open mouth.

Thirteen

'Jesus, Jeanne Louise, what are you doing?' Justin Bricker breathed with horror as she gave up her one turn to the child.

Ignoring the question, she barked, "Call for help. We need blood and lots of it, an IV, and chain, as well as drugs to facilitate the turn."

Justin hesitated, but then pulled out his phone and began punching numbers. He also turned sideways to get past Paul and moved back upstairs as he pressed the phone to his ear.

Free to approach now, Paul moved to kneel on Livy's other side, uncertainty and fear battling on his face. He didn't speak until Jeanne Louise removed her wrist from Livy's mouth and scooped her up. He stood then to follow when she carried the girl into the bedroom they'd used, asking in a whisper, "Will she survive?"

Jeanne Louise didn't answer right away. She set the child on the bed and then turned her on her stomach so that she could examine the back of her head. The wound was as big as it had felt to her hand. She could see right through to her fractured skull.

"I don't know," she said unhappily. It certainly didn't look good. Not only was there the tumor for the nanos to contend with, and her weakened state, but now there was the head wound and the loss of blood.

"Please don't let her die," Paul said quietly. It was a prayer really, a quiet request of God. But Jeanne Louise flinched as if he'd lashed her with the words.

In the next moment, she suddenly raised her uninjured wrist to her fangs and tore into it with even more vicious intent than she had the first. Paul winced and started to turn away, but then forced himself to watch the woman he loved tear a great gaping wound into her wrist. She was doing this for him after all, for him and Livy.

While Jeanne Louise had merely grunted the first time she bit herself, this time a shriek of pain was torn from her throat with the action. But then this time the wound she brought on was bigger, the flap of skin she tore away almost twice the size of the first. She then held this new gash over Livy's injured head and began to squeeze the wound as if trying to get as much ketchup as possible out of a plastic bottle. Paul swallowed at the hissing breath she sucked in as she did it, knowing she was causing herself even more pain. He then turned and hurried from the room, and rushed to the bathroom between the two bedrooms.

Paul felt like he was going to be sick, but that wasn't why he'd come. He ignored the toilet, swallowed the bile in his throat and quickly opened the cupboard door under the sink. A stack of towels sat inside and he grabbed several and then hurried back to the bedroom where Jeanne Louise's wrist had stopped gushing, the wound reduced to little more than a trickle. Still she squeezed at the wound trying to get more of the valuable liquid out.

When she finally gave up on getting any more out, and let her wrists drop to her side, Paul stepped to her side and used the towels to bind first one wounded wrist and then the other, wrapping the towels tightly around each.

"Why did you bleed on her head?" Paul asked quietly as he finished with the second wrist. "Will it help?"

Jeanne Louise shook her head and heaved out a weary sigh. "I don't know. It was the only thing I could think to do. The nanos might be able to heal the head wound. And her skull is cracked, they might be able to get through it to get to the tumor quickly and start to work on it. As to whether it will help or not though . . ." She shrugged helplessly.

"It might help."

Paul turned sharply at that growl, his eyes narrowing on the man with short dark hair now entering the room.

"Daddy!" Jeanne Louise said with relief and hurried forward to hug the man while Paul gaped.

Daddy? The guy had short dark hair, wore jeans and a T-shirt and didn't look a day over twenty-five. But then neither did Jeanne Louise, or any of the other immortals he'd ever met. None of them looked over twenty-five or so. Still ... the guy didn't look like he could be her father, Paul thought, and then changed his mind on that when the man in question released Jeanne Louise and turned to spear him with a look of cold dislike and said, "Is this the bastard who kidnapped you, Jeanie?"

"Oh ... er ... no," Jeanne Louise said quickly, moving to put herself between Paul and her father. When her father turned a sharp look on her for the lie, she added, "I mean yes, but only at first. I'm not being held against my will anymore. He's my life mate, Daddy. Or he was," she added dully, her shoulders drooping unhappily as she glanced to Livy. Swallowing, she glanced back and asked, "Do you have any blood?"

"We only have a couple bags left. Bricker went out to fetch them from the cooler in the van," a woman's voice answered.

Paul shifted to the side to see who this new speaker was, his eyebrows rising as he spotted the tall black woman with short, spiked hair standing behind Jeanne Louise's father. He recognized her at once as the woman in the van at the mall in London. Eshe, Jeanne Louise had said her name was. Her stepmother.

"Only a couple bags?" Jeanne Louise echoed with dismay.

"Nicholas and Jo are only a few minutes away and have more in their cooler, as do Etienne and Rachel. They were searching the small towns along Lake Huron for you too," he explained.

"How did you know we were on the lake?" Jeanne Louise asked with a frown.

"After I spotted you leaving the mall parking lot, a debit withdrawal and credit card transaction popped up," Eshe explained solemnly.

When Jeanne Louise turned to him in question, Paul said helplessly, "We'd already been spotted in London. I figured it was safe enough to get gas and withdraw more money. They knew we were there and I didn't think it would lead to their figuring out where we were."

"It wasn't the cash or gas that told us. It was the raft and water wings," her father said dryly. "Those along with the mosquito repellent suggested the beach to us so we concentrated on searching the waterside towns on either side of London."

Paul felt the blood slip from his face. Christ, he'd bought them at the gas station, not even thinking . . . He'd brought these people here with his own actions. He'd ruined everything himself. His gaze slid to Jeanne Louise but she wasn't looking at him now. She stood, face turned away and hands clenched. Hating him for blowing it for them, he supposed miserably.

Silence reigned in the room for a moment and then Jeanie's father moved to the bed to peer down at Livy. Mouth tight, he asked, "Bricker said you used your turn on her?"

"I didn't have a choice," Jeanie said quietly. "He scared her and she fell down the stairs. She was dying."

"What does that matter? She was already dying," he growled and Eshe moved up behind him, putting a hand on his arm.

"She's the daughter of her life mate, Armand," Eshe said softly. "She loves the child. It was her choice. She wasn't forced."

"No, just kidnapped and emotionally blackmailed," Armand Argeneau growled, casting another glare Paul's way.

He shifted uncomfortably under the look, thinking the guy definitely acted like a father. He himself probably would have been pissed at the way things had played out if he was Jeanne Louise's father. He'd made a mess of everything.

"What is it?"

Jeanne Louise's tense question drew Paul from his self-flagellation as she moved up beside her father to peer down at Livy.

Paul moved to the foot of the bed to get a look at his daughter as well, concern claiming him as he did. She still lay on her stomach in the bed, the gash on the back of her head visible, but looking a little smaller to his eyes. But Paul really hardly noticed that. It was the way that the child seemed to be vibrating on the bed that caught his attention and held onto it.

"Jeanie?" he said in question, a frown claiming his mouth as the vibrating seemed to pick up in strength.

Rather than answer, she bent to turn Livy over and then lifted first one eyelid and then the other. Whatever she saw made her straighten abruptly with dismay, saying, "We're going to need more than a couple of bags of blood and quickly."

"What's happening?" Paul asked.

"She's having seizures," Jeanne Louise answered grimly.

"Why? What does it mean?" Paul asked at once.

"It means the nanos are already working on her brain," Eshe answered, moving around the bed to the side opposite Jeanne Louise and bending to place her hands on Livy's arm and leg even as Jeanne Louise bent to do the same on her side. Armand moved to the end of the bed, shoving Paul out the way so that he could lean over and brace Livy's legs, placing his hands on her ankles and pressing them down on the bed. It freed the women to move their own hands to her shoulders and arms.

"What are you doing? Why are you holding her down like that? She—" Paul paused as Livy's seizures turned into thrashing. He immediately moved back to the bed to try to help hold her down, but froze, horror zipping through him when blood began to squirt from her mouth.

"Dear God," he breathed. It was as if he'd stepped

into the movie *The Exorcist*, only it wasn't green vomit spewing from his beloved daughter's mouth.

"She's bitten the end of her tongue almost off," Eshe said sharply. "Armand—"

She didn't bother to finish whatever she was going to say, Jeanne Louise's father had already released Livy's legs and hurried to grab the wooden tray off the bedside table. He didn't bother clearing it first, simply sent the empty sandwich plates and Paul's half full glass of iced tea flying as he grabbed it. Armand then moved around to Eshe's side, snapping off the end of the tray as he went. He handed the smaller piece of wood to Eshe who slid it between Livy's teeth.

Paul watched this silently, but when Livy's teeth clamped down on the wood, he asked shakily, "She bit her tongue off?"

"Not all the way. The nanos will heal it," Jeanne Louise reassured him quickly, and he nodded, but knew they would only do that if she survived the turn. And Paul was very much afraid she wouldn't.

Jeanne Louise had warned him that the turn was violent and an ordeal, but he'd barely listened to the caution, his mind wholly on Livy's being healthy and strong. Paul hadn't imagined anything like this nightmare.

"Here."

Paul glanced around at that word to see the immortal who had caused this rushing into the room with the couple of bags of blood Eshe had mentioned.

"We don't have an IV," Jeanne Louise pointed out, frowning at the bags.

"Slit the end with your nail and pour it into her mouth," Eshe instructed.

Leaving her father and Eshe to try to hold Livy down, Jeanne Louise straightened and took both bags from Justin. The moment she removed them from his hands, Justin stepped up to take her place and help hold Livy down. Ignoring him, she handed one bag to Paul to hold on to and slit her nail across the top of the other. Jeanne Louise removed the wood from between Livy's teeth and tipped the bag over her now unobstructed mouth.

"How long until the drugs, blood, and IV get here?" Paul heard Armand ask Justin quietly.

"Nicholas and Jo should be here any minute. He said they had a couple bags. Anders has six and shouldn't be long either. Garrett—"

"And the drugs and IV?" Eshe interrupted.

"Half an hour to forty-five minutes," he admitted unhappily. "They have to fly them down."

"That could be a problem," Eshe said grimly as Jeanne Louise tossed the first, now empty, bag aside and took the second one from Paul to slit it open. "It will draw the neighbors."

"What will?" Paul asked, moving back to try to help hold Livy down.

Eshe didn't bother to answer. She didn't have to. Livy answered his question herself by beginning to shriek at the top of her lungs.

* * *

Paul woke up with a start and then glanced around with confusion. He was lying on top of the covers on the bed in the second bedroom in the basement, but he hadn't a clue how he'd got there. The last thing he remembered was panic gripping him as Livy began to shriek wildly and thrash like a wild thing.

"My father put you to sleep and laid you in here to keep you out of the way."

Paul raised his head and peered at the man who had spoken. He sat in a chair by the bed; tall with longish fair hair, a solemn face and glowing silver-blue eyes.

"Livy?" he asked, the question uppermost in his mind.

"She's through the worst of the turn. She should come through okay now," he said solemnly.

Paul took a relieved breath, and then asked the other question most important to him. "And Jeanne Louise?"

"She's upstairs feeding. The blood and drugs arrived last night, but she wouldn't leave Livy to feed until she was sure she was going to make it."

Paul nodded, not terribly surprised to hear that. He then asked, "Who are you?"

"I wondered when you'd get to that," the man said with a smile, and then answered, "Nicholas Argeneau. Jeanne Louise's brother."

Paul stared at him blankly and then dropped back in the bed with a muttered, "So you no doubt hate me too."

"No."

The answer made him lift his head again. Eyebrows rising, he asked, "Why not? I kidnapped your sister. And she's used her one turn on my daughter."

"Well, since I've been poking around in your head for the last several minutes, I know you kidnapped Jeanne Louise out of a desperate desire to save your daughter, and that you did your best to not hurt her and to make her as comfortable as possible. I also know she wasn't a captive long, but was willing to stay, that you love each other and that the two of you planned for her to turn you and then for you to turn Livy so that you could be a family. But events have interfered and now she can't turn you."

Nicholas sighed and rubbed the back of his neck wearily, and then admitted, "I don't hate you, Paul Jones. I pity you. I pity both you and Jeanne Louise right now."

"We'll be all right," Paul said gruffly, though fear had slid through him at the words. "Livy will get better, and we'll be a family. Just not for as long as we hoped."

"You really think Jeanne Louise wants to watch you wither and die any more than you wanted to watch Livy wither and die?" Nicholas asked solemnly.

"I'm not dying," Paul protested.

"You're mortal," Nicholas said simply. "All mortals are dying. It may be slower than Livy or someone else with a disease will. You may have twenty to forty years before you go, but that's a heartbeat to us and you *are* dying. Every day takes you closer to the grave, and if the two of you stay together, Jeanne Louise will have to travel there with you and watch you go."

Paul stared at Nicholas, his words echoing in his head. They raised the terror in him that Jeanne Louise might leave him now, that she'd avoid him to avoid being dragged to the edge of the grave with him and watch him be planted in the ground.

"That won't happen," Nicholas said quietly. "You're her life mate. She won't be able to drag herself away from you. She'll cling to you until your last breath, and then be crushed and heart-broken when she loses you, probably withdraw to relive the moments you shared. It's what I did after losing mine."

"You lost your life mate?" Paul asked quietly.

Nicholas nodded. "But I found another."

"Maybe she will too," Paul said.

"She might," he acknowledged. "But immortals can go centuries, even millennia before finding another, and if her next one is mortal too . . ." He shook his head. "She goes through it all over again, the love, the loss, the despair." Nicholas fell silent, his expression sad. He was obviously hurting for his sister. He didn't see much happiness ahead for her.

And it's all my fault, Paul realized.

If he had just stopped to think, and not bought those water wings and the raft on the credit card when he'd got gas at Canadian Tire, her family never would have thought to search the coastal towns . . . and their plan would have gone ahead as they'd intended. They'd be a family.

Aware that Nicholas was sitting unnaturally still, Paul glanced toward him, eyebrows rising when he saw that he was peering toward the door as if listening to something. Several minutes passed that way and then he suddenly stood. "I'm sure you want to see Livy."

"Yes." Paul sat up and swung his legs off the bed at once. When the other man moved to the door, he followed quickly, eager to see both Jeanne Louise and Livy. However, when he followed Nicholas into the next room, Jeanne Louise wasn't there. Eshe alone sat by Livy's bedside.

Paul hesitated, but moved to the bed to peer down at Livy. She looked much better than she had when last he'd seen her, better even than she had in more than a month. She actually looked healthy, her cheeks filled out and rosy, her face peaceful. A small sigh of relief slid from Paul's mouth and then he glanced to Eshe.

"Where is Jeanie?"

"Upstairs," Eshe said, standing. "Nicholas and I have to go up too. You'll have to sit with Livy and change the blood bags. I'll show you how."

"Jeanne Louise?"

Turning from her contemplation of the contents of the refrigerator, Jeanne Louise raised her eyebrows as she peered at her father over the bag of blood stuck to her teeth. After watching over Livy all night she was hungry for both blood and food. Blood was the first thing she'd attended to. Food would be the next. She'd get Paul something to eat too, she thought as she waited for her father to speak. No doubt Paul would be hungry when he woke up. Along with relieved to know Livy was going to make it.

Jeanne Louise still couldn't believe the girl had hung in there and survived the turn. Between the cancer, the blood loss, the gash and fractured skull . . . well, she'd been sure the child's body wouldn't be able to withstand everything. She'd feared she'd die before the turn really even got started.

"Eshe thinks that your bleeding yourself into the open wound on the back of the girl's head probably saved her," Armand said, obviously having read her thoughts. Tilting his head curiously, he asked, "How did you know to do that?"

Jeanne Louise tore away the now empty bag from her fangs and smiled wryly as she admitted, "I don't know. It just came to me."

His eyebrows rose, but he let that go and then moved to sit down at the dining table. "Lucian will be here soon. We have to talk."

Jeanne Louise hesitated, not really eager to "talk." She knew her father hated Paul for kidnapping her. They all did. And they were also no doubt furious on her behalf that she'd given up her one turn. She wasn't too pleased about that herself and blamed Bricker for it.

"It was an accident," Armand Argeneau said solemnly. "Bricker didn't intend for it to happen. He says he tried to slip into the girl's thoughts to stop her when she turned to run, but met resistance. That was probably the tumor."

"Probably," Jeanne Louise acknowledged, and moved to sit wearily at the table. She wasn't really surprised to hear that Justin had found it difficult to penetrate the girl's mind. It had gotten more and more difficult for her to slip into Livy's thoughts with each headache. She suspected the tumor had grown each day and had been starting to interfere. Jeanne Louise had always managed to get through the initial block, but Justin wouldn't have expected it, and may not have been able to push through in the short amount of time he'd had to do so.

"And I don't hate Paul," her father said quietly, proving he'd read that thought too. "I read his mind as I put him to sleep earlier. He loves you. He wanted to be your life mate. It's tragic that it can't happen now."

Jeanne Louise peered down at her hands. She'd been annoyed with her father at first when Paul had suddenly collapsed in the bedroom and she'd realized her father had put him under. But then as the turn had progressed, she'd decided it had probably been a good thing. Livy's turn had been fast and furious and incredibly violent. Probably because Jeanne Louise had bled into her twice, giving her twice the normal number of nanos and giving them two entry points. It was probably better that

Paul hadn't had to witness his daughter in such agony. Jeanne Louise wished she hadn't had to.

"And I know you love him too," Armand continued solemnly. "Which is why we need to talk. We need to come up with a strategy for presenting this to Lucian if you want to save Paul's life."

Jeanne Louise stiffened. "Lucian can't—"

"Lucian does what he thinks is best for our people. Paul kidnapped you, hoping to get you to turn his daughter. Kidnapping is wrong even in mortal law, Jeanne Louise. But Lucian won't stand for a mortal kidnapping an immortal."

"Paul may have kidnapped me initially," Jeanne Louise said carefully. "But as soon as I was fully awake and realized I couldn't read him I was there willingly. And he was only hoping to convince me to turn Livy. He wouldn't have forced me."

"I'm not sure about that," Armand said on a sigh. "Paul was originally hoping to convince you, but he was also desperate. I don't think even he knew what he would do if you refused, or how far he would go."

Jeanne Louise frowned at this news, but shook her head. "It doesn't matter. The problem never came up and Lucian can't punish Paul for something that *might* have happened."

"Lucian might not agree with you on that."

Jeanne Louise glanced toward the door at her cousin Etienne's words as he entered the cottage with his wife, Rachel, and Jo, who was her brother Nicholas's wife, on his heels. The trio had gone out for food and each carried a cardboard tray of drinks and a Tim Hortons bag.

Nicholas and Etienne and their wives had arrived shortly after her father had removed Paul from the room. With the added help available, her father had sent Etienne and Justin to see to the neighbors, to make sure they didn't think anything of the pained shrieks and wails Livy was eliciting and were plainly heard outside. The others had stayed in the room, helping to hold down Livy and keep her from hurting herself as her struggles became stronger.

Even with the added help, it had been hard to keep the girl still and Jeanne Louise had been relieved when the Enforcer Anders had arrived with the drugs and IV. The drugs hadn't stopped the pain for Livy, but they'd made it more bearable and stopped her from thrashing about.

"He can't punish Paul for taking me. I was willing," Jeanne Louise said firmly as Etienne and the women began to unpack the food they'd fetched. Nine sandwiches and nine drinks, she noted, and guessed they hadn't bothered to bring Paul food.

"Anders doesn't eat or drink," Jo said quietly. She leaned sideways in her seat to offer a piece of her sandwich to Boomer with one hand and a pet with the other.

Not being allowed into Livy's room, the dog was apparently mooching for food from anyone and everyone, Jeanne Louise thought, but then spotted his full food dish several feet away. He wasn't going hungry, so perhaps he wanted affection and reassurance as much as food, she decided, and then let go of the concern as Jo straightened and reassured her, "One of the sandwiches and a drink are for Paul."

"Oh," she murmured and smiled at her sister-in-law with gratitude. She liked Jo and was glad the woman and Nicholas had found each other. As if called by her thoughts of him, Nicholas now entered the kitchen on Eshe's heels and Jeanne Louise frowned at the sight of them. "Livy—?"

"Paul is with her," Eshe reassured her at once. "I showed him how to change bags as necessary."

"You were willing after you realized he was your life mate, Jeanne Louise, but not at first," her father said, drawing her attention back to the matter at hand. He then added sadly, "And sweetie, your being willing or not doesn't change the fact that he kidnapped an immortal with the intention of making them turn his daughter."

"She was dying," Jeanne Louise barked with frustration, and then asked grimly, "What would you do to save me or Nicholas or Thomas?"

That brought a moment of silence that she filled by adding, "Besides, he only kidnapped me because Marguerite told him to follow his heart."

"What?" Etienne asked with amazement, head jerking up at the mention of his mother's name.

Jeanne Louise nodded firmly. "Paul was going to try to convince a coworker who would have been easier to get alone, but Marguerite told him to follow his heart, so he took me."

"You were his heart's desire," Eshe said softly, her gaze concentrated on Jeanne Louise's forehead. She was reading her mind, of course, Jeanne Louise thought with a sigh, but didn't fight it. Seeing everything that had taken place could only help her cause. At least she hoped so.

Her gaze slid around the table at the silence suddenly surrounding her, and Jeanne Louise found everyone staring at her, concentration on their faces. They were all bloody reading her. It made her realize that some of her memories were somewhat personal and private and definitely X-rated. Not something she wanted her father and brother to see.

Standing abruptly, she said, "I love him. He's my life mate. I wanted to turn him and have him turn Livy so that we could be a family. I can't have that now, but if Uncle Lucian harms a hair on Paul's head I will stop him, or die trying. If you love me, I suggest you figure out a way to convince him to leave Paul alone." Gathering two sandwiches and two drinks, she added, "Now I'm going down to sit with Paul and Livy. Excuse me."

Jeanne Louise turned and headed for the stairs then, pausing and stepping around Justin Bricker and Anders as they appeared at the top of the stairs.

"Jeanne Louise," Bricker said, catching her arm as she passed. When she paused, he said, "I'm really sorry. I wish I could—" Sighing, he let go of her arm and said simply, "I'll do what I can to help."

Nodding, Jeanne Louise turned away and continued downstairs. She knew he felt bad and her silence wasn't helping. And she didn't want to blame Bricker for the way things had gone. Jeanne Louise knew he hadn't intended for any of this to happen, that it hadn't been deliberate on his part. But while her head was able to reason all this out, her heart wanted to lash out at someone with all the frustration and rage she was forcing down over the way things had turned out. Jeanne Louise was afraid if she said anything at all to the Enforcer, she would pour all that rage and frustration on his head. Maybe with some time . . .

Jeanne Louise grimaced to herself. She very much doubted time would help here. In fact, she wasn't sure anything would.

Sighing as she stepped off the stairs, Jeanne Louise crossed the sitting area to the bedroom where Paul and Livy were . . . or where they were supposed to be. However, when she entered the room, a somewhat forced smile in place, she found the room empty.

Fourteen

Paul hurried around the side of the cottage, his heart in his throat. He'd sat down to watch over Livy as Eshe and Nicholas had left, but moments later had become aware of a terrible need to relieve himself. He'd decided that it wouldn't hurt to step into the bathroom next door. Livy was resting peacefully now, and her blood bag had just been changed. Leaving her alone for one minute shouldn't cause any problems . . . or so he'd thought. He hadn't been gone long, just the amount of time it took to go to take care of the matter and then splash cold water on his face and dry it off. But he'd returned to the room to find Livy missing, the fresh bag of blood torn open and lying empty on the floor beside the bed.

He'd whirled and hurried out of the room then, pausing when he noticed the open screen door that faced onto the lake. While this was technically a basement, the cottage was on a slight incline. The basement was half above ground and a small area had been dug out and reinforced so that a door could be installed along with a short six-step stairwell up to the backyard.

Cursing, Paul had hurried to the door and out, desperate to find his daughter.

It had only taken a quick glance to realize she wasn't in the backyard or on the beach. Now Paul was rushing around the side of the cottage, very aware that the sun was hot and strong and Livy shouldn't be out in it.

A car was pulling into the driveway as Paul came around the front of the cottage, but he hardly paid it any attention. His sole focus was on the two girls by the edge of the road. Livy and Kirsten, standing by the dead bird that they'd thought was just sleeping. Only their focus wasn't on the bird now. Instead the two girls seemed to be tussling, and as he hurried forward, Kirsten managed to push Livy away and ran for home shrieking, "She tried to bite me!"

Livy was off at once, rushing after her with hands extended and fingers clawed. Her fangs were out.

"Oh God," Paul muttered and hurried forward to intervene. He managed to catch Livy around the waist just as she was lunging at Kirsten's back. He immediately swung her up into his arms and held her in front of his face, and then froze at his first sight of her. Her eyes were glowing silver, her fangs were out, she was growling like a rabid dog and there was blood around her mouth, whether it was from chewing open the blood bag or biting Kirsten, he couldn't tell.

"Livy?" he said with amazement, and cried out when she suddenly lunged at him. Paul didn't react quickly enough, wouldn't have been able to stop her. But he didn't have to. She was plucked from his hold before she got to his throat.

Blinking, Paul stared at the man now holding his daughter—tall, fair-haired, blue eyes burning silver, and his body and stance radiating confidence and strength. He was impressive and intimidating.

The man took one look at Livy and she suddenly passed out in his hold. He then glanced briefly at Paul before looking past him and saying, "Handle the mortals, Anders."

Paul glanced over his shoulder to see the Enforcer nod and turn to follow the path Kirsten had taken. He then peered back to his daughter as the blond man shifted her against his chest and eyed Paul.

"Not quite what you were expecting is it, mortal?" he asked grimly. "All you were thinking of was Livy healthy and well. A happy ever after. It didn't occur to you that she'd change. That it might be a nightmare rather than a dream."

"She—" Paul began, and then paused as a very pregnant brunette reached them and brushed her hand along the blond man's arm.

"She's his daughter, Lucian," she said softly.

Paul stiffened at the name. So this was Jeanne Louise's uncle, the man who would decide his fate. The guy was one scary dude.

"He loves her," the brunette continued. "And Jeanne Louise too. What would you have done to save your daughters in Atlantis? And what would you do to save the child I carry now?"

Lucian Argeneau glanced to the woman, taking in her pleading expression, and then turned back to Paul. He wasn't exactly softer, but he was more relaxed suddenly. His eyes no longer seemed on fire, and the power he radiated was now muted, still there, but not raging.

"Livy isn't herself right now," Lucian said quietly. "She's still in the turn. What you just witnessed wasn't really your daughter. She probably wasn't even fully conscious. Once the turn is done and she's recovered she'll be the girl you remember. Mostly," he added dryly, then shifted Livy against his chest so that he only needed one hand to hold her. It freed his other to clasp the brunette's elbow and urge her toward the cottage. "Come."

Paul released a shaky breath and followed. He'd now met Lucian Argeneau. And he was still alive. So far.

Jeanne Louise stared at the empty bed, and then scanned the room as if the father and daughter might be playing hide-and-seek with her, but knew they weren't. They were gone. Both of them and the only thing that made sense was that Paul had grabbed Livy and run rather than risk Lucian's wrath.

She could understand that. She was immortal and a relative and her uncle terrified her. Paul was mortal, presently looked on as Public Enemy Number One by her people, and in a heap of trouble. Jeanne Louise could understand his running. What she didn't understand was why he hadn't taken her.

Swallowing, she turned and moved out of the room, unable to bear being there alone anymore. Moving without thinking, she started upstairs, her mind sluggish and stunned. She had no intention of revealing that he was gone. She'd do what she could to help him make his escape and simply keep quiet, Jeanne Louise decided, but had barely stepped off the stairs onto the main floor when Anders and Bricker were on their feet and rushing past her.

It was then she realized just how stunned she had been at Paul's abandoning her. She'd forgotten that new life mates were very easily read. She probably also looked rather stricken, Jeanne Louise supposed, and that everyone would have wondered why she was back so quickly. She supposed she probably would have helped Paul more by staying downstairs for a bit.

"The blood bag is mangled on the floor beside the bed and the screen door is open."

Jeanne Louise glanced to Bricker at that announcement as he returned from downstairs.

"Anders went after them while I came to report,"

Bricker added, as he crossed to the kitchen door. "I'm going to help him loo—"

Bricker paused abruptly, then pulled the door open and stepped out of the way as Leigh entered with Lucian behind her, a sleeping Livy in his arms. Paul was right behind them, Jeanne Louise saw. She was torn between being happy to see him and upset that he hadn't managed to get away. There was also a little wanting to smack him silly for leaving her behind. Nice mix, she thought dryly, and had to clutch the back of the chair she'd stopped behind to keep from running to him.

Her gaze slid back to her uncle as he passed Livy to Bricker.

"Take her downstairs, hook her back up to the IV and give her more drugs," Lucian ordered. "Take the father with you, and stay until someone replaces you."

Bricker nodded and waited for Paul to lead the way, then followed without comment when he started across the room.

Paul's eyes sought hers as he passed. He offered her a weak smile in passing, but she couldn't respond in kind. Jeanne Louise turned and watched as the two men walked to the stairs and disappeared down into the basement.

Once they were gone, she turned back to find Lucian eyeing her. She could tell by the way his eyes were narrowed that he was reading her thoughts. Knowing she couldn't stop him, Jeanne Louise simply waited for him to finish.

"He didn't abandon you," Lucian announced abruptly after a moment. "Livy woke up and went outside while he was in the bathroom and he went out after her. It was stupid. He should have shouted for help, but the man is used to being on his own and the only one responsible for Livy."

Jeanne Louise's eyes widened and she sagged briefly with relief at the knowledge that Paul hadn't left her. But then she forced herself to straighten and eye her uncle warily. Lucian Argeneau was the true hard case among immortals, and he would be the one to decide Paul's fate, which decided her own. She couldn't afford to be weak now.

"I love Paul, Uncle," Jeanne Louise said quietly when he didn't speak. "He's my life mate, and he loves me too, I think."

"I know he does," Lucian said calmly, not looking impressed by the knowledge.

Jeanne Louise bit her lip, and then added, "I know he shouldn't have kidnapped me, but I was a willing victim the moment I realized I couldn't read him. There were several points I could have left and didn't. I even helped him evade the Enforcers when we returned from dinner and I spotted their SUVs on his street." She straightened a little and added pleadingly, "Surely, as the supposed victim in this, if I don't wish him punished, he shouldn't be?"

When Lucian merely raised an eyebrow at the suggestion, she added unhappily, "I can't turn him now, thanks to Bricker. We can never be proper life mates. Isn't that punishment enough?"

"You can still be together, Jeanne Louise," Lucian said quietly.

"Sure for ten, twenty, maybe even thirty or forty years if we're lucky," Jeanne Louise said bitterly. "A heartbeat out of my life. And during those few short decades I get to watch him wither and die the slow mortal death of aging." Her mouth tightened at the thought, and she said, "In truth, that's probably more punishing than anything you could come up with."

She felt a hand on her shoulder and glanced around to see that her father had moved up behind her to offer his comfort and support. For some reason his offered strength suddenly made it hard to fight back her tears. Turning back to Lucian, she took a shaky breath and said, "Paul's a good man, Uncle. What he did, he did out of desperation, for the love of his daughter. He didn't know our laws, didn't know what he would be asking of one of us and he never hurt me. In fact, he did everything he could to see to my comfort from the start. The only reason you even figured out it was him was because he was concerned with my comfort and refused to put me in the trunk of his car when he switched vehicles."

Nicholas had admitted as much as they'd sat watching over Livy through the night. As she'd speculated, they'd checked traffic cameras around the parking lot where Paul had left her car and switched her to his own. They'd spotted her unconscious in the front seat of his car, got the license number and used that to get his name and address and particulars.

"Fine," Lucian said abruptly, drawing her attention.

Jeanne Louise peered at him uncertainly. "Fine? What does that mean?"

"He lives and keeps his daughter as well as his memories," Lucian said, and then added solemnly, "That's punishment enough."

Jeanne Louise felt her father squeeze her shoulder, but just stared at Lucian.

As expected he wasn't done. "However, the minute, and I mean *the very minute*, that the girl is through the turn I want the three of you on a plane to Toronto. I'll have someone pick you up and take you to Marguerite's."

"Aunt Marguerite's?" Jeanne Louise said with surprise, aware that Etienne had gone still at mention of his mother. "Why?"

"Because she obviously knew what Paul was up to when she ran into him before he kidnapped you, and rather than tell me so that I could do anything about it, she merely gave him a nudge in your direction," he said dryly.

Jeanne Louise's eyebrows rose at these words. With everything else on her mind the memory of that conversation with Paul hadn't been on the top of her memories. Her uncle had done a thorough search when he'd read her mind. That or the memory had been on the surface of Paul's mind for some reason.

"Since Marguerite helped bring about all this," Lucian continued dryly. "She can help with the fallout and at least start training Livy to be an immortal."

Jeanne Louise bit her lip, but nodded in consent. She liked her aunt, and knew Paul did too. And she was sure Livy would love the woman, but . . . "How long do we have to stay with Aunt Marguerite?"

"Until I decide what to do with Livy," he said bluntly.

"Do with her?" Jeanne Louise asked worriedly.

"Well she can't go back to her normal life, can she?" he asked dryly. "She can't go back to her school, can't play all day outside in the sun with friends in her neighborhood, can't live the same life she had before. But she needs an education."

"Yes," Jeanne Louise agreed with a frown. She hadn't really considered that problem.

"And what I decide for Livy depends on whether you and Paul stay together or not," Lucian added, bringing her eyes sharply back to his. Meeting her gaze he said, "I'm not entirely sure you will."

"But he's my life mate," she said weakly.

"And he's mortal," Lucian said quietly. "We're similar in many ways to mortals, but there are differences, Jeanne Louise, and every minute you spend with him will make those differences clearer to you. He's weaker than you physically, more fragile. He'll get ill, or he'll hurt himself, and even if by some good luck he doesn't, he'll age and wither . . .

I'm not entirely sure you can stand by and watch that. It will most likely tear you apart inside. And if he is injured and dying, I'm not positive that in that moment you will be able to resist saving him with a turn as you did Livy." He paused and then added grimly, "And if you did that, you'd be forfeiting your own life. Until I'm sure you won't do that, I want someone around to protect you from yourself."

"I . . ." Jeanne Louise paused and frowned, unsure herself if she could stand by and watch Paul die.

"Of course, the two of you parting leads to other problems," Lucian continued. "It's difficult for a mortal to raise an immortal. Children pick up skills like reading and controlling mortals faster than adult turns, and faster than their conscience and sensibilities form. Paul trying to raise her on his own would be like a monkey trying to raise a child. Before this year is out, she'll be running circles around him, controlling him and doing what she wants if an immortal isn't there to stop her. I won't allow that either. I have no desire to hunt down a child rogue my niece turned."

Jeanne Louise bit her lip. She hadn't considered any of this in that moment when she'd turned Livy. She hadn't considered anything but saving the girl, for Paul, but also for herself, because she'd come to love the sweet little blond child.

"So," Lucian said quietly, "The three of you will stay with Marguerite until I say otherwise. Or until you part and I make alternate arrangements for Paul and Livy . . . understood?"

Jeanne Louise gave a jerky nod, her mind reeling under the weight of all the problems he'd just made clear to her. She hadn't thought of a single one of them before this, and wasn't happy to have to contemplate them now.

"Good. As long as we're clear," Lucian said and then glanced to Anders as he arrived at the cottage door behind them. Urging Leigh out of the way for the man to enter, he asked, "Everything all right next door?"

Anders nodded. "Livy didn't manage to bite the neighbor girl. I wiped her memory anyway and then checked around to be sure no one else had witnessed the attack."

"Good," Lucian said, and then announced, "I want you and Bricker to escort Jeanne Louise, Paul, and Livy to Marguerite's after the girl's done her turn. Call when it's time and I'll send a plane for the five of you."

Anders nodded, but Lucian had already turned to the others in the room.

"Armand, I'm guessing you'll stay till they leave?" Lucian asked.

"Yes," he said quietly, squeezing Jeanne Louise's shoulder.

Lucian obviously wasn't surprised. He turned his gaze to the other two couples. "Can you bring back the SUVs Bricker and Anders were in?"

There were murmurs of agreement at once. While

Anders and Bricker had been solo, Nicolas and Jo had ridden together as had Etienne and Rachel, but the couples would drive back separately to return the SUVs to Toronto.

Lucian didn't thank them or even comment, he merely nodded, took Leigh's arm, and led her from the cottage without even bothering to say good-bye. No one was terribly surprised, but there was a collective sigh of relief amongst the group once the door closed behind the couple. It was rather obvious how tense they'd all been as a group, as if they'd all been holding their breath and were only now breathing again.

Jeanne Louise, though, wasn't sure she would ever breathe again. She knew she should be happy that Paul wasn't going to be punished, but all she felt was worry, and anxiety and a terrible weight pressing down on her as she contemplated the future. Sighing, she ran one hand wearily through her hair. "I should go tell Paul—"

"Why don't you go get some rest and let me do that?" her father suggested quietly. "While the rest of us took shifts and caught naps, you didn't sleep at all last night."

She hadn't wanted to leave Livy. Jeanne Louise hadn't wanted the five-year-old to wake up hurting and confused to find herself in a room full of strangers. As it had turned out, however, Livy hadn't woken up until after they'd left, and now Jeanne Louise was exhausted. But that wasn't why she was tempted to accept her father's offer. She just didn't think she could face Paul right now without bursting into tears or something else just as weak and ridiculous. Just hours ago she'd been the happiest she'd ever been in her life, sure her future was set, and now that rosy future was a shambles around her and all she wanted was to sleep.

However, her father was pretty angry at Paul over the whole business and she didn't trust him not to use the opportunity against him.

"I'll be nice," Armand Argeneau said dryly, obviously still reading her thoughts. He then added, "I promise."

Jeanne Louise hesitated, but was just so bloody tired and depressed. She needed sleep . . . and time alone to sort out her thoughts . . . and a good cry. Not necessarily in that order. Sighing, she nodded and then simply turned and left the room to head to the master bedroom and the bed that waited there.

Paul was seated in a chair on one side of the bed, avoiding looking at Justin Bricker who occupied a chair on the other. The two men hadn't exchanged a word since coming down here. Bricker seemed lost in his own thoughts, and Paul was just too upset at that point to want to talk. That scene with Livy outside just kept replaying in his head like some horrible nightmare and he was left wondering what he'd done to his daughter.

And it had been him, no matter that Jeanne Louise had turned her. He'd kidnapped her to have her do that. But the blood-covered mad thing that had chased after Kirsten and then lunged for his own throat like some mindless fiend hadn't been his sweet child. And the blond man's words kept playing through his head too.

Not quite what you were expecting is it, mortal? All you were thinking of was Livy healthy and well. A happy ever after. It didn't occur to you that she'd change. That it might be a nightmare rather than a dream.

That was exactly how Paul felt, like his life had become a nightmare, and one he'd brought on himself. The man had then said something about Livy not being herself at the moment and still being in the turn. That she probably wasn't even really conscious, and once the turn was done she'd be the girl he remembered. *"Mostly."* But Paul didn't find that very reassuring. What had the man meant by *mostly?* He kept asking himself that, as well as wondering what he had done to his daughter.

The sound of the door opening caught his attention and he glanced to it, expecting it to be Jeanne Louise. He was actually relieved when it was her father instead. Paul didn't think he could face her right now. He was too upset, and was wondering if immortals were as human as they seemed.

"We're human," Armand Argeneau said dryly and then glanced to Bricker and said, "Go have your sandwich. I need to talk to him."

Bricker stood at once and left the room, leaving the two men alone.

Paul waited until the door had closed behind the Enforcer before glancing to Armand, who was moving around to take the Enforcer's vacated seat. Once the man was seated, he said, "Let me guess. I've been found guilty of kidnapping and sentenced to death."

"No," Armand said quietly. "You've been found guilty of kidnapping and sentenced to live."

Paul stared at him, knowing he should feel relieved but he was just numb at the moment, his thoughts so full of horror and confusion he couldn't feel anything else. "So what are they going to do? Take Livy away from me to be raised by immortals?"

"Is that what you want?" Armand asked.

Paul turned to peer at his daughter. She looked as sweet and innocent now as she had from the day she was born, like the same child he'd been willing to give his life for as recently as that morning. The scene in the front yard had taken him aback though. He wasn't sure who or what she was anymore. Except that she was his daughter, his little Livy. He hoped.

"No," he said finally.

Armand relaxed back in his seat. "Lucian was telling the truth when he said what you saw in the front yard wasn't her. She's still in the turn. Her brain is scrambled at the moment. She wouldn't have been capable of cognitive reasoning or even realize what she was doing. Once it's done she'll be your Livy again."

"Mostly," Paul muttered bitterly.

"There will be some differences, of course," Armand allowed. "She'll be stronger, faster, resistant to illness and even death. And she'll need to feed like the rest of us do."

Paul grimaced at the word *feed*.

"On bagged blood," Armand said dryly. "Though she'll need to be trained in feeding off the hoof too so that if there's ever a situation where she has no access to bagged blood and needs to feed from the source, she can do so without unduly harming or even killing her donor."

"Right," Paul said wearily.

"But there won't be any change in her personality," Armand said quietly. "She'll wake up liking the same things she did before and she'll still love you."

Paul swallowed and nodded, relieved to hear that.

"So, Lucian decided you wouldn't be punished," Armand said solemnly. "He's arranging for you, your daughter, and my daughter to be flown back to Toronto once the turn is done, and taken to Marguerite's."

Paul blinked at this news. "Bastien's mother, Marguerite?"

Armand nodded. "My sister-in-law. The three of you will stay with her while Livy is trained."

"And then?" Paul asked.

Armand hesitated and then said, "That depends on you and Jeanne Louise."

Paul's eyes narrowed at the words. "What do you mean?"

"Whether you decide to stay together or not," he said solemnly.

"I love her," Paul said simply and it was true. While he was confused about the difference between immortals and mortals right now and worried about how it would affect Livy, he did love Jeanne Louise.

"And she loves you," Armand said. "But sometimes love isn't enough and this could very well be one of those times."

"Why?" he asked at once, anger beginning to stir in him at the very suggestion.

"Because you're mortal."

"So I'm not good enough for her," Paul guessed.

For some reason that amused Armand, and then he pointed out, "When I entered the room you weren't even sure immortals weren't a bunch of monsters after all."

"That was just because Livy—" He shook his head, not even wanting to remember her in those moments. "But you said that wasn't her. That she'll be fine."

"So now you think my daughter is the woman you thought she was after all," Armand reasoned and nodded. "She is. Jeanne Louise is smart, sensible, loving, and compassionate. And she loves you. And you're mortal."

Paul stared at him blankly, uncomprehending.

"What do you think she would do if you fell in

front of her and broke your back, or neck, or if you were hit by a car, or just anything of that nature happened?"

Paul frowned. "She'd try to help me."

"She'd probably turn you," Armand said grimly. "She wouldn't even think, she'd just rip open a vein and turn you on the spot rather than lose you. And if she did that she'd be put to death."

Paul sat back in his seat weakly.

"On the other hand, most mortals live their whole lives without deadly accidents occurring and live to a ripe old age," Armand said on a sigh. "And then she'd simply have to stand by and watch you die of cancer, heart disease, or just plain old age."

"People die of old age all the time. It's the natural way," Paul said quietly.

"For mortals it is," Armand agreed. "But Jeanne Louise isn't mortal, and time seems different to us. Because we live so long, time doesn't pass for us like it does for you. Or perhaps it doesn't really for you either."

"What do you mean?"

Armand hesitated and then said, "Twenty years seems like a long time, doesn't it?"

Paul nodded.

"But twenty years ago you were—What? Nineteen?" When Paul nodded, he asked, "Does it really feel like twenty years have passed since then?"

Paul blinked at the question. In truth it didn't. Sometimes he wondered where the time had gone.

"If you stay together, Jeanne Louise will have to watch you wither and die over decades, something you couldn't bear to do even for weeks with Livy," he pointed out.

"You think I should let her go," Paul said solemnly, and felt his heart pang at the very thought.

"No," Armand said. "My daughter loves you. You are her life mate. And she gave up her turn for your daughter after all. She should get something out of it, even if it's just a couple of decades with you." He sighed and then straightened his shoulders and said grimly, "But if you love her, you'll make it clear that you don't ever want her to give up her life to turn and save you. And you'll make sure she never does."

Fifteen

Jeanne Louise murmured sleepily and arched against the body at her back, instinctively thrusting her breast into the hand caressing it. But her eyes opened when she felt a kiss pressed to her neck.

"Paul?" she whispered with confusion.

"I thought you'd never wake up," he growled by her ear, tweaking her nipple for making him wait.

A husky chuckle slipped from her lips, and she shifted onto her back in the bed to peer at him. "Is Livy all right?"

"Mmm hmm," Paul murmured, his attention on the sheet he was tugging down to reveal her breasts. Bending, he pressed a kiss to the nipple of one, mumbling, "She's up and having breakfast with your father and Eshe."

"Oh," Jeanne Louise sighed as his mouth closed

over her nipple. She closed her eyes as he suckled, but blinked them open when he suddenly stopped and lifted his head.

"I love you," he said solemnly.

Jeanne Louise hesitated, the worries that had made her cry herself to sleep earlier rising up inside her, but she pushed them back, and cupped his face in her hands and said, "I love you too, Paul."

He smiled crookedly and bent to press a kiss to her lips, then raised his head again and said solemnly, "Thank you for saving Livy."

Jeanne Louise swallowed and nodded, unable to speak past the tears suddenly crowding her throat and swimming in her eyes. She didn't regret saving the girl, but she regretted losing the chance to turn Paul.

"I know it means I can't be turned, and that we only have three or four decades, but I'll do what I can to make those the best years of your life," he promised.

Jeanne Louise closed her eyes. Three or four decades. So little time.

"I want you to promise me something."

She opened her eyes again. "What?"

"I want you to promise that you will never ever turn me."

"I can't now, Paul," Jeanne Louise whispered, her voice cracking as she made the admission.

"I know. But when Livy fell down those stairs, you didn't even think. You turned her on the spot to save her. I don't want you ever to do that with me, to unthinkingly turn me. You would be trading your life for mine, and I won't have that. I'd kill myself the minute I regained consciousness to save you anyway. So it wouldn't be worth it."

Jeanne Louise stared up at him, tears leaking out of the corners of her eyes and sliding down into her hair as pain welled up inside her. Throwing her arms around him, she hugged him tightly, whispering, "What am I going to do without you?"

"Jesus woman, I'm not dead yet. Don't bury me already," he said huskily, hugging her back. "We have time together. A couple of decades at least, and hopefully four or more. Let's enjoy them and let the future worry about itself." He pulled back to peer at her and wipe her tears away, and then asked, "Okay?"

Jeanne Louise nodded.

"Good," he sighed, and then kissed her to seal the deal.

Jeanne Louise kissed back, and moaned as his hands began to move over her body, his kisses and caresses pushing her worries about the future—and losing him—away for a little while as he made love to her.

"Daddy! Jeanie! Look! I grew new teeth! And look what I can do with them!"

Jeanne Louise blinked her eyes open and stared blankly at Livy as she burst into the room and rushed up to the bed, her fangs sliding out and gliding back into her jaw repeatedly.

"Wow. Well, that's great, honey," Paul said weakly beside her.

"Yeah. Justin and Anders taught me how to do it. Justin says I'm the fastest learner *ever*!" She beamed at the compliment and then whirled away and rushed toward the door yelling, "He said to show you and tell you it's time to get up. We're going on a plane!"

"My daughter the vampire," Paul said on a sigh as Livy disappeared up the hall, leaving the door open.

"She's a cute vampire though," Jeanne Louise said with amusement, and then sat up and slid off the bed as she warned him, "You might not want to use the term *vampire* around the old-timers though. They get kind of touchy about it."

"And who exactly are old-timers?" Paul asked, getting up and following when she headed into the bathroom.

"Lucian, my father, Eshe, Nicholas, Anders, Aunt Marguerite," she listed off as she turned on the shower for the water to warm up. Jeanne Louise then turned and bent to look in the cupboard under the sink to find a washcloth and towel. Old-timers were anyone over a century or two old, and there were many more of them, but those were the only ones he'd met so far. "Oh, and Bastien."

"Right," he said, dryly. "And how am I supposed to tell who the old-timers are? You all look mid twenties to thirty."

She smiled wryly and shrugged as she straightened. "Guess it's best just not to use the 'V' word when there are others around."

"Hmm," Paul murmured, his eyes sliding over her body. "Speaking of that. How old are you?"

"I'll be a hundred and three this year," Jeanne Louise admitted and then stepped in the shower and closed the door. The water was lovely warm and she closed her eyes and turned under it.

"A hundred and three?" Paul squawked, yanking the door open.

Blinking her eyes open, Jeanne Louise peered at him with surprise. "Yes."

"Jesus," Paul muttered, leaning weakly against the shower door.

Jeanne Louise hesitated and then asked, "Is that a . . . er . . . problem?"

"What?" He glanced at her, and then frowned. "Well, no—I mean, I—I guess I just thought you were younger," he finished finally.

Biting her lip, she turned away from him to hide her concerned expression and reached for the shampoo to pour some into her hand. Trying to ignore the sudden awkward silence, she massaged the shampoo through her hair, building a lather.

"You just caught me by surprise," Paul said after a moment, his tone apologetic. "I mean I knew immortals were long lived, I just—"

"I'm considered a youngster by immortal standards," Jeanne Louise said quietly, before ducking under the spray to rinse the soap away. She stepped back out, blinking her eyes cautiously open and murmuring a thank you when Paul handed her the towel to dry her eyes.

"Just how long has the oldest one lived?" he asked curiously. "I mean, I suppose technically the nanos could keep someone going forever but—"

"Some who survived Atlantis are still around," Jeanne Louise interrupted. "Uncle Lucian for instance. Others, like his twin brother and parents, have died in beheadings or volcanic eruptions and such, but there are several around still from the early days."

"Your uncle Lucian is from Atlantis?" Paul asked carefully.

Jeanne Louise paused and peered at him solemnly. "Do not ever joke about him being The Man From Atlantis," she warned. "Thomas did once and he really didn't take it well."

"Right," he breathed, and then smiled wryly. "I somehow don't think you have to worry about that. I don't see your uncle and I sitting around shooting the shit anytime soon."

"Stranger things have happened," Jeanne Louise said with amusement, setting the soap back on the rack and stepping under the water again to let the spray rinse the lather away.

"So," Paul said as she sloshed the water in the places the spray couldn't reach on its own. "You're a hundred and three."

"Almost," she said and then grinned. "I'm an older woman, Paul." Tilting her head, she arched an eyebrow and asked, "Is that a problem?"

Paul let his gaze slide over her body under the spray as he considered her question and then grinned and shook his head and stepped under the spray with her.

"Not at all," he assured her, his arms sliding around her waist. He kissed the tip of her nose and then pointed out, "It means you can't get mad at me if I call you my old lady."

"Ha ha," Jeanne Louise said dryly and pulled from his arms to step out of the shower, twisting the hot water tap off as she went. "Enjoy your shower."

"I—Ahhh!" Paul squawked and quickly began twisting taps as the water turned cold.

"So this is Marguerite's house."

Jeanne Louise smiled faintly at Paul's wide-eyed expression as they started up the driveway. "Uncle Jean Claude had it built. He liked to make a statement."

"Hmm," Paul said wryly, and then glanced at her. "Who is Uncle Jean Claude?"

"Lucian's brother and Aunt Marguerite's first husband. He turned her. Julius Notte is her second husband and her first life mate."

"Her first life mate? Your uncle wasn't a life mate too?"

Jeanne Louise shook her head. "No. He turned her and claimed her as one because she looked like his life mate, who died in Atlantis."

"Hmm." Paul glanced out the window again. "When did your uncle die?"

"1995," she answered.

"Jesus," Paul breathed, and then asked, "How old is Marguerite?"

Jeanne Louise paused to do the calculations. "Seven hundred and forty something."

"Right," he sighed and then glanced to Livy, who was clutching Boomer to her chest and peering excitedly out the window.

No doubt he was thinking his daughter had a long life ahead of her, Jeanne Louise supposed, and then glanced out the window as Anders pulled the SUV to a halt in front of the wide double doors of the house.

"Take them in," Anders said to Bricker. "I'll park and join you in a minute."

Jeanne Louise didn't wait to hear Bricker's answer, but opened her door and slid out. Paul followed, with Livy hard on his heels, and then Jeanne Louise turned toward the house as the front doors opened and Marguerite appeared.

"Jeanne Louise, sweetie," her aunt greeted, managing to look apologetic and happy to see her all at once.

"Aunt Marguerite," she murmured, stepping into the woman's arms and hugging her.

"I'm sorry, sweetheart," Marguerite whispered as she hugged her tightly. "I thought everything would work out. And it may still," she added, squeezing a littler tighter. "Don't lose hope."

"I won't," Jeanne Louise said quietly, but knew it was a promise that would be hard to keep. Releasing her, she then turned to say, "You know Paul, of course, and this is his daughter, Livy. And that's Boomer," she added pointing to the small shih tzu the girl carried.

"Olivia Jean Jones," Livy announced solemnly, shifting Boomer to one arm so that she could hold out her hand to Marguerite.

"Hello, dear," Marguerite murmured, bending to accept the hand. "Do you prefer Olivia or Livy?"

"Livy," she said at once.

"Then Livy it is," Marguerite said solemnly, and then straightened and glanced over her shoulder as a tall, good-looking man with auburn hair appeared behind her. Stepping to her son Christian's side, Marguerite made the introductions, including the dog.

"Ah. That explains why Julius was sent to the kennel," Christian said wryly, eyeing Boomer. "He'd have eaten him alive."

"Julius is Marguerite's dog," Jeanne Louise explained to Paul as she smiled at her Italian cousin.

"I thought Julius was Marguerite's life mate?" Paul said with confusion.

"He is. There are two Juliuses," Christian said with amusement. "One is a dog, and one is my father."

"Long story," Jeanne Louise said when Paul glanced her way.

"Christian, you've met Justin Bricker, haven't you?" Marguerite asked now, gesturing to the Enforcer who stood a little back from the group, looking uncomfortable. Anders approached then and she added, "And Anders."

Christian nodded to the men.

"Now, we should go in. I have sandwiches and snacks waiting, and Caro is eager to meet you all too," Marguerite announced, turning to lead the way inside.

"Caro?" Paul asked, taking Livy's hand and slipping his arm around Jeanne Louise's waist as they followed mother and son into the house.

"Christian's life mate," Jeanne Louise explained. "They're new life mates too. They met in St. Lucia on Julius and Marguerite's honeymoon."

"Christian went on his parents' honeymoon?" Paul asked with amazement as they walked up the hall a few feet behind the others.

"Ah . . . well, not originally. But Marguerite was sure Caro was perfect for Christian so they called and had him fly out to meet her."

"On their honeymoon?" he asked with a grin.

"The things we'll do for our children, eh?" Julius asked behind them and Jeanne Louise glanced around to see him coming out of the office door they'd just passed.

"Oh, hello, Uncle Julius," she murmured and moved back to hug him.

"Hello Jeanie." Julius Notte squeezed her tight and gave her back a quick rub, then released her to offer his hand to Paul. "And hello to Jeanne's life mate. Paul, no?"

"No," he murmured as they shook hands and then said, "I mean, yes. Hello."

Julius smiled and put an arm around each of them

to usher them up the hall. "We know the troubles that have befallen you. Family is important. We do our best for our children. You are welcome here."

"Thank you," Paul said sincerely, and Jeanne Louise noticed that he relaxed quite a bit. It was only then she realized how tense he'd been before and understood that he'd been worried about how her relatives would receive him. It was understandable, of course. After all, her father and brother hadn't been pleased with the whole "kidnapping and using her one turn on Livy" business. But Julius had just said he understood and didn't hold it against Paul and she tightened the arm she had around her uncle in gratitude. She'd liked her Aunt's life mate from the start, but every time they met she liked him a little more.

"Oh, nobody told me you were here. I would have come to greet you too."

Jeanne Louise glanced into the living room they were entering at those startled words and smiled at Christian's life mate, Caro, as she hopped up from where she'd been curled on the sofa, reading.

Setting the book on the table, the blonde hurried forward to offer Jeanne Louise a hug and be introduced to Paul and Livy and then they all went into the dining room to eat. Jeanne Louise had been worried about their staying here, but Marguerite knew Paul, and Julius, Christian, and Caro were as welcoming as could be. He seemed to fit right into the group. In fact, if anything it was Bricker and Anders who seemed uncomfortable as they had their meal. Jeanne Louise could understand that, they were basically there as babysitters for her and Paul. Not really guests and not really welcome, at least not by her, though Marguerite was as warm and welcoming with them as she was everyone and her husband, son, and daughter-in-law followed suit. Still, Jeanne Louise didn't think they were necessary, and the Enforcers were short staffed as it was lately. Surely they had better things to do.

She was wondering about that when Anders turned and answered the question for her, saying bluntly, "Yes, we are short staffed, but Lucian wants us to stay until he figures out the way the land lies."

"Meaning?" she asked with a frown, not liking that turn of phrase.

"I believe Lucian is concerned that you might try to turn Paul despite having used your one turn," Julius said quietly. "After all, he has a life mate and knows how valuable they are, and that losing them, even to time, is not something easily accepted."

Jeanne Louise stared at him silently and then sat back in her seat. "So what? You guys are going to live with us for the next forty years or so to make sure I don't turn him?"

"Jeanie won't do that," Paul said solemnly. "I made her promise she wouldn't."

Silence reigned around the table briefly, and then Marguerite cleared her throat and stood up. "If everyone is done, I guess I should show you to your rooms. Julius, if you'll show Anders and Bricker to their room, I'll show Jeanie and Paul where they're to stay."

"Of course." Julius stood to lead the two men away.

Once they were gone, Marguerite smiled at Jeanne Louise. "Shall we?"

Jeanne Louise forced a smile and stood as well. The expression became more natural, though, when Paul stood up beside her and took her hand in his. He glanced to Livy then and held out his hand, and the girl hopped off her chair, scooped up Boomer from where he'd been sleeping by her feet, caught him under one arm and slipped her free hand into her father's. They followed Marguerite out of the room as a family.

"Jeanie, Mirabeau is bringing clothes from your apartment, and Paul, Lucian arranged for your and Livy's things to be gathered and brought as well. They should be here sometime this afternoon," Marguerite announced as she led them upstairs. "If there's anything else you need, we can make a trip to your places tomorrow."

"So we aren't prisoners?" Jeanne Louise asked dryly.

"What?" Marguerite glanced around with true surprise. "No, of course not. You're our guests. We're going to help with Livy while the two of you decide what you want to do. You have a lot of things to work out . . . whether you want to live together or marry. Where you'll live if you do marry. Where it's best for Livy to live. If you should move to where she can attend school, or if you want to stay here in Toronto and have her tutored and so on."

"There's a place Livy could actually go to school like a normal kid?" Paul asked with surprise.

"Port Henry," Marguerite said nodding. "It's relatively immortal-friendly and Lucian's been working on making it more so, so that our children can have a more normal childhood. Most immortal children have been raised alone over the years with no brothers or sisters in their age range to socialize with. He's been trying to convince immortals in teaching and other useful fields to move to Port Henry so that our children can attend school with others like themselves and have friends, attend dances, and so on."

"That would be nice. Where's Port Henry?" Paul asked with interest.

"On Lake Erie, a little less than an hour the other side of London from where we were staying," Jeanne Louise answered, wondering if Paul would want to move there for Livy. It would mean giving up her position at Argeneau. Giving up on trying to resolve the problem of her uncle and cousin feeding on bagged blood she'd been working on for so long.

Or not, she thought suddenly. After all, Uncle Victor, her uncle who had the genetic anomaly, was in Port Henry. It might be useful to have him handy to test things on. Paul might even be able to continue his work there if they set up a lab for both of them.

"Here we are." Marguerite stopped halfway up the hall and opened a door, then gestured them in. As she followed them into the pretty blue room with a king-sized bed and sitting area, she said, "And this door leads into the en suite bath."

They followed her to peer into the room as she crossed the white and blue bathroom to another door.

"And this leads to Livy's room," she announced, thrusting the door open and leading them into a pretty rose-colored room with two double beds. Turning as they followed her in, she smiled at Livy and asked, "What do you think?"

"I got two beds," Livy said with awe as she entered the room, and then she set Boomer on the floor and whirled to run to her father. Grabbing his hands, she squeezed eagerly and begged, "Can I have Shelly sleep over? We can each have our own bed and everything."

"Sweetie, I think you're squeezing your daddy's hand too tight," Jeanne Louise said, catching Paul's pained expression.

"Livy, why don't we go take Boomer outside?" Marguerite suggested. "He would probably like a run around the yard about now, don't you think?"

Livy glanced toward her and then released Paul's hand and ran over to the woman, stopping to scoop up Boomer again on the way.

"Thank you," Jeanne Louise murmured as her aunt caught Livy's hand in hers and led her from the room. She then turned to look at Paul's hand, frowning as she saw the way it was swelling. The girl didn't know her own strength yet. "We'd better put some ice on that."

"It's fine," Paul said, tugging his hand from hers. "She wants to have a sleepover."

"Paul, we should really ice your hand," Jeanne Louise said with a frown.

"She can't have a sleepover, Jeanie. Shelly is mortal. Livy might get hungry in the night and gnaw on the poor kid."

Jeanne Louise left his hand for now and glanced at his face. "Paul, she won't do that. She wasn't herself when she went after Kirsten. She isn't going to run around attacking people. She'll have access to bagged blood when she's hungry. She won't go after other children."

"How can you be sure?" he asked with a frown.

"Because she knows it's wrong," she said quietly.

Sighing, Paul nodded and ran his uninjured hand through his hair. "Good. Thank you."

Jeanne Louise nodded, and then sighed and said, "But you're right. She can't have a mortal over for sleepovers. They might see something they shouldn't."

"Right," he said wearily and winced as he un-thinkingly ran his injured hand through his hair this time.

"Come on," Jeanne Louise said firmly. "We'll put ice on your hand."

"It's fine. Don't fuss," Paul said, but allowed her to drag him from the room.

Sixteen

Paul rolled over in bed, reaching automatically for Jeanne Louise, and blinked his eyes open when all he found was empty bed. Cold, empty bed. Frowning, he sat up and glanced around. The room was silent and still, no Jeanne Louise. Grabbing his wristwatch off the bedside table he checked the time, grimacing when he saw that it was just after two in the afternoon. Jeanne Louise shouldn't be up yet. Stifling a yawn, he slid out of bed and made his way to the en suite bathroom for a shower.

Twenty minutes later Paul was showered, dressed, and had brushed his teeth and hair. Feeling somewhat alive now, he made his way out of his and Jeanne Louise's room, pausing to look in on Livy as he passed.

"Hmm," he muttered when he found that his daughter was up and gone too. Both girls were early birds this morning. Shrugging, Paul pulled the door closed and continued downstairs. He glanced in each room as he headed for the kitchen in search of coffee, pausing when he spotted the men of the house all congregated around something in the living room.

"What's up?" Paul asked, moving into the room.

"The television isn't working and there's a big game on in fifteen minutes," Julius said with irritation.

"Big game?" Paul asked, crossing to join them.

"Soccer," Christian said, frowning as he pushed buttons on the remote, bringing up screen after screen of static. "Italy's playing."

"Hmm." Paul glanced from the remote to the television screen, but said, "I thought you guys slept during the day?"

"Italy's playing," Christian repeated.

"Right," Paul said with amusement. Apparently, soccer took precedence over sleep. "Do you know where Jeanne Louise and Livy are?"

"They went shopping with Marguerite and Caro," Christian answered and then gave the remote an irritated shake. "Damn thing."

"Let me see," Paul said, taking the remote. The men all turned to him expectantly as he hit menu, then a couple more options before selecting "view signal." "Huh."

"What is it?" Julius asked.

"Well, your signal is pretty low, it looks to me like the satellite is misaligned," he explained. "We had a storm last night, the high winds probably shifted it or something."

Christian groaned. "We'll never get a repairman out here before the game starts."

"You don't need a repairman," Paul assured him, handing back the remote. "There are a couple of screws you turn, is all, one for up and down and one for side to side. I can adjust it. Where's the satellite?"

"On the roof," Julius said with a frown.

"I'll do it," Bricker announced, turning to head out of the room.

"You can't go out there," Paul said, catching his arm to stop him. "It's sunny out. Besides, I know what I'm doing." Turning back he asked, "Do you have a ladder, Julius? I'll just climb up and—"

"I don't need a ladder," Bricker said, pulling free and continuing out of the room.

Frowning, Paul hurried into the hall after him. "Bricker. It's sunny out. I can do it without taking damage. You can't."

"Jeanne Louise is already pissed at me about Livy. She'd never forgive me if anything happened to you," the Enforcer said grimly. "I'll do it."

"Let him do it," Julius said, when Paul opened his mouth to argue. "He can hop up there, adjust the satellite and then hop back down. It won't take a minute."

"Yeah, but I can do it too," Paul said irritably. "I might need a ladder, but at least I know what I'm doing."

"True, but he'll survive if he falls off the roof. You might not," Julius said calmly, then patted his back. "Come, you can help me get beer and snacks."

Paul scowled. "Get the snacks? Of course. I'm mortal. Good only for women's work, right?"

His host paused and turned back, eyebrows raised. "Do I look like a woman to you?"

Sighing, Paul relaxed and grimaced. "No. Of course not."

"Good. So come help me." Julius turned and continued up the hall and Paul reluctantly followed the older immortal into the kitchen. He was still irritated that they wouldn't let him up on the roof. He was mortal, not handicapped.

"We know that," Julius said mildly, retrieving bowls from the cupboard, and then turning to the pantry to fetch a couple varieties of chips. "But we aren't going to take chances with you. You are Jeanne Louise's life mate."

"Yeah," Paul muttered, and then heaved a sigh. "So where's the beer? I'll fetch it."

"I'll get it. You put the chips in bowls, and grab the dips from the refrigerator," Julius said, tossing him the chips and then moving out into the garage.

Mouth tightening, Paul opened one of the bags and dumped its contents into one of the bowls, then did the same with the others. It seemed even fetching beer was too taxing for a mortal to these men.

Rolling his eyes, he moved to the fridge in search of dips. Paul had never been much into sports, but there was nothing better to do, and he supposed it was a way to bond with Jeanne Louise's uncle and cousin.

"And I know how to dog-paddle too. I'll show you," Livy announced to a seemingly enthralled Caro, who had turned sideways in the front passenger seat to listen to Livy's happy chatter. Now the girl turned to Jeanne Louise, who sat in the backseat beside her and asked, "When can we go to the beach again, Jeanie?"

"Not for a bit, pet," Jeanne Louise said apologetically. "You have some more training to do before we can do stuff like that. And when we do go, it will have to be at night. You have to stay out of the sun from now on, remember?"

"Oh, right, cause I'm a vampire like in that movie with the flying cows," Livy announced with a grin.

Jeanne Louise glanced quickly to Marguerite in the driver's seat, catching her wince at the "V" word.

"Flying cows?" Caro asked with confusion.

"Yeah, 'cause they were vampires too from the vampire boy and his family feeding on them," Livy explained. The explanation didn't clear the confusion on Caro's face. Jeanne Louise didn't understand any better but supposed it was a movie the girl had seen.

"Here we are," Marguerite announced, bringing an end to the discussion of flying cows and vampires.

Jeanne Louise glanced around to see that they were pulling into the driveway. Marguerite hit the button to open the garage door, and then pulled straight inside and out of the sun.

"Wait for the garage door to close, sweetie," Jeanne Louise said when Livy reached for the door handle on her side.

"Oh, right, 'cause I can't go out in the sun anymore. I'm agergic to it," the girl said, sitting back impatiently.

"Allergic," Jeanne Louise corrected, turning to watch the garage door's progress. She wasn't allergic, of course, any more than the rest of them were, but it was the easiest explanation and one Livy could give to mortals if the subject ever came up around them.

"Okay," Marguerite announced as the door finished closing. She then hit the button to open the trunk as they all got out.

"You're back."

Jeanne Louise looked toward the door to the kitchen as Paul stepped out to join them.

"Daddy, we went shopping and Jeanne Louise let me get ice cream and chocolate for dessert," she announced gleefully, throwing herself at his legs and hugging him tightly.

Jeanne Louise walked around the car, biting her lip guiltily under Paul's arched eyebrow. "She was so good a treat seemed to be in order."

"Uh-huh," Paul said dryly, hugging and kissing her quickly as she reached his side. Then letting the matter drop, he said, "You two were up early."

"I heard Livy up and about in her room and got up to check on her," Jeanne Louise said with a shrug as she slipped out of his arms to move back to the trunk, where Caro and Marguerite were lifting out groceries. Joining them, she glanced over what was left. The two women had gathered all the bags, leaving a large package of toilet paper, a large bottle of water for the water cooler, and four cases of pop.

"Livy, can you manage this?" Jeanne Louise asked, lifting out the twenty-gallon water bottle.

"Yep," the girl said cheerfully taking it from her.

"Livy honey, let Daddy get that," Paul said with a frown, moving quickly forward.

"That's okay, Daddy. It isn't heavy," Livy said swinging the bottle from one hand as she skipped past him to the kitchen door.

"Jesus," Paul muttered, turning away to continue to the car.

"She's strong now, Paul," Jeanne Louise said with amusement, tossing the large package of toilet paper at him, and then turning to lift out the four cases of pop. Propping them on one hip, she closed the trunk, and then shifted the cases back to both hands, and led the way toward the kitchen asking, "So what did you do today?"

When he didn't answer, she paused and glanced back in question. Paul was still standing by the trunk, the toilet paper package clutched in his hands.

"What's wrong?" she asked, and then, worry sliding through her as she noticed his pallor, she added, "Are you not feeling well?"

"I'm fine," he said quietly, moving around the car now to follow her.

Jeanne Louise hesitated, but then continued on into the kitchen. She set the pop on the counter, and then glanced around in time to see Paul set the toilet paper on the table on his way out of the room. She frowned after him.

"Grocery shopping again? This is the second day in a row. I'll start thinking you're a shopaholic."

Jeanne Louise gave a start at that greeting from Paul as she entered the kitchen with a couple of bags in hand. She smiled when she spotted him seated at the dining room table.

"I think shopaholics generally buy clothes, shoes, and jewelry and stuff. Not kidney beans and tomatoes," she pointed out with amusement, and then explained, "Aunt Marguerite asked me to make my famous 'Smokin' Hot Chili' for supper. She and Julius have been telling Nicholas and Caro about it for a while I guess and want them to try it. I agreed before I realized she didn't have everything we'd need for it."

"Smokin' Hot Chili, huh?" Paul asked with amusement, standing to join her and slipping his arms around her waist. "Made by a smokin' hot woman."

"Mmmm, aren't you a smooth talker," Jeanne Louise murmured just before he bent to kiss her.

"Jeanie, my stomach hurts."

Jeanne Louise and Paul broke apart at that complaint from Livy and both turned to move to the girl as she paused in the kitchen doorway, rubbing her stomach unhappily.

"Where's the pain, muffin?" Paul asked, reaching her first and scooping her up in his arms.

"My belly," Livy said unhappily, wrapping her arms around his neck.

"Does it hurt like when you had the flu, or is it a sharp pain like someone hit you?" Paul asked worriedly.

"She's not sick, Paul. She won't get sick anymore," Jeanne Louise reminded him gently. "She probably needs to feed."

"Right," he said wryly. "I guess I forgot."

She smiled slightly and lifted the bags she still carried onto the counter. "Sit her at the table, I'll put these down and get her a bag of blood."

"I'll get it," Paul said, sitting Livy down at the table and telling her, "You'll feel better as soon as you've had some blood. Daddy will get it."

Jeanne Louise smiled faintly and turned to the bags on the counter to begin emptying them. She took the hamburger and turned toward the fridge, but when she found Paul bent over in the open door, reaching for the blood on the bottom shelf, she couldn't resist pinching his bottom.

Startled, Paul jerked upright, slamming his head on the freezer compartment as he straightened.

"Oh God, I'm sorry," Jeanne Louise said with

dismay, tossing the hamburger on the counter and moving to his side. "Let me see. How bad is it?"

"It's okay," he said with a laugh. "I just bumped it, honey."

"Let me see," she said feeling guilty for causing the injury. Pausing in front of him, she made him bend over so she could get a look at his head.

"It's just a bump, Jeanie," he said quietly. "The skin isn't broken or anything."

Jeanne Louise let her breath out on a sigh, and released him to straighten, but searched his eyes as he did, looking for signs of concussion.

"I'm fine," Paul said firmly, taking her by the arms and turning her away. "Stop worrying."

Biting her lip, Jeanne Louise allowed him to push her gently back toward her bags, then recalled the hamburger and turned to pick it up and put it in the fridge. Her gaze slid to Paul as he handed Livy the bag of blood. The moment the girl took the bag, he turned away and headed out of the kitchen, saying he was going to go take a shower.

Jeanne Louise watched him go and then glanced back to Livy as she popped the bag to her fangs. The girl was a pro at it after just a couple days. She was a fast learner though. Anders and Bricker had been taking time out to train her, as had Marguerite and Julius, and they all said she was bright and quick and would learn quickly. She could already bring on her fangs on her own, and keep them from coming out even when hungry, even when blood was waved under her nose. They figured she'd be able to read and control minds sooner than they'd first thought, perhaps before school started in September. Not that Livy would be attending school. At least not unless they moved to Port Henry. Jeanne Louise and Paul hadn't discussed that yet though. They'd only been here two days and there was plenty of time for that.

"The boys are teaching Paul to play soccer."

Jeanne Louise glanced up with surprise at that announcement from Caro as she entered the kitchen. "What?"

Caro nodded and came to steal one of the pieces of carrot Jeanne Louise had just cut. Her chili had been such a hit the night before that she'd offered to make dinner again tonight. It made her feel like she was contributing while they were here.

"Seriously?" Jeanne Louise asked. She knew from conversations she'd had with Paul that he didn't care much for sports.

"Seriously," Caro assured her. "I think it's a male bonding thing."

"I hope the boys aren't too rough on him," Marguerite said with concern. "Jeanne Louise, maybe you should go remind my son to play nice with Paul. They're not used to playing with mortals and might get carried away."

Nodding, Jeanne Louise set down the knife she'd been using and hurried for the back door.

"They're out front," Caro said, bringing her to a halt.

"Thanks," Jeanne Louise said, whirling to head the other way. She came out the front door to see that they were indeed playing on the lawn in front of the house. She supposed it was to avoid trampling on Boomer and Livy, who were presently running around in the backyard while Marguerite watched them from the dining room table.

It was late at night, after nine. The sun was no longer visible, but the sky was still glowing with its light and the air still hot and muggy. Jeanne Louise stepped off the front step and crossed the driveway that ran around in front of the house to reach the grass. She had no desire to simply yell the caution to her cousin, suspecting it would embarrass Paul.

Jeanne Louise approached the area where the men had set up their nets, watching the game underway as she went. It looked as if it was Nicholas, Julius, and Paul against Anders and Bricker. An unfair division since it was uneven, or it would have been were Paul immortal, but he wasn't and he was having trouble keeping up with the others. They definitely weren't going easy on him because he was mortal. The others were racing toward one net, Christian in control of the ball, kicking it ahead of him as he ran. Julius was on his right side keeping pace and Bricker and Anders were approaching quickly while Paul lagged behind. And then Anders suddenly burst forward and managed to scoop the ball with one foot, sending it flying sideways toward Bricker. The younger immortal leapt up and stopped it with his head, then whirled as he came back down and began kicking it back the other way, charging toward the other net.

Paul was between him and the net in question, and tried to stop him, leaping in his way and trying to kick the ball back the other way, but it all went wrong somehow. Paul misjudged where he needed to be and Bricker crashed into him. Jeanne Louise heard the thud of their heads making contact from where she stood and cried out in alarm. She broke into a run as Paul started to fall.

The men were all surrounding Paul when she got to him. Jeanne Louise pushed between Anders and Bricker to drop to his side, fear clutching at her throat as she spotted blood. Paul sat on the ground, head tilted back and thumb and forefinger pinching the bridge of his nose, trying to stop it from bleeding.

"Are you all right?" she asked with alarm.

"It's okay. Just a bloody nose," Paul muttered.

"It looks broken," Jeanne Louise said anxiously.

"It's not broken, Jeanie," he said quietly. "I'm all right."

"But it looks broken, and if it's broken it could get infected and—"

"Dammit, Jeanie," he snapped.

She sat back on her haunches with surprise at the harsh bark.

Grimacing, Paul shook his head and said more calmly, "It's not broken. I'm fine. Stop fussing."

"Of course," Jeanne Louise said stiffly and stood up.

"Jeanie," he said on a sigh as she started away

back toward the house, where Caro stood in the door watching.

Jeanie just kept going. She hardly heard Christian's murmured, "We'll be more careful with him, Jeanie. Sorry."

"Is he all right?" Caro asked with concern as Jeanne Louise reached the front step.

"Yes," Jeanne Louise said quietly, and continued into the house to return to cutting her vegetables. She wasn't even going to look out a window to watch and be sure he didn't get hurt again, Jeanne Louise vowed. And she would try hard to forget that he was out here banging heads with immortals who apparently had wood between their ears, she decided grimly.

Jeanne Louise had finished cutting up the vegetables, poured them along with beef stock into a pot and was stirring the beginnings of her stew when the sound of the door opening caught her ear. She glanced up, but then lowered her head again quickly when she saw that it was Paul.

"Hey Paul," Caro greeted him lightly. "Who's winning?"

"The other side," Paul muttered, grabbing a glass out of the cupboard and moving to the water cooler. He set his glass on the small shelf under the spout and pressed the button, then pulled it out and gulped half of it down before glancing toward Jeanne Louise, and then it was only to say, "The bottle needs changing. Where does Marguerite keep the replacements?"

Jeanne Louise hesitated, then set down her spoon and moved toward the door to the pantry. "I'll get it."

"I wasn't asking you to get it. I can get it. Just tell me where it is," Paul said sharply, following her.

"It's no trouble," Jeanne Louise said grimly, tugging the door open and stepping into the garage. "Just go back to your game. I'll replace the bottle."

"God dammit, Jeanie!"

She stopped abruptly at the shout and then turned slowly as Paul stepped into the small room and closed the door. Sighing, he leaned back against the door and shut his eyes before saying wearily, "Jeanie, I can't do this."

"Do what?" she asked warily.

He opened his eyes and said solemnly, "I can't handle you treating me like a child."

Jeanne Louise frowned and then forced a nervous laugh and moved in front of him, her hands sliding down over his chest, one drifting farther down to cup him through his jeans as she leaned up to nibble at his ear and whisper, "I hardly think I treat you like a child, Paul."

"Not in bed," he said grimly, catching her hands and urging her back. "That's the only time you don't treat me like a child."

Jeanne Louise stared at him uncertainly. "I don't understand. When do I treat you like a child?"

"The water jug," he said quietly.

She shrugged her shoulders unhappily. "I was just trying to help. They're heavy and—"

"For me," Paul interrupted. "But they aren't for you or Livy, I know," he said wearily. "But they aren't so heavy I can't carry them." Sighing, he ran one hand through his hair. "You're overprotective of me, Jeanie. You don't want me to do anything dangerous, or carry anything heavy. I suspect if I let you, you'd wrap me in cotton batting and keep me in the house all the time."

"I'm just . . ." When Jeanne Louise paused helplessly, he pulled her into his arms and held her tight.

"It's bad enough that your uncle and the other men treat me like a girl, but I can't handle you doing it too," Paul said in a pained voice.

Jeanne Louise hesitated, and then wrapped her arms around him. "We're just worried about you, Paul."

"I know," he said unhappily. "And why wouldn't you be? I'm the weakling here. The fragile one. And you're all stronger, faster, and smarter than me."

"We may be stronger and faster, but we're not smarter," Jeanne Louise said at once, trying to pull back. "You're smart, Paul."

"Then why didn't I see what your uncle and father did?" he asked quietly, letting her pull back finally. "Why didn't I see that we wouldn't work like this?"

"We can work," she said at once, desperation entering her voice.

"No, we won't," Paul said solemnly. "We can't. Because I'm asking you to do what I couldn't."

Jeanne Louise shook her head with confusion. "I don't—"

"I'm asking you to watch me die," he said solemnly. "Jeanie, you treat me exactly like I treated Livy when I found out about the tumor, even before she grew thin and weak. You're worried and protective. You're having to watch me die just like I was watching Livy die, only you're going to have to watch and worry for decades rather than months. And you have no hope of saving me." He let his breath out on a sigh, and then said, "I was selfish enough that I was willing to let you suffer the worry and misery of it. I wanted it even though I knew it would hurt you every day to see me age, wither, and die. And I'd probably still be selfish enough to make you do that . . . except for how weak and useless it makes me feel."

"I'll try not to make you feel weak and useless," Jeanne Louise said quietly and when he started to shake his head, she said more strongly, "I will. I wasn't thinking about how you'd feel. I'll let you be a man, Paul. I'm not saying I won't worry or fret, but I'll try to check myself before I speak, and let you carry heavy things and I won't try to stop you from doing things you're perfectly capable of."

"But no one else will," he pointed out gently. "They'll still treat me like the weakling I am in comparison to them."

"Then we'll leave," she said. "We'll go to your house. I can train Livy myself."

"Will they let us?" Paul asked uncertainly.

"They'll have to," she said firmly.

Paul stared at her uncertainly, and then nodded

and pulled her against his chest for a hug, and Jeanne Louise let her breath out on a sigh. But she was troubled. Just the thought of losing him had raised such panic in her . . . and she was going to. She might be lucky and he'd live to eighty. She might have forty years with him. But that was barely a heartbeat to her people. She was one hundred and two years old, almost one hundred and three. Just a baby to her people. She could live to be a thousand, two thousand, even three thousand years old. Her time with him would be a mere blip in her life, and then she would spend the rest of her years alone, living on her memories. It could break her.

Seventeen

'My, you look comfy in there.'

Jeanne Louise opened her eyes and smiled as Paul settled on the side of the large whirlpool tub in his master bedroom and leaned to scoop up a handful of the bubbles surrounding her. They had left Marguerite's house three days ago. No one had tried to stop them. They had all seemed to understand, and so far they hadn't heard from Uncle Lucian, though she was sure they would soon.

Jeanne Louise had expected that Bricker and Anders would have to go with them, but they hadn't. Instead, they'd returned to the Enforcer house, leaving she, Paul, and Livy to head out on their own. Jeanne Louise suspected she could thank her aunt for that. Marguerite had a way with Uncle Lucian.

So far things were going well. Or at least all right.

Jeanne Louise had managed to force herself not to fuss so much, clamping down on the urge to intervene and carry the heavy things, or worry . . . at least out loud. But it had been hard, much harder than she'd expected, Jeanne Louise acknowledged. "Did Livy get off to sleep all right?" she asked.

"Dropped off like a dream," Paul said with amusement, and then pointed his hand toward her and blew at the bubbles on his flat palm, sending them drifting toward her. She chuckled when they landed on her cheek and drifted down to join the others around her breasts.

"This is a big tub," Jeanne Louise pointed out softly.

"Big enough for two," Paul agreed with a grin.

"So why don't you join me."

Paul grinned. "You just want to see me strip."

"Darn right," she assured him and arched one eyebrow. "So. You gonna do it?"

Chuckling, he stood and headed for the door, saying, "Nah. We might both drown in the tub when we fainted, or at least I would," Paul added wryly. "Besides, I had a shower before making dinner, remember? I think I'll go build a fire in the fireplace in the bedroom and wait for you." Glancing over his shoulder, he added, "Don't take too long. I might fall asleep waiting."

"I'll keep that in mind as I soap every inch of my body here all by myself," Jeanne Louise taunted with a sad moue.

"Don't forget to rinse. Soap doesn't taste good

and I plan on licking every inch of you when you get out," he teased right back.

"You can try," Jeanne Louise said on a snort of laughter. That darned life mate shared passion made such efforts impossible at this stage of the game.

"I intend to," Paul assured her. "And I will keep trying until I succeed. It might take a decade or two, but—" He shrugged. "I'll have fun trying."

Jeanne Louise chuckled at the claim and picked up the soap and washcloth, now eager to clean herself and get out of the bath.

Paul was whistling under his breath as he opened the grate to the fireplace. Turning toward the log holder, he started to bend to collect a couple, but then paused as he saw that there was only one in it. He almost didn't bother with a fire then. It was summer, the air-conditioning was on for heaven's sake. They didn't really need a fire. It had just seemed a nice romantic gesture, a bottle of wine, a fire, soft music . . . Mind you, the air-conditioning was good when you were clothed, but it could get a bit chilly when they were all naked and sweaty.

Paul shifted briefly on his feet and then turned and headed out of the bedroom. He'd cut a couple logs, and build a small fire. Just big enough to set the mood, offer ambient lighting and to take the chill off. He wanted to make tonight special. Things had been a bit stiff and awkward between them since his blowup at Marguerite's after playing soccer. Paul knew Jeanne Louise had only been worrying about him, and felt bad for what he'd said that afternoon. It was true, of course. He did feel like the weak one in the relationship at times. But then he was, physically, and knew it. Unfortunately, her coddling and fussing just made it worse, but Paul knew she coddled and fussed because she cared. They would work it out. They had to.

Frowning at the desperation of his own thoughts, he jogged lightly downstairs and headed up the hall to the kitchen. Boomer was immediately rising from his spot by the back door, tail wagging and whining.

"You want out for a bit?" Paul asked the dog as he stopped at the kitchen closet to retrieve the small axe he kept inside.

Taking the frantic tail wagging and yip as a doggy yes, Paul smiled and closed the closet door, then led the animal to the back door, warning, "It's a short run only, buddy. I'm splitting a couple logs and then I'm back inside whether you're ready or not, so make it quick."

Boomer burst out of the door before he had it fully open. Chuckling under his breath, Paul followed him out and then moved to the left to the large stump with several more logs laid out beside it. They were the remains of a tree a winter storm had taken down six months earlier. Fortunately, it had fallen away from the house or Paul would have had the beginnings of a terrarium in his kitchen.

Grimacing at the thought, he picked up one of

the logs, set it on the stump, and set to work. He'd split it in half and had set one half back on the stump, holding it upright with his left hand while swinging the small axe with his right when Boomer caught him by surprise and jumped on him from out of nowhere.

The action startled him, jerking his body and putting his aim off. The axe had gone through the pad below his thumb and sunk itself in the wood before he registered what had happened. The pain began a heartbeat later, slamming through him like a sledgehammer as the blood began to gush.

Cursing, he slid his hand out from around the axe and clutched it to his chest with his other hand, instinctively holding it up as he hurried for the house.

Jeanne Louise stepped into the bedroom and let the towel she'd wrapped around her drop, then blinked and glanced around with surprise. Paul wasn't there.

"Well, hell," she muttered, bending to pick up her towel and wrap it around her again. So much for her grand entrance, she thought wryly. He'd probably gone for wine or something, she thought moving farther into the room and then pausing when she saw the open grate in front of the fireplace. Her gaze slid to the lone log in the log holder and then she turned and crossed the room to the sliding glass doors to peer out. Sure enough, there he was, splitting logs, she saw, and then glanced to the side as she noted Boomer rushing toward him. She saw it happening, but didn't see it coming. Boomer raced excitedly to Paul, lunged eagerly up to brace his paws on Paul's leg. Paul glanced around with a start mid-swing, his arm going a little wild and then glanced sharply back to what he was doing as the axe landed.

For one second he didn't move and she wasn't sure if everything was all right or not, but then he released the axe, raised his gushing hand and clutched it to his chest as he rushed for the house. Heart in her throat, Jeanne Louise hurried from the room and rushed downstairs, arriving in the kitchen as he reached the sink and turned the tap on. Her gaze slid over the trail of blood from the back door and then she grabbed a dish towel and rushed to his side.

"Let me see."

"It's fine," Paul muttered, holding his hand under the water. "It didn't hit bone. It just got the fatty pad under my thumb."

"It's bleeding badly, Paul. Let me see," she insisted, not willing to take no for an answer.

"It's fine, Jeanie," he said grimly, but let her pull his hand out from under the water and examine the wound.

"It's not fine, you need stitches," she said firmly, wincing as she took in the open gash. Jesus, he had missed bone, but by a hairsbreadth. And he was bleeding like crazy. She wrapped the towel around the wound and tied it tight, ignoring the pained way he sucked in a breath. She had to stop the bleeding. "You have to go to the hospital."

"Yeah." He sighed. "Can you watch Livy while I—"

"You are not driving yourself to the hospital with one hand. Especially not after losing this much blood. You could pass out."

"There you go, fussing again," he said with irritation.

Jeanne Louise ground her teeth together. "Sit down," she said firmly. "I'll get dressed and grab Livy and we'll head right over."

She ushered him to a chair at the table, saw him seated and then raced out of the room, using immortal speed rather than the slower more mortal speed they tried to incorporate around mortals. Jeanne Louise was back in the bedroom, tugging clothes on before most mortals would have reached the stairs. She didn't worry over much about what she put on, just grabbed up the clothes she'd been wearing earlier and slapped them on, grabbed her car keys off the bedside table, and then rushed into Livy's room and scooped her up, slipping into her thoughts to keep her sleeping as she did.

She was back in the kitchen a moment later and carrying Livy out into the garage, aware that Paul had stood to follow. Jeanne Louise buckled the child into the backseat, straightened and closed the door, then turned and offered Paul a steadying hand as he made his shaky way to the front passenger seat. He didn't protest her assistance. Not that she would have cared if he did at this point. He was weaving like a drunken sailor, the dish towel wrapped around his hand soaked through with blood. She saw him in the seat, buckled him in quickly, then slammed the door and ran around to the driver's side.

Jeanne Louise hit the garage door opener before her behind was even fully on the seat. Only then did she pull the door closed, and do up her own seat belt. By the time she started the engine, the door was open and she simply backed out.

They were both silent as she drove them to the hospital. Jeanne Louise was biting back her worry as her gaze shifted anxiously from the road to Paul's pale face. He was still bleeding, the red liquid now dripping from the towel to his lap. She saw that and drove faster, her lips sending a silent prayer that he didn't bleed to death on her before she got him to the hospital.

Jeanne Louise pulled right up to the emergency entrance, slammed the car into park and leapt out to hurry around and open his door. The fact that he was still sitting there looking a little dazed and confused rather than opening the door and getting out himself wasn't a good sign, she decided as she ushered him out of the vehicle. Slamming the door, she hesitated briefly, but then opened the backseat and quickly unbuckled and lifted Livy out. She'd never forgive herself if someone tried to carry the girl off. Chances were the attacker would end up a bloody mess in the backseat now that she was an immortal, but Jeanne Louise didn't want Livy to have to go through that.

Catching her up in one arm, she used her other hand to usher Paul forward and into the hospital. He was shuffling his feet, leaning heavily into her hold. He was also turning gray and Jeanne Louise was worried sick.

"Ma'am, you can't leave your car there," a uniformed security guard announced, moving toward them.

"The keys are in the car. Park it and bring them to me," she ordered, knowing her car could block the way of an incoming ambulance.

The man turned and headed out of the hospital, helped on his way by a mental push from her. Jeanne Louise then glanced around at the people in hospital greens who were available and took control of the one who had "Doctor" on their name tag. She slipped into the man's mind and sent him out of the glass enclosed reception cubicle and around to open the doors for her as she ushered Paul forward.

"He was splitting wood and cut himself with the axe," she said abruptly as she urged him into the inner sanctum of the ER. "He's lost a lot of blood."

A nurse rushed up with a wheelchair and Jeanne Louise urged him into it, and then followed as they wheeled him along a row of examination rooms.

The nurse glanced from her to the doctor Jeanne Louise was still examining, and then said a bit nervously, "We don't usually allow anyone but patients back here."

"But you'll make an exception in my case," Jeanne Louise said grimly, dividing her concentration between doctor and nurse now.

"Of course," the nurse said pleasantly, turning Paul into a room and wheeling him up to the examination table. "Do you think you can stand up, sir?"

Jeanne Louise set Livy in the chair by the door, noting the child was waking. She could only control so many minds at once. Sighing to herself, she murmured soothingly to the girl and then turned and walked over to Paul. Jeanne Louise lifted him out of the wheelchair and set him on the table as easily as if he were a child, but no one said anything. Paul was too woozy and weak to really notice and she still had control of the nurse and doctor.

Leaving the doctor and nurse to their work, Jeanne Louise moved back to stand beside Livy and took a moment to send the just waking child back to sleep. She then watched silently as the doctor unwrapped the bandage and asked Paul questions. One of them was what blood type he was.

"O," Jeanne Louise answered for him when he frowned with confusion.

The doctor glanced at her, but didn't ask how she knew. She supposed he assumed she was Paul's wife and privy to such information, which was fortunate. Jeanne Louise could hardly tell him that after a hundred years of drinking blood one began to recognize and differentiate between blood types and since she'd been drinking Paul's for several days a couple weeks back, she knew.

The nurse rushed off to get blood while the doctor finished unwrapping the towel and took a look at the wound. He was cleaning and sewing it up by the time the nurse returned and began to set up an IV with both blood and a clear fluid she supposed was sugar water or something else to help replenish his liquids.

Jeanne Louise remained silent and still through all of it. Her eyes taking everything in and her heart racing.

"You were lucky, Mr. Jones," the doctor announced as he finished with stitching him up and turned his attention to bandaging the wound. "You only nicked the metacarpal bone of your thumb, but you managed to hack into the vein too. A couple more minutes and you would have bled to death."

Paul grunted at this news. He was starting to come around a little, the blood and fluids already doing him some good. Jeanne Louise on the other hand felt sick. Her stomach felt like it was eating itself and she felt woozy.

She'd nearly lost him. To a stupid accident. How many more times would she have to go through this before she finally did lose him? How many more rushes to the hospital? How many fevers, colds, pneumonias . . . ?

The mortal body was so fragile compared to an immortal's. This wouldn't be her last scare if she stayed with him. It was just the first of many until she finally lost him. Because she would. One trip to the hospital would be the last and she would be alone again. She didn't think she could stand that.

"Just lie back for a bit and relax," the doctor said, patting Paul's arm. "Once the IVs are done, we'll check you again and probably release you."

"Your keys."

Jeanne Louise glanced to the side to see the security guard beside her.

He told her where he'd parked the car as he handed her the keys, and then added, "Doris in reception said to ask you to come back out front and give us his personal information and health card number and everything."

Jeanne Louise glanced to Paul to see him digging his wallet out of his jeans pocket with his good hand. When he passed it to her, she took it without comment, scooped a still sleeping Livy up again and left the room.

As she followed the security guard back to the emergency area it occurred to her that Paul had wanted to drive himself to the hospital. He'd even got annoyed that she'd insisted on driving him, calling it fussing and coddling again. After his upset with her the other day, his annoyance had almost made her let him drive himself. If she had, he'd probably be dead now. He'd have grown woozy and crashed and never made it to emergency in time.

Her insisting had saved his life. Jeanne Louise suspected he wouldn't thank her for it though. It was another example of her fussing and coddling and not letting him "be a man."

"A mortal man," she muttered under her breath. The problem wasn't that he was a man, but that he was mortal. She was going to lose him, her mind screamed. If not today, then somewhere down the line and today's panicked little journey had been the first of possibly many. Why? Because he was determined to prove he wasn't weak so would take stupid chances.

Not that she thought that today's accident was an effort on his part to prove his manliness. But he would insist on lifting things that were too heavy just to prove he was strong, and he would—

Jeanne Louise cut herself off abruptly as she realized what she was doing. She was building a case, painting the future, giving herself an excuse to get out. She didn't need an excuse. The simple fact was, he was already lost to her. It was just a matter of when and how he actually went. She didn't want to stand around and wait and watch for it to happen. She couldn't bear repeated scares like tonight. Her heart couldn't take this. And it would only get worse as she became more bonded to him, as he inveigled his way into her life and heart.

She had to get out, get away from him, and try to rebuild her life without him. She'd been content, enjoying what life had to offer. Surely she could be that way again and—

And what? Wait for another possible life mate to appear on the scene. Unless he was immortal, he could never be hers either.

Livy shifted sleepily against her, nestling her face against her neck, and Jeanne Louise closed her eyes briefly, her footsteps faltering. She wouldn't be just leaving Paul, but Livy too. She'd come to love the little girl as much as she did the father, and the idea of giving them both up was gut wrenching, but she didn't know what else to do. Staying would kill her . . . slowly.

Jeanne Louise sighed wearily and continued on to the emergency desk, then opened Paul's wallet to find his health card. It flipped open to reveal a picture of a perfect, beautiful blonde. Jerri, his wife. He still carried her picture two and a half years later. How long would she carry his in her head?

Grimacing, she handed over his health card and answered Doris's questions the best she could.

Paul shifted in his sleep, banged his hand against something and was abruptly awake. Opening his eyes, he peered around the living room and then sat up on the couch.

Jeanne Louise had settled him there with a snack and drink on returning from the hospital, and then had taken Livy back up to bed. Whether she'd returned or not, he couldn't say. He'd fallen asleep shortly afterward, exhausted by the night's events. Of course, the pain killers the doctor had given him had probably helped to knock him out.

Rubbing his face with his good hand, he listened briefly to the silence in the house and then stood and shuffled out of the living room and into the kitchen. He paused in the doorway though, when he saw Jeanne Louise seated at the dining room table, leafing through a magazine.

"You're awake," she offered a tense smile as she glanced his way. Standing, she moved into the kitchen, asking, "Are you hungry? I made bacon, scrambled eggs, and toast. There's coffee too."

"Sounds good," he admitted.

"Go sit down and I'll bring it to you," she suggested, grabbing the oven mitts and slipping them on before opening the oven to reveal the food warming inside.

Paul moved to the table and sat down. "How long have you been up?"

"I haven't been to bed. Night walker, remember?" she said lightly, setting the food on top of the stove and fetching a plate to begin transferring a portion of each item to it. She then returned the rest of the food to the oven and took the time to fetch him a coffee and glass of juice as well.

Paul watched silently as she carried everything to the table on a tray. There was something wrong. He sensed that much. She was too wound up, her movements too jerky, and she was serving him like he was an invalid.

"Eat," she said lightly. "You have to rebuild your blood."

Paul picked up the fork she'd also provided and

began to poke at the food. It looked and smelled delicious, but he was distracted with what was going on inside her head. "Is there—"

"I'm glad you're awake," she interrupted. "I didn't want to leave while you were sleeping, but was hoping to get home before the sun was fully up."

"Home?" he asked sharply, lowering the fork to the table again. His gaze focused and stayed on her, noting the way she was avoiding looking at him.

Jeanne Louise hesitated, avoiding his eyes, but then suddenly met his gaze and sighed. "You were right yesterday. This isn't going to work."

Paul sat back in his seat. Silent. Waiting.

"I can't—" She paused and swallowed, cleared her throat, then tried again. "I love you, Paul, and Livy too, but I can't do this. I'm going to lose you one way or another. If not to some stupid accident, then to cancer, or a heart attack, or just plain old age. And the longer I'm with you the more crazy I'll make you with my fussing and . . . the more it will hurt when I do lose you." She paused and peered at him pleadingly. "I can't do this."

He nodded and cleared his throat. Now Paul was the one avoiding her eyes. He wouldn't beg for her to stay. Couldn't ask that of her. Because he understood. Asking her to stay was asking her to stand by and watch him die. If she were mortal, it would have been different. But she wasn't. It was like wanting to be with a goddess. A beautiful, strong, brilliant being of light and glory. While he was a mere man. He couldn't ask her to stay. It was self-

ish to expect her to. But it was hard not to. Losing
Jerri had been painful as hell, but losing Jeanne
Louise would be harder. Because she wouldn't be
dead and in the ground beyond his reach. Although
he would be eventually.

"What about Livy's training?" he asked finally.

"I called Uncle Lucian last night. He said he'd
make arrangements," Jeanne Louise said quietly
and something in her voice made him glance her
way finally.

Had she sounded disappointed? Had she hoped
he'd protest, beg, and plead? Should he? Or was
that selfish?

"I should go," she said abruptly, moving to collect a packed suitcase beside the door to the garage.
He should have noticed that, he thought with a
frown. It would have given him some warning,
prepared him. Maybe he would have known what
to do then, what to say.

"Uncle Lucian will contact you in the next couple
of days with arrangements to help Livy," she said
quietly as she opened the door to the garage. Glancing back, she peered at him silently for a moment,
and then murmured, "Have a good life."

He thought he caught the sheen of tears in her
eyes before she turned away, but then she was
walking out the door into the garage and closing
it behind her.

Paul listened to the sounds of her moving around,
then the slam of the door, the car starting and the

garage door opening. He heard her pull out and after a pause, the sound of the door closing again and wondered idly if she would mail him the garage door opener. Then his hand jerked out and sent the plate of bacon and eggs smashing to the floor.

Eighteen

"When is Jeanne Louise coming to see us again, Daddy?"

Paul paused in front of the trunk he'd just opened and stared blindly at the groceries inside. When was Jeanne Louise coming to see us again? *Never* was the answer. She'd backed out of their lives, unable to handle watching him age and die, leaving him alone. He understood. He hadn't been able to stand helplessly by and watch Livy wither away and die either, but damn, he missed her. If only . . .

If only? Paul's mouth twisted at the words in his head. If only what? If only she hadn't turned Livy? He didn't want that. He loved his daughter and wanted her alive. So he supposed it was if only the Rogue Hunters hadn't arrived when they had. If only that Bricker fellow hadn't scared the kid into running, so that she'd fallen and been mortally wounded so that Jeanie had been forced to turn her? So that they could have carried through their plan for her to turn him and let him turn Livy?

He supposed. But "if only" didn't matter. What had happened had happened, and now they had to live with the results.

"Huh? When is she coming, Daddy?"

Paul sighed and glanced to his daughter, frowning when he saw that she'd lifted four cases of pop out of the trunk as if they weighed next to nothing. "Honey, let Daddy take those. You—"

"It's okay. They aren't heavy," she assured him and moved toward the door to the kitchen.

As he watched, Livy shifted the heavy cases to one hand to open the door with the other, and then stepped out of the garage and into the kitchen.

"Jesus," Paul muttered and turned his attention to gathering several bags of groceries in each hand. He managed to get all of them out, and was about to close the trunk when it suddenly slammed shut for him. Paul turned to peer at his daughter silently. She'd returned without his noticing, probably that vampire speed. And somehow she'd closed the trunk. She must have leapt up a couple feet to reach it, she was too short to do so otherwise, but she was smiling at him now looking like a normal, happy five-year-old rather than some strange hybrid vampire.

"So how come Jeanne Louise doesn't come see us anymore? I like her. Doesn't she like us anymore?"

Paul's shoulders sagged with defeat and then he

knelt before her, setting their grocery bags down so that he could give her a hug. "Yes, she loves us a great deal, and that's why we don't see her anymore."

"But that doesn't make sense, Daddy," Livy complained. "If she loves us—"

"Sweetie, do you remember how upset and worried I was when you were sick and I thought you were going to die?"

Livy pulled back to peer at him solemnly, and nodded. "Yes. You were scared."

Paul's eyebrows rose at her wisdom. He had tried to hide his worries and fears, but apparently she'd seen right through them. "Yes, I was. I knew it would hurt to lose you because I love you. And now Jeanne Louise feels that same way."

"But she won't lose me. I'm not sick anymore," Livy pointed out.

"Not you, sweetie, me."

Her eyes went wide and scared. "Are you sick, Daddy?"

"No," Paul assured her quickly. "But I'm not like you and Jeanne Louise. I'm mortal. You remember how Marguerite taught you about being an immortal and how you'll grow up, but won't grow old? And how you won't get sick, or die?"

Livy nodded.

"Well I am mortal. I will grow old and eventually die, and Jeanne Louise is afraid of having to watch that. She'd miss me too much."

"I don't want you to grow old and die, Daddy,"

Livy said at once. "Who will bandage my booboos and tell me I told you so when I make myself sick on too much candy?"

Paul's lips twitched at the words, but he assured her, "Honey, I'm not going to die for a while yet. You'll be grown up when I do."

"But I don't want you ever to die," Livy said at once. "Maybe I can make you a vampire like Jeanne Louise did to me. Then she would come see us again and you would never die and we could be a family."

"Would you like that, Livy?"

Paul glanced sharply to the side at that question, then stood and stepped protectively in front of his daughter when he recognized Lucian Argeneau standing in the doorway between his kitchen and garage. "What are you doing here?"

"The front door was open," Lucian said with a negligent shrug, stepping down into the garage and revealing Leigh, Nicholas, and Bricker crowded in the kitchen doorway behind him.

"We rang the doorbell," Leigh said apologetically. "But the door was open and when there was no answer we decided we'd best investigate."

"I let Boomer out after I put the pop in the kitchen," Livy said with a grimace.

And hadn't closed the door properly as usual, Paul finished in his head. Christ, the kid must have moved like the wind to put the pop away, let the dog out and come back to close the trunk for him in the few short seconds it had taken him to gather the grocery bags in his hands.

"Why don't we all go inside and sit down?" Leigh suggested, rubbing her extended belly uncomfortably.

Lucian was immediately all concern. "Are you tired? Do your feet hurt, love? Come, we'll sit down in the dining room while Paul gets his groceries."

The others made way as Lucian tried to usher Leigh back through the kitchen, but she refused to move and murmured, "Let's wait for Livy."

Paul glanced behind him, intending to collect the grocery bags he'd set down and escort his daughter inside, but Livy already had the bags in hand and was moving around him toward Leigh and Lucian.

"Hi Aunt Leigh. Hi Uncle Luc," she greeted cheerfully as she approached them.

Lucian Argeneau actually cracked something resembling a smile for the girl while Leigh ran a hand gently over Livy's head as the young girl drew abreast of them.

"Did you bring Jeanne Louise with you?" Livy asked, stopping.

"No," Lucian growled, scooping the child up, groceries and all in one arm, leaving his other hand to take Leigh's arm and urge her into the kitchen, as he said, "Not this time, cupcake. But I'm sure you'll be seeing her very soon."

Paul stared after them helplessly. Lucian Argeneau had called his daughter cupcake. And Livy had called him Uncle Luc. And his half pint daughter was carrying groceries he'd barely been able to manage, and doing so as if they weighed nothing.

As to the claim that they would see Jeanne Louise soon . . . Well, that was just cruel when he knew that wasn't going to happen.

"You gonna stand out here all day or what? Lucian isn't the patient sort."

Paul blinked and scowled at the immortal who had scared his daughter down the damned stairs and nearly killed her. Justin Bricker. He didn't respond to the man's words other than to start grimly forward. He didn't want to blame the man for his woes. After all, it had been an accident. But if he hadn't scared Livy, she wouldn't have fallen and Jeanne Louise wouldn't have had to turn her on the spot and forgo her hoped for plan of turning him and his turning Livy. Paul blamed the bastard whether he wanted to or not. If not for the otherwise seemingly nice hunter, he'd have it all right now.

"I'm sorry about that, Paul," Bricker said quietly as Paul drew abreast of him. "I didn't expect the kid to freak like that and take a header. And I couldn't get into her head to stop her. I did try when she turned to run, but I couldn't get in quick enough to stop her. I think the brain tumor caused some resistance or something."

Paul let his breath out on a sigh, his shoulders sagging as his anger slowly drained out of him. Jeanne Louise had commented at some point that it was a little harder to get into Livy's thoughts then most, that she had to make a full concerted effort to manage it, and she suspected it was the brain tumor that caused it. Paul supposed that was what the man was talking about. It had been an accident. He'd tried to save her. Life was full of such unhappy events that were really no one's fault, just fate fucking with you.

"Yeah, fate's a bitch at times," Justin muttered, obviously reading his thoughts. Placing a hand on his shoulder, he urged him into the kitchen, adding, "Lucian brought us all here because I want to make up for it though. I offered to use my turn to turn you for Jeanne Louise."

When Paul stopped abruptly to gape at him, he smiled wryly and added, "And for Livy too, of course. The kid's a cutie. Can't have her moping around and blaming me for eternity after you grow old and die."

"You are not turning him, Bricker," Lucian said irritably from the other end of the room. "Now you two get over here. I'd like to settle this before Leigh goes into labor."

"I'm not due for another month, Lucian," Leigh said with amusement.

"You're one of those people who are early for everything," Lucian growled, offering his wife an affectionate smile to soften the words, and then he scowled at Paul and added, "While Mr. Jones here appears to drag his feet about everything." He arched his eyebrows and gestured to the empty seat at the table. "I'm waiting."

Paul moved toward the seat, but Bricker was right at his side, saying, "I thought we were coming here so I could turn him. It was after I said I would yesterday that you started making arrangements for this visit."

Lucian rolled his eyes. "Did you think you were the only one to make the offer? Marguerite offered too. And Nicholas's Jo offered as well," he informed him dryly, and grimaced. "Every bleeding heart in the family with a free turn has offered."

Paul's eyes widened at this news. Hope beating to life in his chest. He could be immortal, have Jeanne Louise. That hope died with the man's next words.

"But I'm not letting any of you do that. Your one turn is too precious to let you give it away for someone else's life mate."

Paul sighed and sank down in the chair at the table. The man was right of course. The way Jeanne Louise explained it, if Justin gave up his turn he might one day meet a life mate and not be able to turn her. It would leave him in the same position Jeanne Louise and he were in right now. As for Jo and Marguerite . . . well, they might have their life mates already, but immortals could die. What if they found themselves widowed? And then found another life mate who was mortal? They too would be right where he and Jeanne Louise were now. His conscience wouldn't allow that.

"Jeanne Louise's original hope was to turn you and let you use your one turn to turn Livy," Lucian announced, drawing his attention back to the man. "You knew that?"

"Yes," Paul admitted on a sigh. "We had discussed it."

He nodded. "And you agreed to it?"

"Of course," Paul said at once. Good Lord, who wouldn't agree to that?

"Because you wanted to be immortal?" Lucian asked.

Paul blinked at the question with surprise. "Hell no. I'd rather neither Livy nor I were immortals. Everything has changed for her. She can't go back to school next year. Can't run around carefree in the sun. She can't see her friends or play with the kids in the neighborhood for fear of accidentally revealing what she is. And I sure as hell don't want to lose my family."

"And yet you agreed to the turn," Lucian pointed out.

Paul sighed and rubbed his forehead, he felt the beginnings of a headache ruffling through his thoughts. "I agreed for two reasons. One, because becoming immortal was the only way for Livy to be alive. If I could have found another way to cure her or save her I would have jumped at it and allowed her a normal childhood."

"And you?" Lucian asked. "If you could have cured her another way would you have bypassed becoming immortal too?"

"No. Because it would mean not having Jeanne Louise. I'd give up everything in my life for her . . . except my daughter and her happiness."

Lucian was silent for a moment, his gaze sharp

and focused on his forehead and then he nodded and turned to Livy. "You were saying maybe you could turn your dad and make him immortal like you and Jeanne Louise so you could be a family. Did you mean it? Would you turn your dad if you could?"

Paul stiffened at the question. "Just a damned minute, she's five years old. She can't—"

Lucian silenced him with a look. Actually a look and some mental tinkering, Paul decided when he tried to speak again and found he couldn't. The bastard was controlling him.

"Livy?" Leigh prompted gently, brushing the hair back from the girl's face. "Would you use your one turn to turn your father?"

"Uh-huh," Livy said simply, and leaned into the woman. "I'd like Jeanne Louise to come back. Daddy was happy with her. She made me happy too. And I don't want Daddy to die."

"Right. That's what we'll do then," Lucian announced, standing up.

Paul tried to rise and protest, but couldn't do either.

"Leigh, honey, why don't you take Livy out to the car. I'll be out in a minute."

Leigh nodded and stood, taking Livy's hand to lead her out of the dining room.

Paul watched them go, more confused than upset now. He'd thought they were going to try to make the girl turn him. It seemed not. He was relieved and disappointed all at once. He wanted to be turned, it would give him all he wanted, Jeanne Louise and Livy both. A happy family. He just didn't want Livy to have to do it or to lose her turn to do it.

"What kind of sick bastard do you think I am?" Lucian snapped with disgust the moment the two females were gone. "I wouldn't make a five-year-old child rip her wrist open to turn her father."

Paul blinked at that comment. "I—" He paused, surprised to find he could talk again. Lucian had removed his control over him. "Well then, why did you even force her to answer such a question?"

"Because she had to say yes," Lucian said dryly. "She had to verbally give up her one turn to you in front of witnesses."

"She's five years old," Paul said with amazement. "You can't hold her to that."

"I can, and I will. But I will be doing the turning for Livy," Lucian said simply. "I will physically do the turning, but it will count as her one turn."

"No," Paul said firmly. He couldn't take his daughter's turn and possibly leave her in a similar untenable position in the future, faced with a mortal life mate she could never claim.

"Don't you want Jeanne Louise?" Lucian asked simply.

Paul paused. Seriously tempted. He could have Livy and Jeanne Louise. He could have it all, everything he could have wanted, a beautiful vibrant wife and a healthy happy daughter. A future that seemed as rosy as could be. In fact, he would have had it all. Instead he'd lost it all.

"You still have Livy."

Paul glanced up with a frown. "Yes of course," he muttered. Frowning at his own thoughts. Of course, he hadn't lost it all. He still had Livy. A month ago that would have been enough. Why didn't it seem like enough now? Why did his life seem so meaningless without Jeanne Louise in it?

"You could always forfeit your one turn to your daughter," Lucian said calmly.

Paul peered sharply at him. "What?"

"Livy is forfeiting her turn to turn you. Once turned, you have one turn of your own. You can forfeit it here in front of witnesses, giving it to your daughter. It means should Jeanne Louise die and you find a life mate who is mortal . . ." He shrugged. "You're out of luck. But Livy will still have her one turn for her own life mate. Understood?"

"Yes," Paul breathed, his hope rising again. Dear God, he might have Jeanne Louise after all.

"So do you want to be turned?" Lucian asked firmly.

"Of course. I—" Paul's words were cut off when Lucian's wrist suddenly slapped across his open mouth. The immortal's other hand clasped the back of Paul's head to keep him from trying to back away from it. The actions were so fast it took Paul a moment to realize what was happening and

then he became aware that blood was gushing into
his mouth.

"Swallow," Lucian said dryly. "I am not biting
myself again for you."

Paul stared at the man blankly. He hadn't even
seen Lucian bite himself this first time. Damn
these bastards moved fast, he thought with amazement even as he automatically did as ordered and
swallowed. He breathed quickly through his nose
to keep from gagging as he swallowed the thick,
tinny liquid, and then swallowed again, and again.
It seemed to go on forever before Lucian suddenly
took his arm away and released his head.

"The turn has started. You will be immortal.
Now . . ." Lucian raised his eyebrows. "Will you
give up your one turn to Livy to use as she wishes?" •

Paul nodded without hesitation.

"Say it."

"I give up my turn to my daughter to use as she
wishes," Paul said dutifully his voice husky.

"Good." Lucian glanced to the other two men.
"Nicholas, help Bricker strap your new brother-
in-law down. Your father is bringing Marguerite,
Eshe, Julius, and Jo out with IVs and drugs and
whatnot. They should be here soon. Leigh and I
are taking Livy to Wonderland so she doesn't have
to hear her father scream."

Lucian turned and left the room then and Bricker
glanced to Nicholas, one eyebrow arched. "Wonderland?"

"Lucian's always loved amusement parks," Nicholas said wryly, moving to collect a small pile of chain Paul hadn't noticed curled in the corner. "Unfortunately, Leigh likes them too."

"Why is that unfortunate?" Bricker asked with surprise.

"She's due next month. You don't think he's going to let her anywhere near the rides do you?" Nicholas asked with a bark of laughter, beginning to unravel the chain with Bricker's help.

"Oh right," Bricker said with a grimace. "Hell, she'll be lucky if he lets her walk through the park and doesn't insist on a wheelchair or carrying her." He glanced to Paul and then patted the dining room table. "Hop on, Paul. Let's get you buckled in for the ride."

"On the table?" he asked blankly.

"Lucian suggested it when we first entered the house," he said with a shrug, and then patted the table, pointing out, "Sturdy wrought iron base, thick hardwood surface. Less likely to break than your bed, and easy to clean up the mess afterward."

"We'll move you to your bed after the worst of it's over and you're done thrashing and molting," Nicholas assured him soothingly.

"Molting?" Paul asked, his voice rising.

"Well, just one of the terms we use for it," he said apologetically. "During the turn your body pushes out impurities and stuff the nanos decide you don't need. It can get pretty messy. Much easier to clean surfaces like this though. So . . ." He nodded to the table. "Up you get."

Paul hesitated, but then gave in and climbed onto a chair and then sat on the table and swung his legs up. As he lay down, he glanced to Nicholas and murmured, "I know you're Jeanne Louise's brother. But we aren't married yet. Why did he call me your brother-in-law?"

Nicholas smiled faintly as he bent to offer one end of chain to Bricker under the table. As the two men straightened and began to shackle each end to his wrists, he said, "You're as good as married according to our customs. I'm sure Jeanne Louise will insist on a ceremony soon enough, but basically you're her life mate and you've been turned. It's a done deal as far as we're concerned." He glanced to him and smiled. "Welcome to the family, brother."

"Thanks . . . I think," Paul murmured weakly.

"It's not exactly a done deal," Bricker pointed out as the two men moved down to the foot of the table. "There's still the agony and shrieking to go through." He paused to bend and accept the chain Nicholas passed to him under the table, and then straightened and continued, "But it's never killed anyone . . . well, not anyone I've seen turned anyway." Pursing his lips he eyed him solemnly, and then asked, "You don't have a heart condition or something we should know about, do you?"

Paul's eyes widened, but he shook his head.

"Good, good." Bricker patted his leg again, and then began to attach a shackle to it, adding, "I'm sure it will be fine then."

"Good thing too. Jeanie would never forgive us if we killed off her life mate."

That dry comment came from the door and drew Paul's attention from the two men presently shackling his feet. He eyed the fellow leaning nonchalantly in the door.

"Thomas." Nicholas snapped the shackle around Paul's ankle, gave it a testing tug, then stood and crossed the room to hug the other man. Pulling back, he asked, "What are you doing here?"

"For some bizarre reason Uncle Lucian thought I should be here for the big turn. He had an Argeneau plane collect me and Inez this morning and fly us over," Thomas explained grinning.

"Inez is here then?" Nicholas asked.

"Are you kidding?" Thomas grinned. "She wouldn't let me fly off without her. Besides, Bastien thinks he might have a position for her here in Canada and wants to talk to her about it."

"So she's at the office?" Nicholas asked, turning to lead him to the side of the table and Paul chained to it.

"No. Bastien wants to see her tomorrow so she came with me today. She's out front. A car was pulling in as we were entering the house so she stayed to see who it was and either send them away if they're mortals, or greet them if they're one of ours." He peered down at Paul. "Is this him, then?"

"Hmmm." Nicholas smiled at Paul and nodded. "He seems a nice enough chap."

"Is he good enough for Jeanie?" Thomas asked.

"Is anyone good enough for Jeanie?" Nicholas asked with amusement.

"Hmmm," Thomas muttered.

"He's a geek like her though," Nicholas commented thoughtfully. "Works in R and D at Argeneau like her too."

"Well at least they can ride into work together," Thomas said wryly. "Although working in the same place they aren't likely to get much actual work done. I suspect they'll be found in broom closets and getting it on in their car in the parking garage for the next year."

Nicholas nodded. "Really, Bastien should just give them the year off."

Paul scowled at the pair of them. "Hello. I'm awake. I can hear you," he pointed out with irritation. "You may not think I'm good enough for your sister, but I'll do my damnedest to make her happy. And we won't be 'getting it on' in the car in the parking garage. I have a little more class than that," he assured them grimly.

"Besides, the parking garage has security cameras everywhere," Bricker pointed out, finishing shackling Paul's second leg and straightening to join the other two. "It's how we knew Jeanne Louise had been taken. Security saw him slip into the back of her car just before she got in."

Paul scowled again, but since that's why he'd been able to assure them that they wouldn't be caught doing the nasty in the car in the Argeneau parking garage, he didn't comment. Judging by the amusement on the faces of the men, though, he didn't have to. They'd probably plucked the thought from his mind.

"Hmm. That's a new one," Nicholas commented suddenly, staring at Paul's eyes.

"Yeah, they usually go to the organs first," Thomas commented, stepping a little closer to the table and bending to peer at Paul's eyes more closely.

"What usually go to the organs first?" Paul asked warily.

"The nanos. Your eyes are flashing silver already," Nicholas explained, and then asked, "Do you have some kind of eye problem?"

"I have late onset keratoconus," Paul admitted with a frown, alarm beginning to ripple down his spine. There was a strange heat building behind his eyes.

"What is keratoconus?" Bricker asked curiously, moving to the head of the table to get a better look himself.

"The cornea, the clear front of my eye, is thinning and bulging outward into a cone shape," he muttered, beginning to blink his eyes as they began to sting. "I wear rigid gas-permeable contact lenses because of it."

"Huh," Thomas murmured. He glanced to Nicholas and then back with a sigh. "Well the good news is, you won't need contacts anymore."

"And the bad news?" Paul asked grimly, squeezing his eyes closed against the mounting pressure there.

"I think you're going to be one of those ones where the turn comes on hard and fast. You—"

Paul didn't hear the rest. His attention was abruptly and completely claimed by pain suddenly shooting through both eyes. It felt like someone had taken two ice picks and stabbed him in the eyes with them. It brought an immediate roar of pain from him and had him thrashing on the table, yanking at his wrists to try to reach his eyes. It was probably better that he was chained though. Paul suspected he'd have done anything, including ripping out his own eyes to bring an end to the agony exploding through him just then. The worst part was, he knew it was just the beginning.

Nineteen

'I'm back.'

Jeanne Louise lifted her head at that cheerful announcement and forced a smile for her assistant, Kim, as the petite blonde entered the lab with a grin on her face and a spring in her step.

"Lunch with Arthur?" Jeanne Louise teased, or at least tried to tease. The words came out a little flat, but then everything about her was flat lately.

"Lunch and other things." Kim sighed happily at the thought of the mortal male who had replaced Fred in security. The two had become rather close rather quickly over the last few weeks. Well as close as an immortal and mortal who weren't life mates could get. "He's the cutest little mortal on the planet. And a good kisser. Good at other things too," she added with a laugh. "I hardly have to slip into his thoughts and show him what to do at all. He likes doing them."

"Hmm." Jeanne Louise lowered her head. The mortal she'd been dating when Paul had kidnapped her had been the same way. He probably still was. She wouldn't know. She hadn't seen him since leaving Paul and returning to her old life. She hadn't really seen anyone since then. Jeanne Louise had been avoiding friends and loved ones like the plague since meeting and losing Paul. And she had absolutely no interest in seeing her old mortal lover.

"Leave that," Kim said moving up beside her. "I'll keep an eye on it while you have lunch."

"I'm not hungry," Jeanne Louise muttered, turning the knob on the microscope until the image reflected in it was a complete blur of color.

"You skipped lunch yesterday too. What's going on? Immortalpause?" Kim teased.

Jeanne Louise managed a weak smile at the joke. It was a play on menopause, their word for immortals who moved past the desire for food and sex. Kim always teased her about that when she got too busy to bother about lunch and in the past she would have laughed. She didn't feel much like laughing lately, but Kim didn't know that. No one knew about Paul, his being her life mate, or her losing him.

"Jeanne Louise?"

She glanced to the girl, and noting the concern suddenly plucking at her lips, pushed her stool back and stood up. "You're right. I should go for lunch."

Kim hesitated, but then smiled and nodded. Her smile, though, didn't hide her concern. Jeanne Louise ignored it and moved to her desk to get her purse. She then headed for the door.

"Jeanne."

Pausing, Jeanne Louise glanced back in question.

"If there's anything I can do to help . . . you know I will, right?" Kim said quietly.

"Help with what?" Jeanne Louise asked with a frown.

She hesitated and then said apologetically, "They say new life mates are easily read, but it's more like they broadcast their thoughts. At least that's how it is with you."

She met her gaze for a moment, and then looked away. "Thanks," she murmured and slid out of the lab.

It seemed it didn't matter that she'd not told anyone. It sounded like she was telling everyone anyway. That explained why people were avoiding her eyes and being especially nice to her lately, she supposed, and breathed out a sigh. She was the tragic figure, a living symbol of what every immortal feared, one who'd found and lost her life mate.

Sighing, she forced her shoulders straight and head up and picked up her step. There was nothing she could do about other immortals being able to read her thoughts, but she didn't have to be the pathetic creature they all thought she was. She had found a life mate and couldn't claim him. It didn't mean she wouldn't find another, hopefully one who was already immortal and not in need of turning.

Just thinking that depressed Jeanne Louise. She didn't want another. She wanted Paul. But not just for a few decades. She already wanted him like no one and nothing she had ever wanted in her life, even her father's love. And that was after just a couple weeks. She couldn't imagine how much it would hurt to have him for a mortal life and then lose him. Jeanne Louise couldn't even fathom the pain then. Better this horrible soul wrenching pain now than complete obliterating agony later. Or maybe any agony later was worth whatever amount of time she could spend with him now, she thought as she reached the cafeteria.

That was the problem, she thought as she collected a tray and moved along the counter on automatic, selecting her usual ham sandwich and juice. Her thoughts kept fluctuating. She yearned to see his smile, hear his laughter, look into his eyes. She craved his kisses, to feel his arms around her, his body sliding against hers. But she knew, deep in her heart, that losing him later would kill her. However, that didn't stop her from driving past his house every night on her way to work, in the hopes of just seeing him or even Livy. She was acting like some sort of junky or stalker and it was starting to scare her. Every night after driving past she cursed herself and felt shame and promised she wouldn't do it again. But that next night, she did it again.

Jeanne Louise blew her breath out on a sigh as she paid for her lunch. She then turned to carry her tray to an empty table, wondering as she went if she could convince her uncle, aunt, and father to do a mind wipe on her. It was dangerous, but if it didn't kill her and succeeded, she'd stop hurting. She wouldn't remember ever having met him, wouldn't have to recall and ache for his kisses, wouldn't know what she'd lost . . .

"You should really try the bacon, lettuce, and tomato sandwiches if you've lost your taste for ham."

Jeanne Louise glanced up with a start at that solemn comment, her eyes widening as she peered up at the man who so obsessed her thoughts. Dressed in jeans and a T-shirt, with dark glasses covering his eyes, he looked ready to head for the beach, and obviously wasn't here for work.

"Paul," she said faintly as her body roared in response to his very presence. "What—?"

Her words died as he reached up and slid the sunglasses off. She stared blankly at the glowing silver green eyes that flashed at her, and stared and stared, unable to process what she was seeing.

"Your uncle Lucian paid me a visit yesterday afternoon," he said quietly and then smiled wryly and added. "Well, your uncle Lucian, your aunt Marguerite, your father, stepmother, two brothers, their wives, and the hunter named Bricker all paid me a visit. You have an interesting family," he added wryly. "I think I like them. They—"

His words ended on an *oomph* as Jeanne Louise

suddenly launched herself from her seat and at him. His arms closed around her at once, holding her tightly as he kissed her, but she pulled back mid-kiss to ask, "Who turned you? How? Why?"

Paul smiled at her frantic questions, but didn't answer right away. Instead, he scooped her up in his arms and turned to stride for the exit before saying, "Your uncle did the honors. He apparently ripped his wrist open, though I didn't see it, then slapped it against my mouth. Most unpleasant," he added with a remembered shudder as he pushed through the doors and started up the hall toward security.

Frowning, he said, "I'm glad you don't have to taste the blood normally. Bagged is definitely better than having to drink and taste it." Scowling at her, he said, "You should have told me that when I offered you my jarred blood. I could have found some straws or something."

"You get used to it," she mumbled, staring up into his beautiful green and silver eyes. He was turned. Immortal. She wasn't going to lose him. Her mind kept singing that song to her over and over, and still she wasn't quite grasping it.

"Anyway," he continued, nodding to Arthur as the mortal security guard rushed to open the door to the parking garage for them. "The next thing I knew I was being strapped to my kitchen table and your entire family was there. Well, except Lucian and his wife. They took Livy to Wonderland and then to their place so she wouldn't have to 'hear her father scream.'" He grimaced as he carried her along the row of parked cars. "Your uncle's a bit . . ." He hesitated, but then shook his head and said, "They still have Livy. He said they were keeping her for a while so that we could get reacquainted." Worry crossed his face as he said that.

"She'll be fine. I know he seems gruff and kind of scary, but Uncle Lucian has a good heart. Children and dogs love him," Jeanne Louise said quietly. "That's always a good sign."

"Hmmm." He paused next to his car and then peered down at her. "It nearly killed me when you left."

"It nearly killed me to do it," she said solemnly. "But it was a matter of self-preservation, Paul. I loved you after just days. I couldn't imagine how strong my feelings would be after decades. And to watch you age and die and know I would carry on for centuries, even millennia alone without you?" She shook her head. "I couldn't do it."

"You still might have to, Jeanne Louise," he said solemnly.

"No, you're immortal now," she said with a smile.

"And even immortals can die," he quietly pointed out. "I could be beheaded in a car accident tomorrow."

She stared at him silently, fear gripping her heart and he set her on her feet and then cupped her face in his hands. "I didn't expect to lose Jerri like I did or as soon as I did. I did love her, Jeanne Louise, as much as one mortal can love another. And when I lost her I thought my life was pretty much over, that all·there was left to do was to see Livy raised and happy. But I was wrong. There was you."

He bent to press a kiss to her lips and then straightened to say, "I love you. I want to live forever with you, but you have to promise me that if I should die in an accident or something, that you won't give up like I did. Like you did when you realized you'd used up your turn and couldn't turn me. There may be a second love waiting for you, and even a third. As long as there is life there is hope. Don't be the living dead like I was until you woke me up."

Jeanne Louise frowned and glanced away, finding it hard to make any promise like that. Instead, she asked, "Why did Uncle Lucian turn you?"

Paul stared at her for a moment, but then sighed and let her change the subject. "Livy gave up her turn to turn me. He did the honors, but it was counted as her turn."

"Oh no," Jeanne Louise breathed, true horror sliding through her to know that her happiness came at the expense of the child's.

"But once he turned me, I gave up my turn to Livy. It's hers now. So it's all good," he assured her.

Jeanne Louise sighed and melted against him. "Thank God."

"Or your uncle," Paul said wryly.

Jeanne Louise lifted her head and grinned at him. "Admit it, you like him."

"He has his good points," Paul admitted reluctantly and then grimaced and added, "The guy really needs to work on his people skills though."

Jeanne Louise chuckled softly and then leaned up to kiss him. It started as a soft brushing of lips, but as always happened soon became more heated and passionate.

Growling, Paul turned to press her back against his car, his body pinning her to it as his hands began to roam. When Jeanne Louise slid one hand down to cup him through his jeans though, he broke their kiss and glanced to the car to open the door.

Jeanne Louise sighed with disappointment, but slid inside when he opened the door and urged her in. It wasn't until she was sitting and realized he was following her in that she noticed that he'd ushered her into the backseat.

"What are we doing?" she asked with confusion, sliding sideways to make room for him to enter.

"What do you think?" he asked on a growl, slamming the door closed and pulling her back into his arms.

His mouth was on hers at once, and Jeanne Louise didn't hesitate to kiss back, but when his mouth began to travel to her ear, she mumbled, "There are cameras in the garage."

"The backseat windows are black. They can't see anything."

She glanced to the windows to see that the side windows were indeed black, but laughed on a groan as his hands found her breasts, and gasped, "But they'll know what we're doing."

Paul broke off to pull back and look at her solemnly. "Honey, anyone who knows we are new life mates knows exactly what we'll be doing for the next year. But if it bothers you, we can go back to my place. Or yours if it's closer."

Jeanne Louise considered the question, but then shook her head and climbed to straddle his lap. "Screw 'em. Let them know. I don't care. They've all been running around pitying me the last couple weeks. Now they can envy me," she added with a grin and kissed him.

For an early Christmas present,
read on for a sneak peek at

LYNSAY SANDS'
delectable romance

"The Gift"

in **THE BITE BEFORE CHRISTMAS**

Available now in hardcover
from William Morrow,
an Imprint of HarperCollins Publishers

Katricia whistled happily as she grabbed dried and canned food and packed it in the two empty boxes she'd found in a corner of the pantry. She wasn't really paying attention to what she was choosing, but then she had no idea what Teddy Brunswick would like—or what she herself would like, for that matter. It had been centuries since she'd bothered with mortal food.

"Katricia Argeneau Brunswick." It had a nice ring to it, she decided with a smile.

"Katricia and Teddy Argeneau Brunswick." Even better, she thought and sighed dreamily as she packed another can in the box.

Damn. She'd met her life mate. Katricia savored the thought. There was nothing in the world more important to an immortal than a life mate. It was what every one of them wanted and waited for, sometimes for centuries, sometimes even longer. Some never found one at all. But if they did, it was the most important moment in their life, finding that one person in the world, mortal or immortal, whom they couldn't read or control and with whom they could share their long life. It wasn't what Katricia had expected when she'd driven up here yesterday from Toronto. Though she probably should have, she acknowledged. Marguerite's matchmaking skills were becoming renowned. At least they were in the family. It was said she seemed to have the same ability that Katricia's grandmother and the family matriarch, Alexandria Argeneau, had possessed. That woman had found life mates for a good number of her children and the others of their kind before her death more than two thousand years ago. They said it had been like a sixth sense with her. Every couple she'd put together had been life mates. Now Marguerite was doing the same.

Still, this was the last thing Katricia had expected when Marguerite had invited her to join the family for Christmas. Especially since she'd said thank you, but no. It had been an automatic response. If she'd thought first, Katricia probably would have said yes, in the hopes that Marguerite had a life mate for her. However, she hadn't thought. Her answer had been automatic and firm. She avoided family gatherings. Actually, she avoided gatherings altogether. It was just too wearying to have to guard your thoughts all the time, so she'd taken to spending more and more time alone, especially the holidays, when all the older relatives got together. It was impossible to guard your thoughts from some of them, and Katricia didn't want one of her uncles reading hers.

The only family function she'd attended in the last decade was the multiple wedding in New York last February. Not showing up would have raised questions, since she lived and worked in New York, but as she'd expected, it had been hell. Concentrating on trying to guard her thoughts while trying to hold conversations with people had been like juggling knives while doing backflips. Impossible. She was sure more than one relative had caught a glimpse of her thoughts. She'd seen a flash of concern in the eyes of a couple of her uncles and even in Marguerite herself as she'd talked with her. Katricia was positive they all had caught how dark and depressing her thoughts were growing.

The thought made her smile. Both the darkness and depression had blown away like smoke in a stiff breeze the minute she'd reached the end of the driveway, spotted Teddy Brunswick, automatically tried to read his thoughts to see who he was and what he was doing there on the road, and found she couldn't. That had been a shocker. And suddenly her last-minute problems with her holiday plans had taken on a different light.

Katricia had been annoyed as hell when her flight from New York to Colorado for some holiday skiing had been diverted to Toronto. The pilot hadn't known what the problem was and Katricia had disembarked from the Argeneau plane ready to rip someone a new one, only to find her uncle, Lucian Argeneau, waiting on the tarmac.

"Bad weather," he'd announced by way of explanation as he'd bundled her into an SUV.

Katricia had been beside herself with frustration, her concentration divided between reciting nursery rhymes, to keep her uncle from reading her thoughts, and the intrusive worry that she'd be stuck with the family for the holidays and reciting those nursery rhymes for days. So, when he'd taken her to Marguerite's and that dear woman had mentioned that Decker had a cottage up north if she didn't wish to spend Christmas with the family, Katricia had jumped at the suggestion like a drowning woman leaping for a life raft. The next thing she'd known she and her luggage had been bundled in an SUV with the directions already on the GPS and she'd been on her way.

Now, here she was, up in the wilds of Central Ontario, snowed in with Teddy Brunswick, whom she couldn't read. Not being able to read a mortal was the first sign of a life mate. As an immortal, she could read mortals as easily as cracking open a book. Not being able to read Teddy had come as a hell of a shock. But a good one. A life mate. Damn, the idea made her sigh happily.

Of course, not being able to read him was only one of the signs, she tried to caution herself. After all, there was the occasional mortal that couldn't be read by anyone. They were usually crazies or people suffering from some affliction or other, like a brain tumor. Then no one could read them. However, Teddy Brunswick didn't seem mentally ill. He could still have a tumor or something, though, she acknowledged unhappily.

She would know soon enough, however. If Teddy really was her life mate, other symptoms would be showing up soon. The reawakening of her appetite for food was one of them, and she glanced curiously at the next box she lifted out and read the label.

"Bisquick."

She shrugged and stuck it in the box, but some of her good cheer was fading as she considered the one problem she could see with this scenario.

Katricia was pretty sure that bad weather hadn't been the reason for her diverted flight to ski country. She was absolutely certain that this had all been some grand plan to put her together with a possible life mate, which was all well and fine. But the snowstorm last night obviously hadn't been part of the plan and could be a problem, she thought with a frown.

Both boxes were now full of food. Katricia set one on top of the other, picked both up, and moved out of the pantry.

While she suspected Marguerite had arranged this meeting, she had no idea if Teddy knew about immortals. Most would probably call them vampires, but it was a term her people didn't care for.

They were not cursed, soulless monsters, chomp-
ing on the neck of every passing mortal. While
they lived long lives and didn't age beyond twenty-
five or thirty, their physiology and need for blood
was scientific in basis . . . and they avoided feeding on mortals now that blood banks were around.
But just because she suspected Marguerite had sent
her up here to find Teddy, it didn't mean he knew
about their kind. Which meant she couldn't risk
telling him the truth . . . that the provisions she'd
been expecting weren't gas and food but gas and
bagged blood. She didn't think he'd take well to
learning he was snowed in with a vampire who
was lacking in blood supplies right now.

HIGHLAND ROMANCE FROM
NEW YORK TIMES BESTSELLING AUTHOR

LYNSAY SANDS

Devil of the Highlands

978-0-06-134477-0

Cullen, Laird of Donnachaidh, must find a wife to
bear his sons to ensure the future of the clan. Evelinde
has agreed to marry him despite his reputation, for the
Devil of the Highlands inspires a heat within her
unlike anything she has ever known.

Taming the Highland Bride

978-0-06-134478-7

Alexander d'Aumesbery is desperate to convince the
beautiful and brazen Merry Stewart that he's a well-
mannered gentleman who's nothing like the members
of her roguish clan. But beneath it all beats a heart as
intense and uncontrollable as hers.

The Hellion and the Highlander

978-0-06-134479-4

When the flame-haired Lady Averill Mortagne braves
an unexpected danger at Highland warrior Kade
Stewart's side, she proves that her heart is as fiery
as her hair. And he realizes that submitting to their
scorching passion would be heaven indeed.

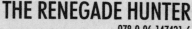